To Lorne —

Enjoy!

Girl With A Past
A Novel

Sherri Leigh James

SHERRI LEIGH JAMES

www.SherriLeighJames.com

ISBN-13: 9781517591328
ISBN-10: 1517591325

*To my partner in all things,
my husband Michael*

PROLOGUE

BERKELEY, MAY 1969

The day I was murdered, I thought all I had to fear was being tear-gassed on campus.

With our faces covered in paisley bandannas, we looked like gangs of marauding outlaws swarming the campus instead of university students. We braved swooping helicopters and air filled with tear gas to get to class on the south side near Sather Gate.

I avoided that side of campus as much as possible, but I had one class in Dwinelle Hall, near Sather Gate. Just outside of the Gate, rows of bayonet bearing National Guardsmen with their faces hidden by gas masks, kept troublemakers off campus. Problem was they couldn't tell just who the troublemakers were. All us hippies looked alike to them.

I crossed Strawberry Creek and was almost back to the relative peace of Northside when I heard the sound of slapping helicopter blades headed straight for my position. I pulled a damp bandanna over my nose and mouth, put my head down, and made a run for it.

Driven by the increasing noise of helicopters, I scrambled toward a grove of redwood trees. I had made maybe twenty feet when my throat and eyes began to burn, tears cutting my visibility. Almost there, almost to the North Gate, when my foot hit a pile of leaves and I slid, landing on my ass.

A strong hand grabbed my arm and pulled me to my feet.

"You okay?" he muttered behind his handkerchief.

He towed me through the trees, into the nearest building. We stumbled down the wide hall to a drinking fountain and splashed our faces with cool water. My back to the wall, I slid to the floor and tried to breathe.

My rescuer plopped down beside me. We both gasped for air, wiped our eyes, and blew our noses. When I could see again, I noticed that even blood shot eyes and a running nose failed to lessen the attractiveness of my new friend. Dark chocolate brown hair curled around his ears and neck; blue eyes matched his faded jeans.

My breathing came easier, easy enough for me to speak. "I'm Lexi." I rasped and extended my hand.

"Derek." He took my hand and held it. "Are you hurt?"

I pulled my hand away and shook my head.

"You fell pretty hard. You didn't break anything?"

"I'll have an awesome bruise on my ass." I drew blonde hair away from my face, tucked long locks behind my ears and into the neck of my fur lined jacket. "I'm okay. Just sick of this routine."

"Yeah. I can dig it," Derek said. "You would think we were causing the trouble."

Certainly Governor Reagan thought we were dangerous criminals—or the enemy. Claiming that the Berkeley campus was "a haven for communist sympathizers, protesters, and sexual deviants" Reagan had sent in the National Guard to deal with us.

How far things had disintegrated since December of 1964.

The party, later known as a "sit-in", in Sproul Plaza had started four and a half years earlier when Mario Savio removed his shoes to climb onto the roof of the police car holding Jack Weinberg. Savio then invited students and faculty to sit down around the vehicle.

Military recruiters, industrial head hunters, and campus organizations set up tables lining one edge of Sproul Plaza just outside Sather Gate. Weinberg had been manning a table for CORE, Congress for Racial Equality, when university police placed him in the car. Thirty-two hours of peaceful sitting by three thousand people while Savio delivered rousing speeches ended with Weinberg being released and the crowd dispersing. The Free Speech Movement born that day on the Berkeley campus soon morphed into an anti-war, anti-establishment movement.

The People's Park crisis that Reagan now responded to with a heavy hand had minimal participation by students or faculty until the National Guard started shooting people. The 1967 Summer of Love in San Francisco had drawn thousands of young people to the Bay Area. Some of the ones who had wandered over to Berkeley from the Haight had camped on a vacant plot of land near the campus and owned by the university. Park inhabitants and local residents began protests when the university decided to clear the site of the campers and vegetable gardens in order to build a parking lot and athletic fields. Thanks to the governor, the National Guard not only brought bayonets, rifles and shotguns, they also filled the skies with helicopters spewing tear gas.

Some of us just wanted to go to class, and graduate.

I stood up and adjusted my book bag on my shoulder. "Thank you for the rescue."

Derek scrambled to his feet, hurried to open the door, and walked beside me out of the building, through the North Gate.

No sign of helicopters, but the smell of tear gas lingered. Masked students and faculty—after years of interrupted campus life—rushed by us attempting to go about their usual business in a war zone.

"Where're ya headed?" He stuck close to my side as I rushed across Hearst Avenue before the light turned red.

Aw, for chrissakes. Yeah, he rescued me, but did that mean I had to be nice to him? Why couldn't I be a bitch without guilt tripping myself? He was exactly the excessively handsome kind of guy I wanted to avoid.

"Thanks again. I do appreciate you helping me." I forced a smile and waved. "Ciao."

I lengthened my stride; maybe he'd give up. I glanced to my left; he was hanging in there. His legs were even longer than mine. I wouldn't lose him easily.

He caught my eye and smiled that charming crooked grin. Oh man, those crystal blue eyes. And dimples.

I couldn't help myself. I returned the smile.

He grinned. "Groovy." He waved at the tables and chairs on the wide patio of the Euclid Café. "Coffee?"

I nodded and followed him to a table.

"Sit, please. Cream?"

I nodded.

"Sugar?"

I nodded again, dropped my book bag next to one of the chairs, and sat down.

He walked to the line of students and faculty waiting to order.

A newspaper left on the table headlined another Zodiac killing. A photo of his latest victim headed the front-page story, a copy of a letter purportedly from the Zodiac was next to the photo.

I couldn't handle any more evidence of our fucked up world that day. I moved the newspaper to a nearby table.

Derek returned with two steaming mugs of coffee before I had a chance to reconsider befriending a stranger. Especially a handsome one. He placed both cups on the table and passed me a handful of sugar packets.

"So . . . where do you live?" he asked.

At least he didn't ask me "what's your sign?" Or "what's your major?" But then the smears of acrylic paint on my bell-bottom jeans might have given my art major away.

"Up the hill." I waved up toward the top of the Berkeley hills.

"Headed home?"

"Yeah. I've got a lot of work to do." I rubbed dried paint off my finger.

"What're you painting?"

"Kinda abstract nudes in landscapes."

He raised an eyebrow. "Like cubist nudes descending staircases?"

"I'm not Picasso or Braque. Landscapes, not interiors."

He flashed that damn smile revealing dimples again. "I'd love to see them."

That I ignored. "What's your thing?"

"Architecture."

"And you escaped the Environmental Design building?" I asked with a smile. "Don't they keep would-be architects chained to their drafting tables? I see people working in there twenty-four hours a day."

"True, too true." He sipped his coffee, and then grinned. "Couldn't hack it, had to get out and find a pretty girl to rescue."

I drank the last of my coffee. "Thank you." I forced a smile.

I wasn't going to violate my new agreements with myself. No more handsome and charming men. Too dangerous for my bruised heart. Women throw themselves at men like this one.

"I really do have to get to work."

He drained his cup and stood up. "May I walk with you?"

I shrugged an "if you want to" and picked up my bag.

The small talk continued as we headed up the hill to the house I shared with a group of close friends plus an assortment of guys who did not officially live there but hung around a lot.

My roommate Carol was about to graduate and already job-hunting. She was beautiful and talented so she would land a position in a fashion house quickly.

Jeff was a law student and my best friend since childhood when we had spent summers at the same camp, playing the same sports.

Dave, a Cal grad, commuted to a job in the city.

All three of them led busy, productive lives.

The others, the hang-arounders, needed to get a life. They used our place as their Berkeley base. All were graduates, and either trust fund babies or wannabes who managed to kill every day fucking around, tripping to the beach, hanging out in the Haight, going to Janis Joplin & Big Brother & the Holding Company concerts in Golden Gate Park or the Grateful Dead at the Fillmore.

Some days I was envious of their freedom. But once I started painting, I forgot everything but the music and the flow of my brush.

Two of the hang-arounders, preppie looking Jamie and surfer Ron, lounged on the front porch swing smoking a joint.

Jamie had actually attended prep school and was one of the trust fund beneficiaries.

Preppie wannabe Ron imitated Jamie's mannerisms, dress, and accent, but his rugged face and his engaging smile charmed both men and women. Jamie's relaxed manner was equally appealing. Both lit up with curiosity when we came up the front walk and climbed the stairs of the entry porch.

"Yo, Lex," Ron said, "Who's your friend?"

Shit. I'd planned to say good-bye and close the door in his face if I had to, but these two guys were going to make it awkward. To make matters worse, another of their group, Tom pulled into the driveway and climbed out of his jeep. Tom, who had actually grown up in the city, affected a cowboy look with boots and a fringed leather vest.

"Can I see your paintings?" Derek asked.

"Ah, shit man, you gotta see her work. It's far-out." Ron jumped up from the porch swing, opened the door, grinned in answer to the scowl I shot his direction, and invited Derek into *my* house before I could think of how to get out of this one.

One of my recent canvasses, a colorful abstract landscape hung above the fireplace in the living room. I followed the four guys into the entry hall and groaned as I watched Ron point out the painting.

"Wow. Cool." Derek directed a nod of appreciation to me.

"I really gotta get some stuff done. Thanks again." I ducked down the hall toward my room as I heard the men introducing themselves. Jeff was exiting his room.

"Hi," I said to him. "If you see Carol, please tell her I need to talk to her."

Jeff nodded his strawberry blonde head. "Sure."

In my room, I dumped my bag on my bed, grabbed a new brush from my desk and headed out to the garden shack I had converted to my studio.

Through open green house windows, I could hear Derek, Tom. Ron, Jamie, and my housemate Jeff in the living room, yukking it up and talking in those low, guttural voices that told me they were passing a joint. Any minute now they'd start discussing the relative merits of Acapulco Gold versus whatever they were smoking.

I loved those guys, but that dope story was getting old.

I closed the rusted, metal-framed windows, slid a Beatles record out of the album cover and set it on the turntable. "*In Penny Lane there is a barber—*" The sweet sounds took the edge off my tension.

Carol cracked the door enough to poke her dark head in. "Jeff said you wanted to talk to me."

"I went to the library after I saw you on campus." I motioned for her to come in. "Know what the symptoms of arsenic poisoning are?"

She shrugged, pulled her long black hair back from her pale face. Seeing how white her face was made my heart ache with concern for my best girlfriend. Carol did her best to hide her soft heart and anxious nature, but I saw through her tough shell.

"Vomiting," I said, "diarrhea, abdominal cramps."

"You're still on that subject!" She walked out; the crooked hinges thwarted her attempt at a door slam.

■ ■ ■

Two male voices sounded as though they were on the brick patio right outside my studio and they weren't discussing dope.

"You asshole, why did you bring that girl to the ranch? A complete stranger, for god's sake?" I recognized Jamie's voice coming through the cracks in the wall. "How could you violate our agreement like that?

"Hold on, you didn't mind her bein' there when she had your dick in her mouth."

I didn't want to hear about their sexual adventures, I turned up the volume. "*Penny Lane is in my ears and . . .*"

"You didn't mind havin' her then." That had to be Tom's voice raised in anger. I remembered how Tom's brown eyes flashed sparks when he was pissed off. Tom was another member of the clique of four who lived on a ranch in Marin County; the ranch that Jamie's family owned.

Something, maybe a body, slammed against the thin exterior wall of my makeshift studio. *"Penny Lane—"* I turned the music down. What the hell was going on out there?

"Get over it. Question now is how the hell do we get rid of her?" Tom lowered his voice, but continued with a hiss, "Found a guy who'll help us with our problem."

What *were* they talking about?

"What exactly do you mean?" Jamie's voice lacked his usual insouciant charm.

The tension level out there was far from the usual for these guys. They were normally laid back, joking and teasing.

"Met this guy at the Monk. He's nuts, but hell, if he gets caught he'll get the blame," Tom said. "I tol—"

"Hey, guys. What's going down?" I smelled tobacco smoke and, because he was the only one of the guys who regularly smoked tobacco, even before I heard his voice, I knew my housemate Dave must be out there too.

"A-ah, not much." The anger in Tom's voice had disappeared. Whatever they were talking about, they didn't want to share it with Dave. That didn't surprise me. Dave had never been an accepted member of the clique, but had he been listening to them?

Maybe I didn't want to know what they were up to. I pulled the windows of the studio shut tighter, cranked up the volume, *"beneath the blue suburban skies . . ."* and set to work determined to get the shade of blue right.

■ ■ ■

The layer of blue paint I had added to my canvas would have to set up before I continued so I headed into the house just before sunset.

"Lex, that Derek's an okay guy," Jeff called out from the living room as I headed down the hall. I turned around to where the gang had congregated on the sofas in front of the fireplace.

"Definitely, he is cool," Jamie said.

I considered giving them some shit about inviting him in without even considering how I felt about it. But, what the hell, they wouldn't get it. And I'd just end up feeling stupid trying to explain.

"Don't you like'im?" Jeff asked. "Isn't he cute?"

"Cute?" Carol said. "Hell, he's a stone cold fox!"

"I don't have time for that shit." Why can't they leave me be?

"Lex, don't get all uptight, remember the conversation we had about you sleeping with more than one guy in your life?" she said, "Sweetie, you don't need to be lonely, let someone in."

"Carol, not now." Un-be-liev-able! She had brought this up in front of all the guys who would no doubt use it to tease me mercilessly. I glared at Carol, but she didn't take the hint. She meant well, she cared, but she needed to learn to censor herself. But then, censorship was not her forte.

"He seems like the perfect opportunity," she continued.

I rolled my eyes and sighed. "Goddamnit Carol."

"He's coming over tonight," Jeff said.

"What? You invited him back?" I shook my head. "You guys are too fucking much." I headed to my room, grabbed a robe, and walked into the bathroom slamming the door be-hind me.

Twenty minutes later, I had washed my hair, put on clean jeans, a tunic top with a low-slung hip belt, boots, and two quick swipes of mascara. No bra of course. I wondered what time he was coming over, but no way was I going to ask.

A chorus of wolf whistles accompanied my return to the living room.

"Yo man, I think Lex noticed that Derek's a fox," Ron cracked as he and Jamie headed to the entry hall. "Ciao," they called as they closed the front door.

I ignored the comment, grabbed the joint out of Jamie's hand and took a hit while I stood admired the sun setting be-hind the Golden Gate. The grass mellowed me out and my end of the term worries about paintings and papers disappeared. I deserved a break.

The sunset's rainbow of colors reflected in the dark blue water of the bay, the entire composition framed by the deep green redwood trees outside the window. I'd give years off my life to capture the magic of those colors on canvas.

Jeff handed me a glass of dark red wine.

"No law books tonight?" I asked.

"Taking a night off. I really do dig Derek. He seems OK." He smiled. "I met someone too. I think you'll like her."

Jeff and I had schemed together not to get too emotionally attached to anyone until we finished school. Unlike our rich friends who had no need to work to survive, we both wrested all we could out of the opportunity to learn. But now, all I wanted was to graduate and get on with life.

I sipped the wine, discovered it wasn't the usual Red Mountain rotgut, held the glass toward Jeff and raised a questioning eyebrow.

"Yeah, she brought that Cabernet over. Pretty good, huh?" Jeff winked.

"Did you find yourself an heiress? Does she know even though you got into Boalt Law, the odds are slim you'll ever pass the bar?" It was safe teasing because Jeff was a hardworking student with a photographic memory. He intended to make the world a better place, one law case at a time.

"Her father is a state senator. That's from their winery," Jeff said.

"Aw, going for the political connections already, huh?"

"Lex, I really like her. And . . . I think she likes me." Jeff had that dreamy eyed look I'd seen on other faces, never his.

Wow, I was about to lose my best friend. I raised my glass. "Here's to your new love," I said, "When do I meet her?"

"Soon."

The doorbell chimed.

"Aaha." He scrambled out of the armchair we'd liberated from the Berkeley dump and bolted for the entry hall, smoothing his strawberry blonde hair in place as he walked.

But it wasn't a girl's voice I heard say hello. "Welcome, Derek. Entrée!" Jeff said.

Derek's tall slender body was backlit by the chandelier in the entry hall as he passed through the archway into the living room. It wasn't until he sat down next to me that I got the full effect of his looks. Short dark brown tendrils curled at his neck and framed his chiseled features. No longer bloodshot, his blue eyes twinkled mischievously.

Maybe Carol was right. Maybe this was the opportunity to broaden my horizons. Try someone new. It had been months since my first lover had broken my heart. My resolve to dedicate myself to my studies with no distractions was melting in the warmth of his smile.

"Hi!" He looked me in the eye. His smile exposed those dimples again. I tried to ignore the sexual tension, like the pull of tractor beams between us, but there was even more: the recognition of a kindred spirit, a person with whom I immediately felt comfortable.

Jeff remained at the door awaiting the entrance of his woman who arrived right after Derek.

Flames on oak logs in the fireplace and in candles on the mantel lit the room. On the stereo Bob Dylan rasped "*Lay lady lay, lay across my big brass bed.*" A tray on the coffee table held two bottles of Cabernet, two more wine goblets, and a dish of pre-rolled joints. The rest of our gang made themselves scarce.

I'd been set up.

I poured wine for Derek and Jeff's new girl, Lauren. Then I sat back, ignored Derek, and studied Lauren to determine if she was good enough for my best friend. I wanted to be sure she really liked him.

She thanked me for the wine in a soft, husky voice.

Her brown eyes seldom left Jeff's tan, freckled face; she hung on his every word. Could she be for real? Light brown hair fell around a delicately featured heart shaped face and grazed her shoulders. She shrugged off a vintage Chanel jacket revealing slender athletic arms visible in her sleeveless turtleneck.

"Do you play tennis?" I asked her.

"Some," she answered.

"She's being modest, she's damn good, plays in tournaments," Jeff said.

"Let's see . . . ski?" I leaned forward so I could watch her eyes.

"Yes," Lauren said.

"Golf?"

"Definitely."

"Bridge?"

"I do okay."

"Sail?"

"Absolutely."

"Hike?"

"Jeff took me on a hike last weekend. To the top of Mount Tam. It was fab."

So that's where he'd disappeared. She was doing pretty well so far. Almost too good. "Like kids?" I knew Jeff wanted several.

Lauren smiled at Jeff. "Love them." They'd evidently already explored these avenues.

"What are you studying?" I asked.

"Art History." She nodded towards my canvass above the mantel. "I hope you don't mind . . . when I saw that one, I insisted that Jeff show me more of your work. Beautiful. Really impressive."

Failing to find a flaw, I thanked her and sat back to discover that Derek had placed his arm on top of the sofa behind me. I feigned being cold and went over to stand in front of the fireplace, a ploy which failed when I realized I had just given Derek the opportunity to check me out from head to foot, which his eyes unabashedly did. He grinned and joined me on the hearth.

The four of us rapped about the subject of which there was ample supply: fucked up politics.

"Them times that're changing, ain't changin fast enough," Derek said with a Dylanesque twang.

"Anybody else think it keeps getting worse?" Lauren asked.

"The worst was when Kennedy and King were killed." I remembered how my hope had died the moment I heard the radio announcer tell us presidential candidate Bobby Kennedy had been shot in the Ambassador Hotel kitchen hallway. In despair, most of us had turned to drugs, art and music for consolation, but, unlike the most discouraged of our generation, we had not "dropped out."

Jeff picked up a joint from the tray, lit it, took a big toke, smiled at each of us in turn, and passed the "relief from our despair" to Lauren. Lauren took a hit, held her breath, and turned to me. By the time the weed had gone around the circle twice, Jeff pulled out a roach clip to avoid any waste.

Ron, the wannabe preppie surfer, had stayed in town to pick up his friend Suzy from the library. Around ten, they joined in the fun.

We smoked, played a few mind games, drank, got the munchies and ordered a pizza.

"Hey, whaddaya think about this Zodiac guy?" Ron asked as he pulled dripping cheese on to the top of the piece of pizza he had lifted from the box.

"I think he's scary as hell, that's what," Suzy said.

"Do ya think he really killed all those people he claims?" Ron asked, looked around the circle of faces as he munched on a bite.

"Why would he say he killed more than he actually did?" I asked.

"Cause he's nuts?" Jeff asked.

"That's obvious from the notes he sends to the *Chronicle*," Derek said.

"I can't look at them. I wish they wouldn't print them on the front page. Those letters creep me out." Lauren shivered.

"Why do they print the notes at all?" I asked. "Doesn't it just encourage the guy?"

"The psycho tells them he'll kill even more people if they don't print them," Ron muttered, his mouth full of pizza.

"Is it true that he kills young lovers?" Suzy asked.

"He seems to have a knack for finding people in compromising positions on their first date," Jeff explained.

"How in the world does he know it's their first date?" I asked.

Everyone in the circle shrugged their shoulders, shook their heads.

"Good question," Jeff said.

"Maybe he follows pretty girls around," Ron said, "waits for them to meet a new guy."

"Oh, that's just too, too horrifying." Lauren shuddered.

"Yuck, yuck, yuck," Suzy said. "Where's the dope? I need a hit."

We smoked some more, and finally decided to dance.

Jeff changed the record to slow, romantic music. Following one dance that was more like standing-up-making-out, Jeff and Lauren wandered down the hall hand in hand. "We're gonna hit the rack," Jeff called out.

Ron led Suzy into the next room where Dave was writing his usual, a business plan. Ron asked Dave for use of his bedroom.

Dave shot Ron a scowl, but was too much of a kiss-ass to say no.

Now we were alone in the room. Derek held me tighter, kissed my neck sending chills down my body.

But I dreaded what I knew was coming; Suzy, the screamer. Suzy's pre-orgasmic groans were shockingly loud when she and Ron had sex; I was embarrassed even before the noises started.

At the first dramatic moan, followed by an even louder grunt, Derek said, "Is that what I think it is? Or I should say, who I think it is?"

"Shit." I nodded.

"You wanta get outa here?" Derek asked.

We climbed into Derek's VW bug, the same model that we all had and headed to his place.

All my friends owned VW Bugs. If their parents insisted they get a new one, the usual routine was to kick a few dents into the fenders and smear it with mud. In Berkeley in the 60's, it wasn't hip to look as though you came from money.

I loved my bug—an early ragtop, black on the outside, red inside, and I had replaced the interior lining with yellow fabric printed with red and black ladybugs.

Derek surprised me when he stopped at a pay phone on Hearst Avenue, made a quick call, and hopped back in the car.

I looked at him questioningly. I was a little freaked, "What's happening?"

"Ah, sorry, just something I forgot."

Derek flipped on lights as we entered a brown shingle craftsman in the flats. I followed him into the kitchen where he stood studying the contents of the fridge.

"Wanna beer?"

"Sure." I glanced around the room. The original kitchen had been updated, walls taken down to create a dining area, and the back wall replaced with sliding glass doors opening onto a deck. Unusually neat for student housing, especially male student housing. A movement in the yard beyond the deck startled me. "Do you have housemates?"

"Yeah, three other architecture students. They're on campus. Chained to their drafting tables no doubt." Derek smiled, handed me a beer.

I tilted the bottle to my lips, took a long swallow. Then I asked, "Did you call to see if they were home?"

Derek looked at me puzzled.

"The phone call? At the pay phone?"

"Oh, that." He bit his lip.

Was that a blush? I waited for an answer.

"I thought maybe someone had come over," he finally said.

"Your girlfriend?"

"No," he said, "nothing like that."

I gave him a faint smile, took another slug of the beer.

"I thought maybe my father might stop by. Seemed like that might be a bit awkward. That's all. He's not. Coming by, that is." He shot me that smile, the one I couldn't resist. "Wanna see my room?"

I giggled and he grinned.

He wrapped an arm around my waist and led me to his attic bedroom with a wall-to-wall bed nestled against a window overlooking the bay.

He patted the corner of the bed. "Come, check out the view."

Could I do this? Carol's voice in my head said, "Do it!"

"That's quite a line." I had to admire the clever set up. "Does this usually work?"

"This does." He reached out and pulled me close until his lips touched mine in a gentle, tentative kiss. I wrapped my arms around his neck and deepened the kiss. He smiled into my eyes, slid my arms off his neck, peeled off my jacket and it hit the floor.

Yes, I could do this; I wanted to do this.

His hand explored the center of my back. His sly smile reacted to my lack of a bra.

He removed my belt, lifted my tunic over my head and eased me down next to him on the bed. His mouth crushed mine. Then he kissed his way down my body and stroked feathery soft touches on my breasts.

My nipples hardened, and a growing warmth traveled down to a yearning between my legs. His mouth followed.

Oh yeah, it definitely worked.

■ ■ ■

I'd finally satisfied Carol's nagging me to fuck someone new so I would realize there were other lovers possible. She insisted I'd get over the one who had broken my heart, and left me gun shy.

But this didn't feel right. I fought back the post-orgasmic emotions, the urge to cuddle. He was too good, too smooth, too practiced. I refused to fall for this guy just because he was a skilled lover. In fact his skill was the very thing that put me off. He was too good to be true, to be true to me that is.

A noise near the front of the house startled me. Probably his housemates were coming home. I had to get out of there. "Take me home please."

"What?" He pushed himself up on his arms and studied my face. "Now?"

"Yes."

"Is something wrong? Did I hurt you?"

"I want to go home." I turned my face to the side; I couldn't look at the hurt in his eyes. Just his ego that's hurt, I told myself. "Please, take me home."

He rolled off me. Turned his back and picked up his jeans.

I gathered my clothes from the floor and scrambled into them. Tossing on my jacket, I threw my scarf around my neck and headed for the door.

Derek followed, grabbed my arm on the landing. "Are you okay?"

"I'm fine." I pulled my arm from his grasp. The twinge of guilt for hurting his feelings didn't out weigh my fear of being hurt again. Didn't so-called liberated women understand why the sex act was called "making love"? "Look, it's not you, that was . . . nice . . . very nice . . . just, just too much for me. I'm not used to going so fast."

"Nice? That was nice? Not mind blowing? Not fab? Or even bitchin?" Derek pulled me around so that he could look in my eyes. "I'm sorry. For me, it was a lot more than nice."

I moved out of his arms, but waited while he dressed.

He held my hand; we walked down the stairs side by side. He opened the door and guided me through the opening with his arm around my waist. "One last kiss." He pulled me to him, brushed his lips across mine, nibbled on my bottom lip, and groaned, "Stay the night, please."

I wrenched away and ran down the porch stairs to the street.

There was a loud bang, a car backfire? A glimpse of a dark figure wearing a black hood, another bang, then something hit my head, slammed it hard, knocked me down, my hand to my head covered in warm fluid, sharp unbearable pain filled my skull.

Then merciful blackness closed in.

Letter to the *San Francisco Chronicle* newspaper received May 1969

PRINT THIS LETTER TOMORROW OR I WILL GO ON A KILLING SPREE ON THE STREETS OF SAN FRANCISCO AND I GUARANTEE 12 DEAD IN ONE DAY.

GOOD CLEAN HEAD SHOT

A NEW LOCK TO MY COLLECTION

WHAT the HELL IS THE MATTER WITH YOUNG GIRLS THESE DAYS? USED TO BE SOILED WOMEN HAD LITTLE CHOICE BUT TO SELL THEMSELVES. NOW THEY CALL IT FREE LOVE!

LOT OF WORK TO DO.

GOTTA PURGE THE WORLD OF THIS FILTH.

ROLL IT

SHOOT IT

MARK IT WITH Z

PUT IT IN THE OVEN

FOR BABY AND ME

ZODIAC

1

SAN FRANCISCO, MARCH 2008

My name is Alexandra Nichols, but everyone calls me Al. Even my dad.

Usually the best way to talk to my father is to visit his office in San Francisco, but that day he was totally into a case he was prosecuting soon. His secretary had done her best to stop my entrance, but I pushed past and opened the heavy oak door.

"Dad, I can't find the Zodiac file. Did your new secretary do something with it?"

"Al," my startled father looked up from the law book on his massive oak desk, "what do you want with it?"

I plopped into one of his leather guest chairs, "To look at it."

"Why?" He removed his reading glasses, studied my face.

I returned his stare, scowling at him. "Do I have to have a reason?"

"Why the sudden interest?" Dad asked, as the chime of a new email caught his attention.

He glanced at the laptop on his desk.

"I don't know . . . I had a dream a couple weeks ago, it's been coming back. Probably from you keeping that file around when I was a kid." I swung my legs over the arm of the chair trying to appear casual. If I told Dad about the nightmares that had gotten worse every night, if I said, "I'm afraid to go to sleep because I'm haunted by this terrifying image of a dark figure in a black hood," he'd be alarmed. He'd want me to "talk to someone."

Especially if I told him I woke up with blinding headaches after each of the nightmares—pain in my head that felt like half of my face had been blown off.

The dreams started my freshman year at Cal and got increasingly frequent and more intense each year. Then, last summer I paid a visit to a great aunt in Pacific Heights. I saw this kid on a bike. He was about sixteen. Strong déjà vu. My heart leapt, then fell. Something about him was familiar. He looked like some one but I couldn't think of who. I watched his dark head disappear as he rode away and my heart ached with loss. I had no clue why I reacted like that, but the dark nightmare got even worse that night.

Now, in my senior year, the headaches that followed the nightmare were so bad I often missed morning classes.

Then again, if I told him, maybe he'd stop looking at his computer and talk to me. "Hey, Dad!"

"What?" He closed the lid of his laptop and leaned back in his fancy black mesh chair.

"When I was little, I used to sit at your desk at home and pretend I was a lawyer."

"Yeah, you sure did." He smiled at the memory of his five-year old daughter playing prosecuting attorney, how I would pick up the phone and mimic his voice and attitude when talking to defense attorneys.

"That file was on your desk for years. I looked for it after dinner when I was over last night and it wasn't there." I could vaguely recall the contents of the folder; I remembered that I felt a strong connection to the incidents.

And my first totally bad headache started while I was looking at newspaper clippings included with the papers. "Mom thought you'd brought it to the office."

"Al, please, there's no need to dig all that up again. It's ancient history."

"Where is it?" I grinned at my father. He was a good guy; all my school chums were hot for him. He still had a full head of strawberry blonde hair, although it got lighter every year. He and Mom spent enough time on golf courses, tennis courts, sailboats, and ski hills to maintain his year round tan.

"I put it away. Decided it was time to get over it." He glanced at the book on his desk.

"Why?" I knew he needed to get back to work, but I persisted. "Why give up on it now after decades of obsession?"

"Don't you have classes today? A painting to work on?" He raised a blonde eyebrow at me. "What are you doing hanging around here anyway? You don't work here anymore. Summer's over."

I swung my legs off the arm of the chair, turned around, and leaned forward. "Dad, I'm like, totally serious. I want to look at your file. I'm taking a criminal anthropology class, it's a good real world example."

"Al, it's time to put all that behind us." He stood, walked to the window and studied the sailboats and ships out on the bay. "If it's a real case file you want, I'll give you one from a closed case, a real one, because that file is not an actual case file. I just collected that stuff. It was my personal file."

"What are you saying?" I joined him at the window. "Why? After all these years?"

He rested his arm on my shoulders. "Al, do you know why I was obsessed with that killer?"

"Yeah. Mom gave me the download. He killed a good friend of yours when you were in college."

"She was my best friend." He looked away, stared at a row of law books on the shelves lining his office.

I nodded, trying not to feel guilty about the sadness on his face.

"I was in my last year of law school. I'd just met your mother. My best friend was shot and killed while coming home from a date," he hesitated. "There was a guy around at that time that was killing young lovers. There was some thought that he, the Zodiac was her killer."

Dad's work dealt with killings all day long, but it was obvious that decades hadn't made this one easier for him. He turned back to the view of the bay

"So?" I would wait as long as necessary. I'd wanted to know what the deal was with this murder from the get-go.

I wasn't going to let his discomfort stop me now. "Yo, Dad tell."

"There was no evidence linking the prime Zodiac suspect to Lexi's murder. In fact there was never enough evidence to indict him for any of the cases." Dad turned around and returned to his desk chair.

"Did you think it was the Zodiac guy?" I sat on the corner of his desk.

"I never thought it was the prime suspect, this Arthur Allen, that shot Lexi."

"Who's Arthur Allen?" I asked.

"A deadbeat. A pedophile. He lived in Vallejo. He was the closest the cops ever came to arresting someone in the Zodiac case. Got warrants to search where he lived three times." Dad leaned the mesh chair back and locked his hands behind his head.

"You don't think he was the guy?"

"No."

I raised an inquiring eyebrow at my dad.

"No, there was a mountain of circumstantial evidence that linked him to the Zodiac, but the fingerprints at the scenes and the handwriting didn't match Allen's."

"Handwriting? From the notes sent to the newspaper?"

"Yeah, the Zodiac wrote these wacko letters to the *San Francisco Chronicle*."

I knit my eyebrows. "How do they know that the killer actually wrote the things?"

"The letters contained info that only the killer and the cops could've known. You know, stuff never previously released to the media."

"So this Allen guy. What was the deal? If there was no real evidence, why was he the prime suspect?"

Dad shrugged his shoulders. "He was the only suspect at the time."

"Why didn't you think he was the Zodiac?

"The reasons for suspecting him could easily have been coincidence. A lot of men wear size ten-and-a-half shoes." Dad sighed and rubbed the back of his head. "Turns out I was right. A few years ago, the FBI excluded him based on DNA tests of the saliva on the stamps of letters from the Zodiac."

"Whatta you mean . . . *at the time*, he was the only suspect?" I asked.

Dad exhaled a long sigh. "In recent years, maybe a hundred people have claimed that their father, or their stepfather, or their uncle was actually the Zodiac. It's gotten so the police don't even want to talk to anybody on the subject."

"So . . . you have theories that you've been working on. That's why you had the file, right?

"Lexi's date went missing the same night. His body was never found." Dad put hands on either side of his head and pushed back his hair. "He could've killed her."

"Yeah?" I said. "So? What about him?"

"Years went by. He never turned up."

"Why would he disappear? Did this Zodiac killer hide other victims?"

"Not that we know." Dad frowned. "There was a Jane Doe who had been moved, she was found around the same time, but police were uncertain about the linkage to other cases. There were some aspects that didn't connect, were different.

In general, his victims were shot or stabbed and left at the scene."

"Per my criminal anthro class, it's a bit weird that the same killer would use both a gun and a knife. Shooting is much less personal than stabbing. Doesn't seem like it was one guy."

Dad shrugged, pursed his lip. "Well, there ya go. Maybe the guy was schizo."

"Or maybe there was more than one Zodiac?" I studied Dad's face to see what he really thought, but he looked down at the law book and his notes. I asked anyway. "And your friend, Lexi? She was shot?"

"Yes." He glanced up at me, and then studied his hands in his lap.

Dad's pain tugged at my heart, but I had to know. "Why have you lost interest?"

He shrugged without looking up. "The prime suspect died a long time ago."

"But you didn't think he was the guy anyway."

"Al, I don't want to talk about this right now, I can't, I've got a case . . . I can't get distracted." Dad leaned over his law book. Knowing him, I figured he didn't want me to see tears in his eyes.

Conveniently for the man who didn't want to talk about the subject, his cell phone rang, and he grabbed it. "Hi! Yeah, I forgot to check with Lauren, I'll have to get back to you. Al's here. Sweetheart, say hi to your Uncle."

I called out, "Hi Uncle!" without asking which one. Dad had a group of college friends that my brother and I had always called Uncle. "Dad?"

"Hold on a sec," he said into the phone. "What?" he asked me.

"Where's the file?"

"In the safe in my study at the house."

"Can I get it?"

"Yeah, okay. Go ahead. Otherwise you'll stay here bugging me the rest of the day, huh?"

He put the phone back to his ear.

2

I loved driving the hills of San Francisco in my vintage rag top bug, but somehow it had freaked Dad out when I bought it. His reaction to my excitement when I found the right yellow fabric with red and black ladybugs to replace the torn head lining was just plain weird. Or so I thought at the time.

The distance from Dad's office to our house was only a few miles, but nearly a half hour drive in afternoon traffic.

Mom should have been home by then. She usually timed her trips to the design center to avoid rush hour traffic. She'd be surprised to see me on a Monday afternoon. I came home on Sundays to get a home cooked meal but seldom during the week.

I drove between the massive square pillars marking the entrance to Seacliff, lowered the car windows and enjoyed the briny aroma of the breezes off the ocean.

China Beach, the one beach in San Francisco safe for swimming, was below the cliff side of the house. "Safe," that is, if one was a fan of water temperatures that barely hit sixty degrees on the warmest summer day.

After my brother and I had left home for college, my parents down-sized from six thousand square feet on Pacific Heights to a four bedroom six bath Italian Renaissance villa in the only San Francisco neighborhood adjacent to the ocean and reduced household staff to day help.

Like most of the houses along the avenue, my parent's was built in the 1920's. Well-mannered lollipop trees lined the quiet street, maintaining a height blocking no house's view, and symbolizing the perfect order that marks the graceful neighborhood.

I punched in the code that opened the heavy wood planked garage door. Mom's car wasn't in the garage.

I bound up the stairs to the kitchen door, punched another code, and hurried through the kitchen and hall to Dad's antique pine paneled study. I opened the pencil drawer of his desk, pulled out a tiny box, and turned it over. On the bottom of the box was a code from which I eliminated the date of my birth, 5-25-1987, so that 5927561896847 became 97-68-64, the combination to Dad's safe.

A hinged colorful oil painted by some old friend of Dad's swung open with the touch of my finger. I used the combo, and extracted the familiar, dingy file folder. Without bothering to close the safe or the painting, I sat down in the worn leather chair that had been Dad's my entire life and opened the file.

It was in reverse chronological order with the earliest items in the back. I flipped to the bottom of the pile of papers. A newspaper clipping folded around a lock of hair caught my eye. I unfolded the dark, fragile paper and stared at a black and white photo of a young woman my age. Long blonde hair fell past her shoulders in what was meant to be her college graduation portrait.

Something in her eyes felt familiar. The headline identified the girl in the photo as Alexandra Johnson. Alexandra? Was I named for her?

I heard a noise from the front of the house. Must be Mom, but it didn't sound like the garage door opening. I heard the tinkling of breaking glass in the front of the house—.

Shit! What was that? The shrill security alarm rang.

I peeked around the edge of the doorway opening into the hall. A dark figure with a gloved hand reached through the broken pane, stretched to grasp the door handle lock, and undid the dead bolt.

I heard a voice, maybe two voices. How many were there? It wouldn't be smart to stick around to find out. On autopilot, I gathered the papers and the lock of hair off the top of the desk, stuffed them back into the file, picked it up and ran.

My car was parked in the front . . . where the break-in was occurring. That wasn't an escape option.

I bolted to the French doors that opened onto the terrace. Wisps of gray fog filled the air.

I ran across the terrace, down the steps to the garden below, and to the trail that led down the cliffs to the beach.

I scrambled down the path of the railroad tie steps, shoving aside overgrown shrubs. A manzanita branch scraped my face and neck.

A sharp, loud noise from the street above scared me into a faster pace.

If only I knew some of the neighbors, I'd know where to go for help.

But I didn't even know how to access all the wall-in houses.

The going was faster once I reached the beach but the sand hampered my run.

A glance up the side of the cliff and a glimpse of a dark figure in the mist quickened the pounding of my heart.

The tide was in. Waves broke on the jutting rocks, blocking access to the adjacent sections of the beach.

There was nowhere to go.

I shoved through tall brush and ducked into the shadows under the overhang of a stone terrace. A brisk, cold wind whipped through my hair and blew sprays of moisture off the water.

I dug my cell out of my pocket. Marginal service. I pushed the speed dial for Dad's cell. When it went immediately to voice mail, I tried Mom next.

I didn't want Mom to come home and happen on the burglars.

Another voicemail. "Mom, don't go to the house. Call the police, stay away. Burglars broke into the house. Stay away." I sent her a text: *"burglars in house."*

I dialed 9-1-1. "I need to report a break-in in progress. And I think I heard a gunshot." I gave the address. "No, I left. I'm hiding below the neighbor's deck. Please tell them to hurry."

I huddled in the cold, damp sand listening for sirens but all I could hear were waves crashing on the rocks pounding in the same rhythm as the pain in my head.

My hands shook as I tried to call Mom again, but now I had no service. I checked the time. It had been less than five minutes since I'd called for help.

I clung to the file folder, wondering why I'd brought it with me in my panic. I used the light from my phone to look at the newspaper clipping again.

My heart jumped when I saw the grainy photo of the male college student who went missing the same night that Lexi was killed. I knew him. But how could that be? Yet his face . . . it was as though I knew exactly how his face felt, the rough texture of his beard on my skin.

Whoa, Al, get real. What *are* you thinking?

I shoved the paper back into the file and stood up. I hadn't heard any sirens but I needed to go back up. Waves splashed into my damp and cold hiding place. The rising tide would soon reach me.

Uncertain as to what I would find at the top, I took my time climbing up the path. Had the bad guys left?

3

I peeked around the full growth of bushes and saw lights flashing. Relieved, I ran to the patrol car.

Two guns held in beefy hands greeted my return to my parent's house. One hand grabbed me, shoved me against the front fender of the car.

"Hey, what're you doing?" I shouted.

"What're you doin'?" Asked the uniformed officer who owned the hand.

I attempted to shake off his hand. "I'm the one who called you."

He ignored my protests as he patted me down. I assumed he was checking for a weapon. He put his hand on the file.

"Hey!" I screamed, "That's my property. Dude, what the hell do you think you are doing?"

"Do you have some identification?"

"It's in the house." I pulled away from his grasp. This time he let go. "I'll show you." I turned to go inside when I spotted Mom's car pull into the gates. "There's my mother. She lives here."

Mom stopped to let an ambulance pass her.

I watched the vehicle pull to a stop twenty feet from where we stood in the street. A cluster of officers stepped back to let EMTs through.

The group of police opened their circle. One kneeling officer stood up and moved aside. A body lay face down on the sidewalk in front of our house. Long tan legs extended from jogging shorts to end in feet clad in running shoes. Blonde hair was colored with bright red at the back of the head.

My world stood still. Who was that?

"Al, what in the—?" Mom slammed the car door then rushed to gather me in her arms. "O my god, I thought . . . maybe that was you." She hugged me so tight I had to struggle to breathe.

But I hugged her back and then waited until she wiped away tears and blew her nose before I asked, "Who is that?"

She shook her head and grabbed me again. I held her while she struggled to get a hold of herself.

Mom can be a bit emotional. My brother and I figure her protectiveness had something to do with the struggle she went through to have us, the number of miscarriages and stillborn babies she endured.

Mom showed her ID, assuring the waiting officers that I was her daughter and not a bad guy.

"Mom, do you recognize the person they're putting on the stretcher?"

"Oh, no, no, please no. I think it might be Kira, Margaret's daughter." Mom pulled her phone out, pushed buttons as we walked toward the ambulance. "Margaret? Are you home? Is Kira with you?" She paused. "Come outside."

Mom hurried to the back doors of the ambulance as the gurney was loaded. I didn't know Kira, but Mom's face and a sharp cry told me it was Margaret's daughter.

A tall blonde hurried from a walled house two doors down and rushed to where we stood. Mom reached out to squeeze her neighbor's shoulder.

"Kira." Margaret caught a sob. "Oh, oh. That's my daughter."

The EMT extended a hand, helped Margaret into the vehicle.

"Margaret, I'll call Sid." Mom assured her friend. She walked to the front of the ambulance. "I'm calling the father. What hospital?" she asked the driver.

The driver told Mom which hospital and that he would let Margaret know her husband had been called.

Mom pulled me with her to Margaret's open gate where she got Sid's cell number from the housekeeper and made the promised call.

"Will she be okay? I asked as we walked hand in hand back down the sidewalk.

Mom choked back a sob, shook her head, "The wound looked bad . . . really bad. But head wounds bleed a lot. Let's pray she'll be okay."

"Is there anything else we can do Mom?" I couldn't stand the thought of how crushing the loss of their daughter would be to Margaret and Sid.

Tears ran down Mom's cheeks. I slid my hand around her waist and held her close while I wiped away my own tears.

We entered the house with the policeman. All appeared normal until we got to Dad's study. The safe was still open. The desk and floor were strewn with papers; every drawer had been ripped from the desk and now littered the floor. Books were helter skelter below emptied shelves.

"How did they get the safe open?" Mom asked.

"I opened it." I explained what I'd done and seen.

"Do you know what they were looking for?" a policeman asked.

Mom and I both shook our heads, indicated we didn't know and were told to leave the area.

"This is part of the crime scene, ma'am. I'm sorry but you'll have to leave the premises."

"We'll wait for my husband in the back of the house." Mom told the policeman who looked dissatisfied that we were not leaving immediately.

"Is she . . . is Kira going to be okay?" I asked the officer.

He lowered his chin, shook his head slowly. "She's going to have a long recovery."

Mom flinched, sighed. My heart fell.

We went into the kitchen and called Dad. When his voice-mail answered, I called his office.

"I'm pretty sure he's on his way home," his secretary said.

I was still shaking.

Mom's trembling hands wrapped me in a cashmere throw, poured each of us a glass of Pinot Noir, and we sat in the seat of the bay window in the kitchen in silence for several minutes. Mom continued to wipe tears and her nose.

So many questions went through my mind. What was going on? Why did that photo trigger my strange reaction?

"Mom. Alexandra Johnson, I mean Lexi, and the boy . . . . man, who disappeared the night she was killed, they look familiar to me. Did you and Dad have photos of them around when I was younger?"

Mom shook her head. A scowl marred her lovely heart shaped face. "Definitely not. Your Dad didn't need any reminders."

"But yet you named me for her."

Mom looked at me. Her brown eyes studied my face for a minute as though she were deciding how much to tell me. "Yes." No explanation was offered.

"Why?" I asked.

Mom shook her head. "I always liked the name Alexandra. And your Dad . . . I guess he wanted to somehow continue Lexi's existence." She hesitated. "I don't really know. I only met Lexi once, but . . . it wasn't the name we had agreed upon, but when we saw you, well, Al just seemed right for a baby who was obviously going to grow up to be a beautiful woman. As you have." Mom gave me a weak smile, squeezed my hand.

"Lauren! Al!" Dad's voice echoed from the garage. "What the hell is going on here?" He bound up the stairs to the kitchen and pulled us into a hug. "What's with the police cars? Are you alright?" His fingers turned my face to examine the scratches from the manzanita bush. "What happened?"

We had just finished filling him in on everything we knew when a Detective Schmidt entered the kitchen and greeted

Dad. "Sir, I'm sorry. We need to seal the crime scene. Come to think of it, I'm sure you understand that." The detective referred to Dad's position as a prosecuting attorney. "Just a few questions before you leave. What would someone be looking for in your safe? Did you have valuables in there?"

Dad jumped to his feet and strode to his study. We heard his exclamation when he saw the condition of the room.

I followed him down the hall. The open safe was now empty.

"Al, what did you take from the safe?"

"Just the file we'd talked about," I said.

Dad described the missing contents of his safe, papers, documents, passports, a half dozen jewelry boxes, and a gun. He answered several more questions for the police.

"Okay, girls, grab some overnight things. We'll go to dinner and spend the night at the St. Francis. That'll give these gentlemen the chance to do whatever they need to do without us under foot."

"Do you really think that's necessary darling?" Mom's husky voice sounded much calmer than I felt, but I knew she was faking it.

"It'll take awhile to process the scene." He wrapped his arms around his trembling wife. "Plus, I don't like the idea of spending the night here with that window broken. Tomorrow we'll have it repaired and have some new locks installed."

"I could just go home after dinner, Dad, back to Berkeley."

"I'd rather you stuck with us until we know what this is all about."

"Sir, if I may," Detective Schmidt addressed Dad. "I'd like to ask Alexandra a few more questions." The detective turned to me. "You opened the safe?"

I nodded.

"Why?" he asked.

"I was looking for some papers."

"Valuable? Something the perps might have wanted?"

"I can't imagine why. It was just a file from an old case that I wanted to use for my criminal anthro class."

He studied my face for a full minute. "One of the neighbors mentioned that you bear more than a casual resemblance to the young woman who was shot—both of you being tall, slender and blonde."

"Oh shit! That's just awful."

4

After dinner with Mom and Dad in the St. Francis dining room, I crawled into the luxury hotel bed with the file folder. Even without the letter to the Chronicle, authorities had seen a connection between Lexi's murder and the Zodiac killer. Hers was just one of the 37 deaths the self-named Zodiac had claimed as his victims. And she had been killed by the same caliber of bullet as other victims also thought to be his.

He had shot and stabbed several young couples. The nutcase seemed to have a knack for spotting and attacking couples on their first date.

The police were sure he'd killed at least four women and three men. There were three more young lovers who had been wounded, but recovered, and several more unsolved cases that could have been the Zodiac's doing.

Early victims had been shot, but later the Zodiac seemed to switch between using a gun and a knife. One Jane Doe, the only one to have been moved from the primary scene, that is, from where she had been killed, was both shot and stabbed.

I flipped through horrible, gruesome photos of mutilated bodies with Z's carved into their flesh. What a sicko this Zodiac was!

Notes in Dad's handwriting and in a variety of inks, evidenced Dad going over this file on several occasions.

At dinner, Dad had asked that I give the file back, forget the whole thing.

No way was I going to do that—now I suspected somebody else wanted the file—or maybe didn't want me to have it. I wanted to know why.

But Dad wouldn't let me keep it if he thought it was dangerous. I tried a diversion. "Maybe there was something else in your safe they were after? I mean, we don't *know* they were after the file, do we?"

Dad shrugged but when we returned upstairs he left the door between our rooms ajar. "Don't hesitate to come into our room if you hear anything," Dad said as he kissed my forehead. "Sleep tight."

"Won't let the bed bugs bite," I responded and, even though my head hurt like hell, I smiled at my handsome Dad as he went into my parents' room.

I wasn't going to sleep tight, or it seemed at all. Every time I closed my eyes I saw the sickening photos of carved bodies, chests with Z's slashed through young breasts. I hated knives. The mere sight of a large, or even small, blade creeped me out.

I read through the file a second time relieved to learn that most of the carving had occurred when the victims were dead, or at least unconscious. Still I avoided the photos of the corpses.

Even the photos of the victims that had been taken before their encounter with the Zodiac made me feel heavy with
grief. They were all so young. And beautiful. Except for the
taxi driver.

I guess I fell asleep during my third time through the
file. I woke with a start to find my face on top of scattered
papers.

A noise, I thought a noise had woken me. Someone was
jiggling the handle of the hotel room door.

"Who is it?" I asked, "Dad?"

No answer.

The door opened two inches, caught on the chain.

Panic hit me. I grabbed the folder and was across the room
before I realized I'd left pages on the bed.

I turned, scrambled to pick up papers. But then lock cutters
appeared in the open crack, the door opened into the room.

I dropped everything, dashed to the door connecting to
my parent's room. I ran into their room, slammed the connecting door closed, and pounced on their bed.

"Dad! Somebody's opened my door."

Dad leaned over, picked up the phone on the nightstand,
and pushed a button. "I need hotel security."

He jumped out of bed, rushed to each door, flipped the
dead bolts, and attached the security chains. He picked up the
phone, "Someone has broken into our connecting room."

As soon as Dad came back to the bed, I fell between my
parents. Mom put her arms around me. Dad put his arms
around both of us. "Security is on the way up."

We waited. Sounds of movement next door grew louder.

Dad responded to a knock on the hall door. "Who is it?"

"Hotel Security, sir. Could you please look at the room? See if anything is missing?"

Dad and I opened the connecting door and looked into the room.

"Did you move the papers that were on the bed?" I asked hopefully.

"No ma'am."

I saw a few sheets of paper scattered on the floor and sticking out from beneath the bed. My overnight bag that I'd brought from Mom and Dad's was upside down, my clothes strewn across the floor.

The file folder was gone.

5

After Detective Schmidt left and Mom had dozed off, I asked, "What's going on here, Dad? Who took your file?"

"Al, your guess is as good as mine. I really have no idea why the sudden interest in that file after all these years."

"Why did you put it away?"

"It seemed hopeless. There's no new evidence and the killer might've died by now." Dad was silent for a moment, then he said, "I was ready to move on."

I slept next to my mother that night while Dad sat guard in the armchair.

I awoke to the sounds of lowered voices talking in the bathroom.

"Take Al to your father's for awhile," Dad said. "He'll be happy to put on extra security at his estate."

"Sweetheart, do you think we're in danger?"

"I don't know. I have a bad feeling."

"What about you? And Steven? Are you two safe?" Mom's quavering voice gave away her fear for her husband and son.

"I have no idea, but I can't walk away from this case—you know my office has been prepping it for months."

"Don't you think we're safe here, in the hotel?" Mom asked.

"After last night?" he reminded her, "Did you notice the break into Al's room? And Kira was shot in front of our house!"

"Maybe we should tell the kids," Mom said.

"No."

"They aren't children anymore. They can handle it."

"What would be the point?" Dad said. I'd never heard Dad take such a serious tone with his adored wife.

"Are you never going to tell them?" Mom was totally serious too.

"Maybe not."

I couldn't take anymore; I had to let them know I could hear every word. And I had to know what the hell they were talking about. "Yo. Dudes. Parents, I can hear you."

Dad came out of the bathroom, shirtless but fully dressed from the waist down, wiping his face with a towel. "Good morning sweetheart."

"Dad, what're you maybe never gonna tell us?"

He ignored my question. "You and Mom are going to spend a few days with Grandpa."

"Dad, I have classes. This is my last semester—I can't miss my seminars." I scowled at my father to let him know I was serious. "I'm not a child. Don't order me around."

"Al, I'm worried about your safety." He buttoned his pale blue oxford shirt.

"Why me? What about you?"

"Because you've had two run-ins with somebody. And because of Kira."

"Don't you think that could've been a coincidence?" I really did not want to think I had been the real target.

Dad shook his head.

"But now they have the file . . . so that's probably the end of it. Don't you think?"

"I don't know what to think, but I don't want to worry about you." He straightened his tie and put on a navy blue blazer. "I gotta run. Gotta be in court this morning." He leaned over to kiss my scowling face. "Love ya, kiddo."

"Da-a-ad! You're leaving? Wait, you haven't told me."

"Bye." He closed the door.

"Mom? Are you ever coming out of there?" I whined.

My mother stuck her head around the edge of the door. "Only if you promise not to torture me into telling you something I can't." She came into the room, her slender body wrapped in a towel.

"Don't be a bitch." I said without thinking.

Mom's brown eyes filled with hurt. "You can call your friends that, not your mother."

The pain on her face brought a sinking sensation to my chest. My mother was such a sweetheart. Caring, loving. I felt like a shit.

"Oh, Mama, I'm sorry." I reached out to wrap my arms around her, but she brushed past me.

She shook her head. "That's not a term of endearment, not in my generation." She brushed something, maybe a tear off her cheek, and hurried into her clothes. "And don't think you can sweet talk me after that."

I knew that tone. Not a chance I would get one hint out of her. I jumped out of the bed. "I have to get to class. Can you drop me?"

"Your dad wants us to go to Grandpa's."

"Not happening," I yelled back at her as I dashed into the adjoining room and into my clothes. I peeked under the bed to look for stray items from Dad's Zodiac file, stretched to pick up a few sheets of paper. Whoever they were, they'd missed a few.

"Can we stop to get coffee?" I yelled into the next room.

"You don't have time for room service?"

"No way."

"Grandpa's?" Mom jammed nightclothes into an overnight bag.

"Definitely not."

She sighed in reaction as she retrieved Dad's pj's from the bathroom floor.

"But your father . . ." Mom said as she emerged from the bathroom. "Please listen to me. You know how difficult . . . Your dad gets grouchy while he's trying a case."

She paused for a moment waiting for a response. When she didn't get one, she tried a different tact. "Whenever I even imagine that you or your brother might be hurt, a pain shoots through my body as though your bodies are still part of mine."

I'd heard about that pain before, but I was doing my best to avoid the reacting guilt.

"Let's go." I stood in her room with my book bag in my arms.

6

We headed over the bay bridge to Berkeley and up Ashby to get coffee.

"Mom, you aren't gonna tell me?"

"What?'

"You know what."

"No." She turned her head briefly to smile at me. "You're right. I'm not. Peet's coffee?"

"Fine." I folded my arms and slunk down in my seat.

I looked at my mother. She appeared to be fragile. In fact, she was tough, a tigress devoted to her family, her charities, and to her children. Her children went way beyond my brother and I to include numerous underprivileged young people whom she had taken under her wing with both emotional and financial support.

Mom turned left below the Claremont Hotel, double-parked on Domingo Avenue and remained in the car, I ran in for coffee and two whole-wheat scones. I absentmindedly watched the traffic out the window while I waited for the coffees.

A blue econo-van pulled around mom's Lexus.

I carried the coffee to the condiments counter and put cream and sweetener in both. When I turned around I saw the same blue van behind Mom's car. Must've been circling the block, looking for a parking place no doubt. Berkeley totally has a parking shortage.

I handed a coffee in to Mom via the driver's side window and climbed into the passenger seat. "Drop me at Bancroft and Telegraph please?" I checked the clock in the dash. "I'm barely gonna make my class."

She nodded, put her coffee and scone in the cup holder, and sped up. "I wish you would consider coming to grand-pa's." She glanced at my face. "What if I waited until after your class?"

"I have three classes and a meeting today. I don't get why Dad . . ." I wasn't sure how to describe Dad's attitude.

"He wants to know you're safe."

"But I don't get what he's worried about. Somebody wanted the file. They got it. End of story. Kira looking like me was just a coincidence. I'm sorry about what happened to her. Unfortunately, it seems she was in the wrong place at the wrong time. Or maybe they shot her because she saw who it was."

"Al, have a little compassion for your dad. He worries."

"He worries more lately."

"I think it's because you're in the end of your senior year."

"And what? He's worried about what I'm going to do next?"

"No," Mom hesitated. Sighed. "I think it has to do with his friend who died. In the spring of her senior year."

"So?"

"You remind him of her, always have."

"That's not my fault," I paused for a moment. "If I went to Grandpa's, would you tell me what you and Dad were talking about this morning?"

She grimaced and shook her head

"Stop here." I waved at the empty loading zone across the lawn from Sproul Hall.

Mom pulled up to the curb and leaned over to give me a kiss. "Turn your phone on whenever you're not in class, please."

"Sure. See ya tomorrow." I kissed her and gathered my books. "I'll pick up my car and my bag from your house in the evening. You'll be home?"

"Of course, especially if you are coming over. But please have your brother bring you." She leaned across the car and smiled at me. "Love you."

"Love you, too."

"Love you more."

I hurried through Sproul Plaza turning once to see Mom drive away.

Oh no. I was sure it was the same blue van. Right behind her.

7

I speed dialed her cell as I rushed to class. Voicemail. Probably buried in her purse.

I made it to Wheeler Aud, slid into a seat and called Dad's cell. Voicemail. Shit. He's in court. I tried Mom again.

The van probably didn't mean anything, a coincidence, but I didn't like it.

Damn, Mom, answer your fucking phone. I left a message. "Mom, there's a blue van following you. I saw it in front of Peet's and again after you dropped me off. Don't go home. Drive to dad's office, to the underground parking and valet. Don't be alone when you get out of that car." God, I wished Mom would text.

The dude next to me gave me a look. The lecture started, but I couldn't concentrate on what the prof said.

Shit, maybe Dad was right, maybe there was some danger. I checked the time. Dad would be on lunch recess in two hours. I could catch him then. But what could I do about Mom?

I slipped out of the auditorium, into the vestibule and called Dad's office. As I listened to the phone ring, I remembered his new secretary, the not-so-bright one. Shit, shit. She'd be no help.

I tried Mom again. Same voicemail.

I went through my speed dial and hit Uncle Dave's number. Another voicemail. Got Mom's friend Carol's voicemail next. I sent texts to all of them, but that gang never checked them. I was pretty sure Mom didn't even know how.

I headed for the bus stop. I could take BART to the city. If luck was with me, I might beat Mom to the house. If it turned out to be a false alarm, I could pick up my car and head back to campus. At worst, I'd miss one class.

What the hell was this all about?

After I'd climbed aboard the bus I realized I could call the policeman who had been at the house the day before and at the hotel. What the hell was his name? Schmidt? I called information and was connected to the SFPD. Eventually I was put through to Schmidt's cell. Turned out he was at my parent's house.

"I think someone is following my mother's car. I hope she's headed home to change, or maybe pack. How long are you gonna be there? Can you wait for her?" I asked.

"Does this have something to do with the case your father is trying?"

"What?"

"The homicide case, the Giacometti case?" Detective Schmidt said.

Maybe that was what Dad was worried about. Had he been threatened?

"Did my father ask for protection for his family?" I said.

"I wouldn't know." He coughed, cleared his throat. "But I'll wait for your mother."

I pushed past two bus surfers, and got off the bus at the next stop. I ran back up the hill to campus, and re-entered the lecture hall just in time to hear the prof say good day. I looked around the room for a friend I could beg notes off.

"I'll catch the next one. Promise." I patted my friend on the shoulder.

We headed to the student center and copied the notes. I checked my email, and called my mother every ten minutes without a response. At eleven forty five, I called Schmidt again. "Is she there?"

"Not yet."

I started the walk to my next class as the Campanile bells pealed "Ragtime". I waited outside the door until noon to try Dad again. No answer. I tried the hotel on the off chance she had reason to return there, but the front desk said that she hadn't.

I sat in class forcing myself to listen. At twelve forty, my phone, the one I'd failed to silence, rang. A glance at the screen showed my father's number. I ran for the door.

"Dad, Dad, do you know where Mom is?"

"You aren't with her?"

"No. I, uh—"

"Goddamnit Al! I told you both to go to Grandpa's."

"Dad, does this have something to do with the case you're on?"

"Al, I'm sending your brother to pick you up. Meet him in front of Kroeber Hall in ten minutes. I want you both in my office in under an hour. I have to see you before I head back to court."

"What about Mom?"

"I'm on it."

8

Steven was seldom prompt so I knew I would be waiting for a while. He often got waylaid by some girl. With his preppie good looks, crystal blue eyes and sun bleached blonde hair, girls hovered around him like moths around a porch light.

I sat on a bench waiting for Steven to drive up on Bancroft and noticed the air had turned cold. I stuck my hands in my jacket pockets and found a wad of papers—the papers from under the hotel bed.

There was a newspaper clipping with the photo of the familiar looking dude, a note in Dad's handwriting, an autopsy report, a letter addressed to Dad—wait, this letter wasn't part of the file. It had this year's date on it. Where had this letter come from? Had I shoved it into the file off Dad's desktop?

I scanned through the text of the letter. Couched in legalese—a threat. A threat to Dad's family.

Oh God where was Mom?

And then it dawned on me. Maybe I knew what was going on.

My hands shook as I punched Dad's speed dial number. "Dad, why didn't you tell us? Goddamn, Mom knew. Steven and I have to go get her."

"Al, not on the phone! Just follow my instructions."

"Dad, they'll kill her."

"Not on the phone," he snapped. "Your line is not secure. Hang up. Turn off the phone. Throw it in a trash can."

"Forget it Dad!" I turned off the phone.

I spotted Steven's car at the curb and raced across the lawn. We had to hurry.

Twenty feet to go to the car, I heard a shot whiz by my ear. I threw myself to the ground.

9

My brother leaned on the car horn with one hand and threw his other arm in the air. "What the hell?" he yelled. He leaned across the passenger seat to open the door.

Spitting mud and grass, I raised myself to my elbows. Without success, I scanned the traffic to see if I could spot the blue van. I searched the windows of the buildings opposite the lawn. No sign of a shooter. I scrambled to my feet, dashed in a crouch for the car.

"What the fuck?" Steven reached over to brush dirt and blades of lawn from my jacket. "What was that about?"

"Get outa here fast!" I yelled.

Steven jerked the steering wheel, punched the gas and forced his way into the stream of traffic to the tune of screeched brakes, honked horns, and screamed expletives.

"Someone shot at me," I said, my heart pounding to break out of my chest.

"With a gun?" Steven's look clearly said that he thought I was up to what he sees as my usual drama queen antics. I'm really not a DQ, but Steven is so damn mellow about everything he makes me look, well, dramatic.

"I didn't hear a gunshot," he said.

"Well, I fucking felt it go whizzing past my head." I wasn't dramatizing. "Where are you going?" I asked as he sped down University Avenue.

"Dad wants us to meet him in the courthouse, in a conference room."

"We have to get Mom. Dad can wait."

"Where do we go?" Steven pulled the car to the curb in front of a shop that sold Indian Saris.

"Head for the city." I punched numbers into my phone to call Detective Schmidt. "Has my mother showed up yet?"

"I take it this is Miss Nichols," the detective answered. "No sign of her."

"She's been kidnapped. Put out an all points bulletin or whatever you call it for a blue van, royal blue econovan with white scrapes on the passenger's side and for my mother's silver Lexus. Steven, do you know Mom's license plate?"

Steven shook his head. He wove around stoned, meandering drivers headed down University Avenue.

"Hold on young lady," the detective's voice grew snappish. "What makes you think she's been kidnapped?"

"My father has received threats," I sucked in a deep breath, exhaled. "I have a copy of a threatening letter he got."

"Your father hasn't reported any such thing, hasn't asked for protection."

"Look, I don't know what the hell is the matter with my father," I yelled into the phone. "But my mother is in danger. Seriously. And someone just took a shot at me."

"What?" That got his attention. "Where?"

"On the Berkeley campus. In front of Kroeber Hall."

"Did campus security notify the police?"

"I don't know if security is aware—"

"Don't tell me you left the scene?" the detective said in a voice heavy with annoyance.

"Of course I left the fucking scene—my mother is—are you gonna help me or not?"

"I'll arrange for your mother to be located. I need you to go back to where you were shot at and show the police where it happened."

"My father wants my brother and me to meet him before he has to go back into court. We're headed to the city."

Steven drove onto the overpass headed for the freeway and the bay bridge. Ahead of us the choppy water of the San Francisco Bay gleamed with afternoon sun but a threatening bank of fog hung out past the Golden Gate.

"Someone is liable to pick up that bullet. That is, if it didn't hit someone." Detective Schmidt's tone of voice indicated patience wearing thin.

"Oh, you're right. Steven, turn the car around." I twirled my hand in a circular motion. "Detective, I need to call my father. Can you go see him before he goes back to court?"

"I'm headed over there, to him. Come to think of it, I'll have an officer from the Berkeley PD meet you outside Kroeber Hall."

Steven shot past the freeway entrance, turned into the Berkeley Marina and flipped a U in the hotel parking lot. For once, midday traffic going up to the campus was light, but in my adrenalin pumped state every second seemed an hour.

I pushed the speed dial for my dad.

"Al, goddamn, I told you to get rid of that phone."

"Huh, yeah, before I got a chance to do that," I paused, "someone shot at me."

I heard his intake of breath. "What?" Dad said.

"I spoke with Detective Schmidt, you know the detective from the house—"

"I know Detective Schmidt," Dad said in his no nonsense tone.

"He said I have to show the Berkeley PD where the shots were fired. Steven's driving us back to campus."

An exasperated, heaving sigh greeted this news.

"Dad?"

"As soon as you've done that, you and Steven are to go directly to your grandfather's. Do you understand me?"

"I do, I do understand, but Dad, I want to help Detective Schmidt find Mom."

"Let me speak to your brother."

"Dad," I continued, "you have to tell me what you know about this. I found the letter."

"The letter?"

"The one that threatens your wife and children if you—"

"Al!" Dad shouted. "We are NOT, not going to have this conversation over a cell phone."

"Fine, then you can just talk to the detective about it. He's on his way to see you." I punched end just as Steven pulled the car up in front of Kroeber hall.

My brother grabbed my arm as I opened the door. "You really were shot at?" He looked freaked, his face paled beneath his tan.

"Yes, I told you." I shook my head and rolled my eyes.

Two police cars were at the curb, four officers and two campus security guards stood in a circle.

I told them everything I knew. A notch out of a tree trunk inches above the height of my head clued the location of the bullet in the flowerbed three feet beyond the tree. A second bullet was dug out of the dirt less than a foot away from the first. Trajectory had all the officers looking at the second floor windows across the street.

After I promised to come to the station the next day to sign a statement, I climbed back into my brother's jeep.

"Where to now?" Steven failed to suppress a nervous grin. "I'm guessing not Grandpa's."

"I've been trying to reach," I took a breath, "Aunt Carol. She's not answering, thought she might know what Mom had planned for the day." I sat in the front seat of Steven's jeep hugging my knees, wondering what we could do next.

I dialed Detective Schmidt who snapped that he would certainly let me know if our mother were located and joined our father in demanding we await his call in a safe location such as our grandfather's estate. I didn't relay his orders to Steven.

"Well, we can't stay parked in this red zone forever. Your cop friends might lose patience eventually." Steven raised both eyebrows in my direction. "So?"

"Let's try Carol's studio."

Steven pulled away from the curb with less urgency this time. "You know what this is about?" he asked.

"Either the trial Dad's prosecuting . . . or the Zodiac. Maybe there's a connection."

"What's Dad prosecuting?" Steven asked.

I shrugged. "Did he tell you anything about that case? Even when I work in his office over summer break, he's very secretive until after the verdict. He never tells me anything about his cases."

Steven shook his head. "Me neither." He changed lanes. "Why do you think this could have anything to do with the Zodiac?"

I explained about the file and yesterday's events.

"You read Dad's file on the Zodiac?" Steven asked.

"Yeah."

"Any mention of anyone else Dad knows in that file?"

"All Dad's college friends. Carol, Mom, Dad, Dave, Ron, Suzy, Tom, Elliott, and Jamie were all interviewed in connection with his friend Alexandra's murder."

"Who knew you were looking for the file?"

"Dad, Dad's new secretary . . ."

"Nobody else?"

I thought back to the previous afternoon. "Dad was on the phone as I was leaving, he had me say good-bye to an uncle."

"Which one?"

I shook my head. "I don't know, I just yelled out hello and hurried out of Dad's office before he changed his mind about letting me get the file."

"Dad can tell us."

"When he gets out of court." I rubbed my arms.

"You're shivering. Are you cold?" Steven asked.

"A little. Mostly nervous." I clenched my teeth together in an effort to stop them chattering.

Steven looked at the lightweight jacket I'd tossed over my T-shirt. He turned on the car heater. "Got a warmer jacket with you?" He nodded at my backpack.

"No."

He stopped at a signal, took off his pea coat, and placed it around my shoulders. "Are you okay?"

I nodded, but didn't relax my bite.

Steven turned the car around again.

"Where are you going?" I muttered.

"To your house, to get you warmer clothes."

We weren't far from my house on Piedmont Avenue, and a warm jacket that fit me would be good. I slunk down in the seat and pulled the pea coat tighter feeling the scratch of the wool on my neck.

I knew I wasn't thinking straight. Or at all. My mind kept going blank, but one wild thought persisted.

"Do you think one of our so-called uncles could've been the Zodiac killer?" I muttered through clenched teeth. My body was really shaking now.

"Na-ah." Steven shook his head, rolled his eyes as if to say, 'here goes the drama again.' "Where did that come from? That's nuts."

"What . . ." I took a huge breath and exhaled before continuing. "What makes you so sure?"

"For one thing, there's that guy that the police thought was the killer, but they couldn't prove it. What was his name? Allen?"

"Arthur Allen." I supplied.

"Yeah, him." Steven brought the car to a halt while a stream of students crossed the street; he turned his head and studied me. "Are you okay? You aren't going into shock, or something are you?" He held out a bottle of water and insisted I take a swallow.

I ignored his question. How the hell was I supposed to know what going into shock felt like? But then, how did I know it was a bullet that went whizzing past my ear? "DNA evidence from the stamps on the Zodiac letters didn't match Allen."

"Don't you think the fact that the killings ended in the seventies would indicate that the guy died?" Steven pointed out.

"Or went to prison for something else?" I said.

"Yeah . . . neither of which would apply to any of our uncles," he said. "As Dad would say, you're barking up the wrong tree with this uncle business."

I shook my head. "No, guess not." My hand continued to tremble as I dug my house keys out of my jean's pocket when Steven pulled his car into the driveway of my house.

"Hold on. I'm coming with you." Steven turned off the car.

I was relieved. Not because I thought bad dudes might be waiting inside, but because the house mascot, a ten foot tall taxidermied grizzly bear, that stood in the curve of the staircase, freaked me out every time I ran past him and up the stairs. The knit Cal cap, the blue and gold striped scarf, and letterman's sweater my housemates had dressed the monster in did nothing to alleviate my fear of his mouthful of sharp teeth and his ginormous paws.

My six-foot tall brother stood at the base of the stairs, dwarfed by the giant bear, but not intimidated. "Hey Oski, ole buddy, how ya doin'?" Steven pulled a play punch at the stuffed creature. "Sis, want me to come up there with ya?"

"I'm okay." Once I got past the grizzly, I was fine. My housemates were all on campus, in class or the library. The house would remain empty and quiet until dinnertime.

In my sun porch bedroom, I tore off my grass and mud splattered jeans, T-shirt and jacket, pulled on clean jeans, a turtleneck, sweater, and down jacket, shoved the papers into my pocket, and swept a brush through my blonde mane. A quick swipe with the electric toothbrush and I was ready to go again.

Ignoring the fucking bear, I ran down the stairs with my attention on my brother. "Carol can tell us about the dudes, our so called uncles, what they were like when they were young. I've always had the idea that Mom wasn't totally crazy about all of them, like she didn't think they were the greatest buds for Dad."

Steven gave me a questioning look. "Really? Wow, that's fuckin' weird. I thought they were everyone of'em real good friends. Come on, those uncles practically raised us." Steven checked the lock on the door as he pulled it closed behind us.

My brother opened the car door for me. When he climbed into the driver seat, I continued. "Mom and Carol are good friends. And we spent a lot of our childhood at her house. But didn't you ever notice that Mom never sent us off by ourselves with certain of the men?"

"Never paid much attention to that." Steven looked at me with surprise in his eyes.

"Well, Uncle Elliott and his wife Nancy were allowed to take us on outings along with their kids. Ron, Jamie, and Tom never took us anywhere unless Mom and Dad were along."

"Maybe they didn't want to take kids without some help."

"No, Mom would discreetly shake her head at Dad and the plans would change to include the whole family."

"You think Mom didn't trust them? Probably just thought they were too careless to be trusted with kids." Steven said.

"They *were* a bunch of druggies." I announced to my brother. But I was already thinking about something else, remembering what had happened yesterday afternoon at my parent's house.

"Did you ever see them doin' drugs? They wouldn't do that in front of kids." Steven said as he drove up the hill on the road that wound around the gleaming white wedding cake buildings of the Claremont Hotel.

"Al, are you crying?" Steven pulled the car off the road to study my tear-streaked face.

"Steven, I think . . . I might be the reason that Kira was shot."

"What?" He handed me a box of tissues. "How do you figure?"

"Clearly I was the intended target. She was shot because she looks like me."

"You don't know that."

"Bro, I'm still being shot at." I blew my nose. "This is all my fault. If I hadn't been stubborn, make that obsessed about the file; I wouldn't have brought on this hell. And I was not very nice to Mom. Oh shit, what if . . . I can't stand the thought that the last time I saw my mother, I was rude to her." I paused for a moment. "I don't even understand my compulsion to find out the truth about this Zodiac."

"Al, get real. How the hell were you supposed to know what would happen? Give it up." Steven pulled into an opening in the line of cars snaking up the curved road.

When we reached the Bay Bridge, I tried Aunt Carol's number again.

"Al, what the fuck is going on?" Carol answered. "I've been trying to reach your mother. She was supposed to meet me for lunch, but she never showed. And I just noticed your voicemails."

"Hey, Carol, I think Mom's been kidnapped."

"Sh-i-i-t," a whisper followed by silence.

"Carol?" I said. "Are you there?"

"Yeah," she answered. "What's this about?"

"Where are you? Can we meet you someplace?" I asked.

"My studio, I'm headed there now."

10

"You know how to get to Carol's studio?" I asked Steven.

He nodded. He pulled off the freeway at the first exit past the bay bridge, drove over the steel grating of a metal drawbridge, and headed for her warehouse studio in India Basin. "Are you still cold?" he asked.

"Just nervous." My teeth were chattering again. "I wish I knew what to do."

"What's the deal with this letter you found?"

"It's from a law firm," I pulled the wrinkled paper from my pocket, and read the names on the letterhead, "From Spegal, Thompson, and Bloodworth. The text sounds like thinly veiled death threats if Dad should release certain information regarding an investigation—"

"Why would a law firm write a letter threatening anything other than legal action?" Steven interjected.

"How should I know?" I snapped, and then felt like a shit. Especially since Steven had been so considerate. I really had to stop being a bitch to my family.

"What does it say exactly?" Steven kept his cool. "What do you think are threats?"

I read a sentence from the middle paragraph. "As the aforementioned holder of such information, as you value the health and well being of your wife and daughter, take precautions to ensure the confidentiality of any information in connection with said investigation. Failure to maintain confidentiality of the materials in your possession will cause our client to take the necessary steps to violate any agreement as to the safety of your family." I turned my head and grimaced at Steven. "Whadda ya think Bro? Sounds pretty threatening to me."

"Okay. Fuck. Yeah." Cool went out the window. The frown on Steven's face deepened. He rubbed his forehead as he glared at the road ahead. "Try Dad's cell again."

I pushed the speed dial with the same resulting voicemail as the last time I'd dialed him.

Steven pulled the vehicle into the parking lot of the sample shop below Carol's fashion design studio. As soon as the car stopped, I opened my door and headed up the stairs. Carol, tension visible in her face in spite of the botox, greeted me with a hug.

Steven dialed his phone as he climbed the flight of steps. "Dad, we're at Carol's studio. Al is freaking out. We can't any of us reach Mom. Please call back as soon as you get this message. We don't know what to do." He pushed past racks of beaded chiffon gowns, paisley multi-hued scarves, tiered gypsy skirts, velvet jackets, bell-bottomed pants, and threw himself onto the tufted leather chair in the window alcove. He continued to dial the phone leaving voicemails and messages at every number he had for Dad.

Carol led me over to the chair across from Steven's and sat down with me. She flung one arm over my shoulders while her free hand brushed unnaturally black hair back from her flaw-less, pale face. "Okay, you two, fill me in."

I pulled the letter from my jacket pocket, put it in her hand and waited while she read it.

When she looked up at me with a puzzled expression, I explained as much as I knew about what had happened in the last twenty-four hours. I was halfway through my explanation when she stood and began to pace the hun-dred-foot long concrete floor. As soon as I quit speaking, she walked over to the offices at the end of the space and told her staff, all except her assistant, to take the rest of the day off.

"What's this cop's name?" Carol asked pulling an iPhone from her pocket.

"Schmidt." I answered. "Detective Schmidt. Here's his number." I held up my phone.

"Detective Schmidt?" Carol asked into her cell. "This is Carol Huntington, I'm a close friend of Lauren Nichols and her family. I'm here with her children. Do you have any—" Carol stopped speaking. "I see. Yes, please do keep us in-formed." She collapsed next to me on the tufted black leather. "Nothing new."

No one spoke for a few minutes.

"When did you eat last? How about some tea?" Carol walked over to her office where her assistant was loading a purse with phone and items from a desktop. "Barb, get us some tea please."

We sipped steaming green tea in silence.

"How about showing me where you got shot at?" Carol suggested.

"What good would that do?" Steven said.

"Well, it's better than sitting here, doing nothing. I'll drive, just in case someone is following your car." Carol said. "Maybe we can spot something the Berkeley PD wouldn't recognize as a clue."

"Carol, I was hoping you would tell us about Dad's college friends—what they were like back in the day." I said. Now that the adrenalin had eased up, dread swept over me at the thought of returning to that lawn. Not to mention how tired I was.

Carol grimaced, stared at me without answering.

Steven explained. "You see, Al has a theory that all of this has to do with the Zodiac case."

Carol paled and looked away.

I remembered that the girl who was killed was a close friend of Carol's. And now another close friend of hers was missing. Carol was tough, a formidable businesswoman, but this had to be the last thing she wanted to discuss.

I pressed forward anyway. "I think, make that I *know* there is a connection between Mom's disappearance and what happened to your friend in 1969. Someone is very afraid of being found out, that someone has to be connected to Dad in some way. The only person besides Dad who knew I was interested in his file on the Zodiac killer was whichever

Uncle," I used my fingers to mime quotation marks around "uncle", " was on the phone with Dad when I was in his office. He could've heard that I was getting the file out of the safe. He would've been the only other person who knew I was after the file."

"You want me to tell you about your father's friends?" Carol asked.

"Yes."

"I really didn't know them well at the time. I was Lexi's friend since nursery school. She and Jeff needed another housemate. There was a fire where I was living and Lexi recruited me to move in with them."

"How did Lexi and my dad know each other?"

"They were great pals, best friends. They had been counselors together at summer camp as high schoolers, at a place on the lake where they'd been campers while in grammar school. Lexi taught arts and crafts, Jeff tennis and golf."

"So you didn't know my dad until you moved in?" Steven asked.

"Oh, we'd met several times over the years before then."

"What about his friends?" I asked.

"I knew *about* them, and I'd met them on a few occasions."

I raised an eyebrow at her. "About them?"

"Lexi talked about them. And a couple of them, especially Jamie, were rather infamous. Big man on campus types."

"How's that?"

"Jamie," Carol sighed, "Jamie was killer good looking, outrageously charming and self-confident, and Rich with a capital R. He'd been to all the right prep schools, traveled extensively.

He was way more sophisticated than most Cal students, not to mention that half of the buildings on the campus were named after of his family."

I thought about "Uncle" Jamie, he was still killer good-looking, charming, and sophisticated. And totally dedicated to making the world a better place—hardly a playboy, he had been married for decades. And no way a killer. At least, it didn't seem likely.

"What about Uncle Dave?" I asked.

"Now Dave was practically the opposite of Jamie." Carol hesitated, "Oh, he was good-looking too, in a way less well groomed way."

That's funny, because now Uncle Dave is always meticulously groomed, his dark hair perfectly cut and styled, his slim body stylishly dressed, and he is widely traveled—in his own jet.

Carol noticed my doubtful reaction. "He's maybe changed the most of any of them." She looked at me thoughtfully. "Funny thing about Dave, I never got a sex vibe from him." Carol grimaced. "And, you may not believe it, but I used to get plenty of attention."

"I'm sure you did. You're hot." I wasn't being polite; my aunt Carol was amazingly attractive.

"For an old lady." She smiled at me.

"Hot for any age," Steven said.

She was still slender, dark haired with a perfect smile, and with enough bucks to have regular botox and whatever else including veneers plus her personal trainer in her at-home gym. She'd be hot into her nineties.

"Whatever. Back to Dave, he's like asexual. Not gay, not straight. No girlfriends, no boy toys. But he and I never hit it off even platonically." Carol stood, paced. "You know, I've got a photo album around here somewhere, shots taken at a party shortly after I moved into the house."

Carol bellowed toward her assistant's desk who was still packing her tote to leave, "Barb, where's that album we used for the Fall Collection? Get it out will ya?" Her attention returned to Steven and me. "Dave and your father Jeff were the poor boys in the clique. I shouldn't put it that way. Dave only wanted to be part of the clique. The others never actually took to him. Dave was driven, ambitious without limit. Obviously tired of being poor. Hanging with rich people can do that to ya."

"My dad wasn't ambitious?" Steven asked.

"In a different way, in a want-to-make-a-mark-on-the-world kind of way. And, frankly, marrying your mother made money less of an issue."

Steven looked at Carol with surprise. "Were all the rest of 'em rich?"

Barb handed a purple leather album to Carol. The mostly black and white photos inside had yellowed with age.

Carol opened to a page in the center. A large colorful group shot showed smiling faces of my dad, five of my uncles, Carol, and Lexi all jammed together on a worn sofa, all eight hamming it up for the camera. Lexi and Carol were seated in the middle, surrounded by young men three to a side. The girl's mini skirts showed off svelte legs. Their heads leaning together contrasted Carol's long dark hair with Lexi's blonde cascading tresses.

On the far left, Jamie's slender elegance draped over a thick sofa arm. At the opposite end, Ron's lanky frame mimicked Jamie's insouciant lounge. Next to Jamie, Dad grinned, his strawberry blonde hair tousled and longer than I'd ever seen it. Towards the center, Tom's arm draped over the shoulders of both girls. On the other side of Lexi, Dave did indeed look less meticulously groomed, his hair long and as messy as Dad's. In contrast to the rest of the group, Elliott looked stiff and uncomfortable. He never had learned not to try too hard.

"Wow, amazing album Carol." I looked at her wondering who keeps an album of their druggie college days in her office.

Carol blushed, "I use the photos of that time for inspiration." She looked at me, challenging me to say something more about her album.

When I was quiet, she admitted she had built her career on the elegant bohemian look adapted by the wealthy hippies of San Francisco. There was something about the carefree self confidence, the "coolness" of the young rich that still sold like hotcakes to those less self assured.

"May I have a copy of this photo?" I asked. "Please."

Carol slipped the corners of the 8 x 10 from the black guards that held it in the album. "Barb, copy this please." Carol stood, picked up her coat. "Can we go then? Before rush hour?"

"I want to know everything you can tell me about the people in the photo," I said.

"I promise to tell all—in the car, on the way." Carol slipped a cropped sable jacket on over her jeans.

Barb returned with the photo. I clutched it to me. I was convinced someone in that photo knew where my mother was.

11

We loaded into Carol's Jag; I sat next to Carol so that I could pump her for info.

"So we covered Jamie, and Dad's next in the photo, then there's Tom and Elliott, were they both rich?"

"Elliott, yes. He and Tom both came from upper middle class backgrounds, prep school, professional parents, fathers were doctors—surgeons maybe, I'm a little vague on those details. But the one thing I know was that Tom came from an old family, early San Francisco money. No longer lots of dough—but enough."

I looked at Tom in the photo. He was good-looking, only slightly shaggy light brown hair gently curling around his ears, wearing cowboy boots. He was tall enough to keep his arm on the girl's shoulders and still slouch low in the seat.

Carol took a quick glance at the boy, Tom, who sat next to her on the sofa. "Well connected, knew everybody who mattered, attended the right kind of deb balls—in those days there were "wrong" ones, can you believe it? That world seems so strange now."

It was almost painful to look at Elliott's discomfort in the photo. Chubby, his cheeks looked full and pimply. "Was Elliott rich?"

"Oh yeah, but he was one of those awkward rich kids. Over protected, nerdy as hell, no cool, shy, stiff and uncomfortable in his own skin. Except for the huge trust fund, he was the opposite of Jamie." Carol said, then drove in silence for a few minutes.

I could tell she was considering whether to tell us more. "Hey, Carol, please don't worry about saying the wrong thing about any of these guys. Mom's life maybe at stake."

She cleared her throat, "Elliott was short, shorter even than Dave. I've learned not to trust short men. They tend to be manipulative and mean, as though they want to cut everyone down to their size." Carol took a deep breath and exhaled. "I mean, how dare he have such a chip on his shoulder? He had every material advantage, wealth, a high priced education, but he resented Jamie for having everything Jamie had. Elliott seemed to think that Jamie had what Elliott lacked—loving parents. Which wasn't even true, you know. In fact, Jamie's mother lived on the opposite coast and his father was always abroad. But Jamie had an insouciant charm, a self-deprecating confidence that drew people to him, while Elliott had a self-assertive lack of confidence that repelled all but his oldest friends. I actually always wondered how he had become friends with that gang."

She wasn't holding back anymore. And I'd never realized before that Aunt Carol had a thing for Uncle Jamie.

"And Ron?" I asked while she was on a roll.

"He was a weird one. No connections, no money, but he never let on. Imitated the rich ones. He married money— twice. He did a good job of looking rich. Ya know . . . blonde and always tan. The preppie layers of clothes. He learned a lot from Jamie. He was fun, joking, playful, acted like he didn't have a care in the world. But it had to be a strain trying to keep up with the others."

"Carol, I imagine it's hard, but . . . would you please tell me about Lexi?"

She sucked in her cheeks. The only sound she made for a full minute was a deep sigh. She opened her mouth as though to speak, but then closed it and concentrated on traffic. "I loved her the way one loves someone who really gets you. Do ya know what I mean?"

My heart answered her with a deep ache, a longing for such a friend again. I nodded. In the silence while we both fought back tears, I wondered at my reaction. Again?

"Al, the strange thing is . . . you remind me of her. The way ya accepted me from the first moment. I'm not usually terribly popular with children. Lexi would've said it's because I'm a bitch." She stretched her mouth into a sad smile. "But you." Sigh. "As a toddler, ya tossed your curly blonde locks with excitement, ran across the lawn, and jumped into my arms smothering me with kisses." She failed to stop the tears. "Oh, fuck, hand me a damn tissue!"

She wiped her face, blew her nose. "I do love ya kiddo!"

"I love you too, Aunt Carol." I grinned, wiped my own tears, and sniffled.

There was not a word from Steven in the back seat. I was tempted to look to see if my tough guy bro had teared up, but then Carol continued.

"Lexi was an amazing artist. Like you, actually. At times she lived in another world, a world full of her paintings, and color. She was obsessed with color. She could go on about the colors in a sunset, or a rainbow, the ocean, or a forest, until I was ready to scream. But she did make me see a colorful world that I'd been oblivious to." Carol pounded her fist on the steering wheel. "There was no damn reason, no fucking reason for anyone to kill her. She always saw the best in people, ignored shortcomings. It used to drive me crazy sometimes, she was such a Pollyanna."

I smiled.

"You know, after she was supposedly killed by a serial killer, I researched the subject thoroughly—it's been a secret obsession of mine." Carol said.

"Why do you say supposedly?" I asked.

"No one was ever caught, tried or convicted." Carol hesitated as though she were deciding if she should voice her thoughts. "Serial killers used to be called "stranger killers" because most murderers kill for a motive rather than for thrills. I've never been totally convinced that Lexi was a stranger to her killer."

"What?" Steven broke his silence.

"A couple of her friends were, still are, strange enough to be serial killers."

"Who?" he asked.

"I've got a list of serial killer characteristics. You can look at it and see for yourself." Carol said.

"I read a file Dad had about the Zodiac. Douchebag was wacko and wrong. Nobody who could even pretend to be normal could be that messed up," I said.

Carol gave me a quick glance. "You might be surprised. Sometimes they can seem pretty normal and the characteristics aren't all that weird."

"Give me an example of a characteristic." Steven asked.

"Portly," Carol said.

"Fat?" Steven asked.

"Ever seen pictures of John Wayne Gacy? That kind of pudgy."

"Like Elliott?" I asked.

Carol nodded and pulled the car up to the curb in front of Kroeber Hall. I glanced at the spot where I had waited for Steven earlier in the day, but looked away. A chill ran down my spine. I let Steven do the talking.

"That's where it happened." Steven waved toward the middle of the lawn. "She was on the bench, then she saw me I guess." Steven looked to me for confirmation, I nodded and he continued, "She stood up and started to run towards the car when all of a sudden she collapsed onto the grass, scared the hell out of me, but then she jumped up, ran to the car and hopped in."

"And the police? What did they find?" Carol asked.

I had to answer; Steven had waited in the car while I spoke with the Berkeley cops. "They found two bullets," I managed to choke out.

"In the grass?" Carol asked.

She was strangely curious about this shooting. I nodded an affirmation to her question.

"Show me." Carol opened her car door.

I really didn't want to get out of that car, but she stood waiting on the sidewalk.

"Al, I'm going to park the car legally this time." Steven said as he slid into the driver's seat. "You okay?"

I nodded, but I wasn't okay. My heart was in my throat.

"Hey, you don't have to do this." Steven leaned across to the passenger window. "Aunt Carol, I don't think—"

"It's okay Steven. I've gotta do it some day. Might as well get it over with." I opened the car door and put one foot at a time on the sidewalk. I took a deep breath and stood up.

My heart pounded, my eyes teared. What the hell? I had to stop overreacting. After all, I hadn't gotten hit by the bullets. But now that adrenalin was no longer coursing through my veins, my legs felt like lead weights, and my headache was back with a sharp pain. I dragged myself over to where Carol rubbed the raw scar on the tree branch.

"Yeah, that's how the cops found the bullets. One of them hit the tree." I said.

Carol drew me into her arms and hugged me until it hurt. "Oh my god, thank god you're okay." She brushed my hair back and kissed my cheek.

I nodded, but I didn't feel okay. "Aunt Carol," I whispered, "We've gotta find Mom. Don't you have any ideas?"

She shook her head. She held me close while she spoke in my ear. "I just can't imagine that any of the people we know could have had anything to do with this. You are like, well for me, you're the closest thing to a daughter I'll ever have, and

I think all of your uncles feel the same way about you. The thought of losing you . . . or your mother. It's unbearable." Carol shuddered as she squeezed me tight enough to hinder my breathing.

"We've been through that once, it was hell, the worst —" She choked, then hesitated before continuing. "We each blamed ourselves for encouraging her, hell, fucking pushing her to go on that date. If I'd just let her stay locked in her studio . . . it was my fault." Carol sighed again. "I guess everyone involved felt the same. But really it was me, I made her go. Anyway, our mutual guilt drew us all together. We became like a family, the realization that one of us could be gone, just all of a sudden disappear from our lives. Facing the fact of one's own mortality is especially hard when you are young, when life is just beginning, but having a contemporary die brings the fact of death home." She released me and shook her head.

We linked arms while we walked to the bench. My knees shook, I sat down just as Steven walked around the corner of Kroeber Hall. Carol released my hand to wave at him.

I'd forgotten to tell him something that could be important.

I stood and ran to my brother.

And the unthinkable happened.

I had twenty feet to go to reach him when I heard a shot whiz by my ear and seconds later felt something slam into the side of my head.

12

Where was I? My eyelids felt glued shut, my limbs heavy, yet I was floating out of touch with my body in a cloud of fog.

I concentrated, tried to pick up a hand, but something was attached to it. Could I lift a finger? The effort to move made me aware of the intense pain shooting through my head.

Elevator bells chimed; phones rang in the distance. Voices muttered nearby. I couldn't make sense of what they said. Too much work. I was too sleepy.

I drifted back to the dream.

I had misjudged the rock outcropping overhead on the trail above me and slammed my head right into a few tons of granite. Shit that hurt! I spun in black and stars, grabbed a bush that had managed to grow in a crack, and prayed I wouldn't tumble down the rocky cliff. A hundred feet below, waves crashed against jagged crags embedded in a narrow strip of sand. Screams from the beach were faint, nearly drowned in the undulating roar of the breakers.

My friend Jeff and I had been climbing down the cliff face to join a party on the beach in Big Sur when we heard a sharp yell followed by cries for help. Jeff who had some emergency medical experience opted to continue the climb down, but had sent me back up to the road to get help. Without Jeff calling out each foot placement, I was fighting the urge to sit down, frozen in place by fear. Rock climbing, particularly without any safety gear, or expert guidance scared the shit out of me.

The stars floating around my head gave me an excuse to rest at least until the spinning stopped. Afraid the black that drifted in and out of my consciousness would lead to a fall, I laid down on the warm dirt ledge.

On the edge of my awareness, Jeff's faint, insistent voice called my name. I wanted to answer, if only the whirling would slow down. I knew I had to hurry. I had to get up.

13

BERKELEY, ALTA BATES HOSPITAL, MARCH 2008

"Al, Alexandra." Jeff squeezed his daughter's hand, whispered her name as though he could call her back to them. "Alexandra."

Steven couldn't believe how fucked up this was. His sister lying there, her face as white as the hospital bedding and bandages covered her blonde head. Tubes ran out of her mouth, across her nose, and out the top of her hands. The hum of machines attached to her arms and chest drowned her occasional moan.

Dad had said, "Thank God she's still alive," and seemed unaffected by her comatose state. Spending his adult life prosecuting murders had hardened him. Steven vowed anew not to be cold like his father.

"Where the hell is Mom?" Steven asked again.

Jeff shrugged, but his hands shook and the strain on his face belied his attempt at casual. "Not answering her cell." Maybe he wasn't as coldhearted as Steven thought.

"I've been trying to reach her all afternoon." Steven said. "What's going on? What's this about, Dad?"

Jeff shook his head, but he looked relieved when Carol and Dave burst into the room distracting his son from further questioning. The four exchanged silent, gentle hugs.

Carol tiptoed to the bed and whispered, "Is she going to be okay?"

Dave put his arm around Carol and whispered in her ear. She turned to Jeff and Steven with tears running down her botoxed face. She slid her hand down Steven's face and then embraced Jeff. "Have you found Lauren yet?"

"No," Jeff said.

The four stood together eyes on Al's pale face, listening to the hum of the machines.

"When was the last time you guys ate?" Carol broke the silence.

"This morning," Jeff answered even though he'd only grabbed coffee on the run to court.

Carol glanced out the window at the darkening sky. "Let's get some food."

"She's been moaning, trying to tell us something." Steven returned to the chair next to the bed. "I'll stay here."

Steven's father, his Uncle Dave and his Aunt Carol tried to persuade Steven to go with them but he held his ground.

Dave and Carol were not a couple. In fact they'd probably run into each other in the lobby, but they were both, each in their own way, extraordinarily successful.

Dave had turned what had started as a waterbed company into several furniture manufacturing and distributing businesses spending weeks at a time flying on his plane throughout south East Asia checking on his companies. He was today, as always, dressed in a dark, impeccably tailored, suit, his grooming perfect in every detail from the trim of his light brown hair to his buffed fingernails.

Aunt Carol had never given up her hippie ways. Instead she had built a career on designing bohemian chic clothing and home accessories. She had changed out of her bloodied clothes into a rose velvet vest over a full paisley skirt, a silk shirt and ankle boots, with her signature scarf tied around her black hair. Indian style.

"We'll bring you a sandwich," offered Carol.

"Fine." Steven wasn't feeling hungry even though he'd been about to eat lunch when his father called and told him to leave immediately to pick up Al on the edge of campus.

Oh man, did that scene blow. He couldn't close his eyes without seeing blood erupt from the side of his sister's head. She was running towards him, totally freaked even before the shots, on a mission. If only he had some idea of what she was on to. For sure, it had something to do with Mom.

14

BIG SUR, JULY 1968

Familiar voices brought me back from dreaming of Big Sur. I wanted to tell them I was okay, but even the thought of trying to speak made my head hurt unbearably. Slipping back into the world of dreams, even a nightmare, was easier.

The heat of the glaring sun intensified against the granite and dirt, where I was sheltered from the ocean breeze by the cliff and the rocky over hang. My heart pounded nearly out of my chest when I awoke to find my legs draped over the side of the ledge, my ears filled with the sound of the waves crashing below. I scrambled to my knees, fought hyperventilating. "Breathe in through your nose, out through your mouth." I mentally chanted until I stopped freaking out.

I licked lips gritty with dust, wiped sweat from my brow, rolled my sleeves down over arms that were already stinging with sunburn. If only I'd asked Jeff for some of the water he carried in his backpack. Thinking of Jeff, usually my best friend, I cursed him for leading me down what he called a shortcut from the easier trail climb. With great care, I braved turning my head to look up the mountain face. I had no idea how to climb up from where I was. Faint, familiar voices from the beach below reminded me that I had no choice.

I grabbed a handful of a manzanita bush, pulled myself to my feet, and stretched for an outcrop within my reach. Hot granite stung my palm digging into tender skin. I pulled myself up the face with constant reminders not to look down.

An eternity later, I crawled onto the shoulder of the road and wondered what to do next. My limbs shook as violently as my heart throbbed. I clambered to my feet and stumbled along the dry, dusty edge keeping as much distance between the cliff and myself as the hot asphalt allowed.

A multi-colored VW bus wandered around a bend in the road. I waved both arms in broad X's and the vehicle, covered in hand painted peace signs, pulled next to me on the roadside.

"Can you take me to the ranger station?" I asked.

When the two bearded young men stared at me without responding, I added, "Well, at least to the nearest phone?"

"Sure." The bearded one in the passenger seat grinned. He opened the sliding door to the rear compartment; a cloud of marijuana wafted out the opening and engulfed me as I climbed in. I perched on the edge of a homemade wood framed bed.

"I think Nepenthe's got the closest phone," I gasped. The smoke didn't help me to catch my breath or clear my head.

The two guys sat motionless, the driver checking me out in the rearview mirror, the passenger turned to face me.

"Look, there's been an accident. Someone, a girl, fell down the cliff, landed on the rocks below," I wheezed.

The beards nodded, but didn't move. "Shi-i-it." The passenger muttered.

"I . . . we need to get help." When that failed to elicit any movement, I slammed my fist into the back of the driver's seat. "Turn this fucking thing around!" I pointed to the road behind us, "Help is that way! The closest phone is at that restaurant you passed, back there. It's a couple, maybe three miles."

The driver slowly rotated the steering wheel to the left, and pulled into the lane just as a sports car whipped around the corner, smoothly corrected course to miss the lumbering van. A pang of regret, if only I'd been pickier about what vehicle I'd flagged down.

We chugged along, jolted from gear to gear, never exceeding fifteen miles an hour.

"We kinda need to hurry," I suggested, but nothing changed. I sighed, resigning myself to the long minutes it took to reach the restaurant parking lot. The bus rolled onto the decomposed granite. I jumped out the side door and ran up the timbered path beneath shading oaks.

I reached the rustic patio overlooking the ocean and grabbed the arm of the nearest waiter, "Help me please. A girl fell on the cliff over there," I waved down to the beach south of the patio. "I need a ranger."

Blue green eyes beneath sun-bleached blonde hair studied my face for the seconds it took to absorb my meaning. Then he turned and strode through glass doors to the interior of the restaurant. I hurried behind him.

He leaned across the rough wood counter, pulled a black phone toward us, and dialed a single digit. "Mare, give me the ranger station." He handed the receiver to me.

I listened to the ring and looked down at my body, at the dust and blood on my legs beneath once white shorts, smears on my tennis shoes, and felt the sweat and dirt on my face, I noticed curious patrons looking me over.

I didn't fit in the hipster chic, glass and redwood structure that hung on the cliffside overlooking the ocean. We seldom ventured inside this establishment. Lemonade on the patio was the best I could usually afford. The one time Jamie had treated the whole bunch of us to dinner here, we'd spent the afternoon showering in a cold waterfall and getting ready for a big night out.

I told the rangers what I knew. "Yes, there are three VW bugs parked on the other side of the road, I'm not sure of the distance, maybe a hundred feet from the top of the trail."

In the process of telling them, I realized I didn't actually know much. Who had fallen? Was it my friend Carol? Or one of the dates with Jamie or Ron or Tom?

"She fell . . . hurt . . . rocks," I remembered hearing above the sound of waves breaking.

Blonde-with-amazing-blue-green-eyes unwound his white apron; "I'll drive you back to the spot so you can show the rangers." He handed me a paper cup filled with lemonade.

It was the most delicious liquid to ever hit a dry mouth.

He took my arm, guided me down the steps and into a topless jeep. As he backed out of the staff parking, he turned to offer me his hand. "I'm Ted." His blue green eyes held mine for a few seconds.

"Lexi." I wiped my hand on my filthy shorts and reached the tips of his fingers, expecting sparks to fly. A previously unexperienced flow of desire traveled down my arm through my body to below my tummy and made me look away in embarrassment.

"Tell me when we get there," Ted said.

Even his voice elicited a sensual response.

I pulled back long strands of hair that blew across my face, and concentrated on the side of the road, uncertain that I could locate the right spot. "There!" I shouted over the sound of the jeep and the wind. I saw the cars on the left side of the road and figured this had to be the point that jutted out above the beach.

Ted pulled over to the shoulder; I slid off the seat and down to the gravel. Then I peeked over the edge while Ted turned the vehicle around and parked on the opposite side of the road.

He joined me in pacing the top of the cliff. "What happened?" he asked.

"I'm not sure. My friend and I were halfway down the trail—" I saw him look me up and down, most likely noting the evidence that I had been off the trail. "Well, actually, Jeff and I took a shortcut, and we heard shouting from the beach that someone was hurt, from falling down the face, I think."

"Who's Jeff? Your boyfriend?"

"No, a friend. A friend I grew up with."

"Are you staying down there?"

"Some of our friends are. We just came for the day. Uh, the evening." I thought about the way I had pictured the evening going. We'd sit around the driftwood campfire, drinking beer, smoking a joint or two, and speculate about the secrets of the universe while toasting marshmallows for s'mores. The sky brilliant with stars, the moon reflecting on the ocean, the heavens perhaps revealing knowledge we hadn't learned in our university classes. Well, not gonna happen that night.

"Where did you come from?"

"We left Berkeley this morning. Jeff and I both have to work tomorrow night, the rest planned to spend the weekend." I heard sirens on the road north of us, then the slapping of helicopter blades overhead.

A yellow fire truck followed by a smaller yellow vehicle forced us to move out of the way. The first fireman, clad head to toe in yellow, greeted Ted as he jumped from the side of the truck. "Hey, Ted, what's happening?"

"Down this trail." Ted pointed to the start of the path down. "Someone's hurt."

Another yellow clothed man removed his jacket and pulled a backpack from the smaller vehicle. He nodded at Ted, and followed two firemen down the trail. A radio crackled, answered by a ten-four. My heart leapt at the sight of the men who remained behind, readying a body basket.

"Want to go down?" Ted nodded toward the beach, held out a hand.

"As long as you don't suggest a shortcut." I ignored his hand and headed down the trail, carefully placing one foot in front of the other in the sandy dust.

We stuck to the trail and it would've been easy, if slow going, had I not been freaked about what we would find at the bottom. Halfway down, we moved aside to allow two of the rescue team and the basket to pass us.

I climbed over rocks to the sand and caught a glimpse of long black hair tucked into the basket. No one but my best girl-friend Carol had hair as dark as shiny coal. I moved closer. Her normally porcelain skin was statuary marble white, her green eyes, closed. A clear mask sat over her mouth and nose and a tube ran to a canister that sat on her chest.

I pushed through the onlookers. "Is she going be alright?" I demanded of the rescuer.

He looked me in the eye, nodded and then continued to lace up the basket in preparation for hauling her up the cliff face.

I hurried to Jeff's side. "Jeff, what's the matter with her?"

"She hit her head. And I think she may have broken her arm and wrist trying to catch herself."

"She's unconscious?"

Jeff grimaced, nodded.

I climbed over a ribbon of rock, sloshed through a tide pool, and stood next to Jamie. I punched his upper arm. "How could you let this happen?"

"I had nothing to do with this. I was unpacking gear, I didn't even look until I heard her scream." Jamie moved to put his arm around my shoulders, but I ducked out of reach.

I felt my eyes pop with anger. "You left her up there?" I hissed.

"I came down with June. Carol and Dave teamed up. They were a few minutes behind us and goin' slow. June and I both have some mountain climbing experience, so we offered to carry the packs." Jamie groaned, "I shoulda gone behind them. I was, fuck, just impatient."

I looked over at Dave. "What happened?"

Dave shrugged, shook his head. "I think she tripped." He looked at his feet and kicked a little sand. "I don't know," he muttered.

Elliott spoke up, "She fell about ten, maybe fifteen feet. She tried to break her fall with her arm, but she landed on her head anyway." Elliott frowned, hesitated. "She was moaning earlier. Lexi, I think she's going to be okay."

Carol was loaded into the basket that had been attached to pulleys at roadside. Firemen guided it up the face of the cliff. My stomach jumped into my throat as the basket dangled from the red ropes and twisted out of their grasp once.

I couldn't watch.

If Carol had been conscious she would've been screaming her head off. She hates heights and would never have agreed to this outing if I hadn't bullied, bribed and begged with dogged persistence.

Had I killed her?

■ ■ ■

A radio on the hip of a fireman packing up equipment crackled. He turned to Jeff, "Where do you want her taken?"

"Closest hospital," I blurted.

"Well, closest is Community, Eskaton in Monterey is a few miles farther."

"Community in Pebble Beach?" Jamie asked.

"The closest hospital is what, is that thirty, forty miles away. Are you kidding me?" I tried not to scream.

"Yes miss, that's the closest." He turned to Jamie, "You know Community?"

Jamie shrugged. "Only because of the fame of the architect, and I've heard about the all private rooms thing."

"Then you know it's kinda . . . well, it's not cheap."

Jamie leaned close to the fireman, "I will take full financial responsibility," he murmured.

"You'll have to come do the paperwork then," the fireman announced.

"Right." Jamie dug car keys out of his short's pocket and tossed them to his date. "June, darling, will you drive the girls home please?" He nodded at the other two girls, dates of Elliott and Tom. "Jeff, you will bring Lexi with you guys to the hospital?" He grabbed a sweatshirt from his mummy sleeping bag, picked up a small pack of personal items, and followed the fireman up the hill.

15

PEBBLE BEACH, JULY 1968

After loading the cars, and making two stops for directions, we finally found the damn hospital. It looked more like a small Kennedy Center than a hospital.

"That's because it was designed by the same architect, the same year," Elliott explained. "Edward Durell Stone. Won a bunch of architectural awards."

"Impressive, I hope that means they're good," I said.

We piled out of the two cars, found the emergency room waiting area, and elected Jeff to speak with the medical staff. Thanks to his EMT training as a lifeguard, he would understand their lingo better than the rest of us. He stood next to Jamie at the reception counter. Jamie signed his name with a flourish at the end of a pile of papers.

"They'll let one family member at a time into the exam room," Jamie explained when he and Jeff returned to where the rest of us sat clustered on a leather clad window seat.

"That won't be me as I already made the mistake of admitting I'm not . . . a family member that is," Jeff said.

With Jeff's strawberry blonde hair, and tanned, freckled skin, there was not a chance he could pass for Carol's brother.

We looked from one face to another. Jamie with his year round tan and blonde hair looked nothing like Carol. Nor did blonde Ron. Pudgy Elliott didn't even faintly resemble my slender, elegant friend. Tom's hair was light brown, his eyes brown, his body tall and sturdy. Dave had dark hair, was tall and slender—but Carol was not at all fond of him. In fact, she claimed he gave her the creeps. Carol barely knew any of the guys. A couple of them, she was to meet that day. That left me, but she and I were a contrast in opposites.

"What if we just told them the truth? That none of us are related, but I've known her all her life. What do ya think?" I asked.

Jeff shook his head.

"Jamie's paying. Doesn't that give him any privileges?" Ron asked.

"I think Lexi should just go in there as though she has every right to be there. Ignore any questioning regarding your relationship." Jamie smiled at me. "I'll run interference if need be."

Yeah, I'll just be like Jamie. Calm and confident; like I own the world. Which, of course, he almost does.

And I don't. Never mind that, I told myself as I pushed past the receptionist and demanded to know where Carol was. No one answered, so I walked in like I owned the place.

The first white clad nurse I asked glanced at me before hurrying down the hall. I peeked in an open doorway and caught a glimpse of a wall of windows overlooking a spectacular fountain court. The room was empty.

The next room was buzzing with activity. I slipped in behind the medical personnel and watched two men clad in white coats study two x-rays and confer with a nurse. A guy in green scrubs cut away Carol's sweatshirt while a nurse attached a tube to each arm, and one attached to her nostrils.

I turned my head until I thought they were through cutting and poking, I hate anything sharp.

When I turned back, a second nurse was checking vitals; a man pulled open her eyes and shone a small flashlight into each one.

I remained quiet, trying to make sense out of their conversations.

The two conferring doctors turned to leave the room. I stepped in front of them.

"Is she going to be okay?"

Both men looked at me with surprise. "Time will tell," one said as they brushed past me.

The nurse who had been part of their conversation had a better bedside manner. She smiled and touched my arm, "The prognosis is good. She has a broken wrist, a compound fracture of her forearm—"

"People don't die from broken arms," I blurted.

"No, the problem is she also has a severe concussion."

A squeak escaped my mouth. "How do you treat that?"

"She'll be closely monitored."

I jumped at the sound of Carol's bed being moved behind us.

"What are they doing? Where are they taking her?"

"We need more x-rays." The nurse studied my face. "Take a deep breath. Here, sit down in that chair and put your head between your knees." She led me to an armchair and sat me down. "Most likely your friend will be fine. But when someone has been unconscious for more than thirty minutes, it sometimes indicates severe brain injury."

"What does that mean? Is she going to die?"

"She may require surgery if there is swelling. Even in the best case, with traumatic brain injury, we'll keep her under observation for twenty-four hours." She looked at my dusty clothes and body. "You have time to get cleaned up and eat something before you see her. But you must wait outside that door." She nodded at the door I had brazenly entered.

Dazed, I wandered back to the waiting room.

"Well?" Jeff asked.

I spotted Dave with his back to us, looking out the wall of windows at the fountain in the courtyard.

"Damnit, Dave, what the hell? What happened?" I blurted.

"I told you, she tripped." Dave watched the water spout into the air.

"Were you in front of her—to break her fall?" My fists pounded his back. "Turn around! You tell me now. How did you let this happen?"

"Lexi, calm down." Jeff pulled me off Dave. "What did you find out?"

I repeated what I'd heard the doctors say, "Traumatic brain injury, possibly severe."

Dave remained looking out the window. Elliott and Tom sank back down on to the leather-clad bench. Ron leaned against the wall; for once he found nothing to joke about. Jeff pretended to hug me, but he was actually restraining me from pulverizing Dave.

Jamie moved to stand next to Dave as though he, too, were watching the fountain. Just loud enough for all of us to hear, Jamie asked, "What *did* happen?"

"I was in front of her most of the way. But when we got near the bottom, she pushed in front. Like she was excited to get onto the sand, into the water. I saw her trip. There was nothing I could do."

16

Steven looked up from his book when his father entered the room. "Dad, she's been saying stuff."

"Like what?"

"Asking for Carol. Asking if she's going to be alright."

Jeff rubbed his forehead. Steven could tell his father had one of his headaches. He looked like shit: his eyes red, and his gray face gaunt. Even his freckles were pale. His hair was a washed out tint of its former strawberry blonde.

"Dad, did you eat?"

Jeff shook his head and stared at his pale daughter lying in the hospital bed. With her usual lively animation gone, she was a sleeping beauty. The wisps of blonde hair that had escaped the emergency room razor trailed below a white crown of bandages. How he wished she were back to her usual ass-chewing self, calling him on every imperfection in his behavior.

"Has there been any ransom—" Steven started to ask.

Jeff shook his head again.

"Dad, it's been more than ten hours since any of us talked to Mom. She's not answering her phone or texts. It's not like her to ignore us for that long. I feel like I should be out looking for Mom, but I wouldn't know where to start."

"The police are on it, and I've got an investigator that Tom's law firm uses looking for her, also." Jeff said.

"Maybe I could talk to people around Bancroft and Telegraph. I'm sure that'd be where Mom would've dropped Al off. But I hate to leave her here alone."

"I'd rather you stay here with the policeman outside this door. I'd like to know that at least you two are safe. I'll get an investigator over there," Jeff said.

17

GOLDEN GATE PARK, SUMMER OF LOVE, 1967

The fog burned off by mid afternoon. I stripped off layers of sweaters and a jacket, down to my T-shirt and denim sailor pants, and wadded up my clothing to make a pillow. The warmth of the sun was worth the popped out freckles on my arms and nose. The heat awoke the sweet smell of the freshly mown lawn. From the makeshift stage, Janis Joplin's voice rasped out, *"Call on me, darlin', just call on me."*

The glutted streets of San Francisco emptied pedestrians into the park. Noting the growing audience, I stretched a blanket full size to mark our territory until my companions returned from their foray into the Haight in search of maryjane and liquid refreshments. Smoke from weed and incense drowned the sweet smells of the lawn and ocean breezes.

"Ciao, Lexi," I heard Carol say as she stood over me.

"If you're going to San Francisco," Carol's off key attempt at John Phillip's song preceded something damp and fragrant landing on the face I had turned to the sun, *"be sure to wear some flowers in your hair."*

I sat up to adjust the wreath of flowers onto the crown of my head. "Groovy." I grinned and loosened my braided hair into waves. "Where are the guys?"

"There are a lot of half-naked women dancing in the street over at the corner of Haight and Ashbury." Carol sunk to the blanket folding her legs Indian fashion. Pastel flowers on her tunic and in her jet-black hair set off her dramatic coloring. Oblivious to admiring stares, she lit up, took a toke, and passed the joint to me.

This had been our summer of liberation. Prior to this summer, we females depended on the men in our lives to provide the dope while we provided the food. The stereotypical roles of the sexes were a long way from broken down, but Carol and I were beginning to see the possibilities. A couple of the men in our circle were even starting to cook.

I fought back disappointment that Dave, Elliott and Ron had ditched us. I wanted Carol to get to know the guys in my circle of friends.

I handed the joint back to her and used my now free hands to remove my sandals. A few more hits, and we both stood to sway to the tunes. Hundreds of raised arms undulated like the tentacles of a mega sea anemone.

The constant succession of bands eager for an audience kept us moving to the sounds of Big Brother, the Grateful Dead, Country Joe and the Fish, the Who, Credence Clearwater Revival, Iron Butterfly, and Jefferson Airplane until late into the night when Joan Baez sang us down. Carol and I finally crashed onto the blanket and snoozed to *"Oh, where have you been, my darling young one?"*

"Lexi, wake up!" Carol's hand shook my shoulder. "It's creepy here."

I raised my head, opened my eyes. Wisps of mist drifted through the black moonless night as fog rolled around us. The cold mist muffled scattered voices. "Shit. What time *is* it?"

"Late." Carol looked and sounded pissed. "And we've been abandoned."

"They probably couldn't find us in the crowd." I offered as I gathered clothing, bags, and the blanket.

"Pul-eeze, stop making excuses for them." Carol snapped. She tossed her wilted floral crown onto the ground. "We shouldn't've come when we found out it was just those three going."

I considered what excuse she might buy, but she wasn't fond of any of them. I couldn't offer anything she would see as a redeeming quality.

"Guess Ron changed his mind." Carol pulled a sweater over her head.

"About what?" I shoved an arm into my jacket, fastened my sandals.

"I heard him say you meet the prettiest girls at Barry Goldwater rallies."

"He might have a hard time finding one of those around here." I slung my stuffed bag onto my shoulder. "Let's us find a bus stop." I headed for the edge of the park.

Carol grumbled but she followed.

The lawn was damp. The bellbottoms of my Navy surplus jeans flapped wet and cold against my ankles. I barely avoided tripping over sleeping bodies in the dark and mist.

Carol was right. The murky place was creepy in the middle of the night.

Ahead a street lamp almost lit a break in thick bushes ringing the meadow.

I checked to see if Carol had kept up. "Come on."

"You better know where you're going." She pulled her purse strap onto her shoulder.

Even though I could barely make out her silhouette, I knew she was giving me her pissed off look. "Fulton Street is right through there." I motioned.

"Through those bushes? I don't see any street. And it's really black in there."

I ignored her whining and slugged ahead. When I reached the edge of the bushes, I waited for her to join me and we stepped into the dark brush.

Dead center in the gloomy thicket of blurred shadows of shrubs, a dark figure wielding a knife suddenly blocked the gap. A voice muffled by a black mask and hood, cackled a malicious laugh. Without a word, the figure motioned at Carol's purse with the knife.

I slipped the strap of my bag off my shoulder and dropped it on the ground. Knives petrify me.

The dark figure slashed the glinting knife at both of us in one long swoop and bent to pick up my bag.

Carol swung her heavy leather handbag hard, hitting him on the side of his head. Before he could recover, she knocked the knife from his hand.

The black clad figure was barely my height, but built like a man.

I kicked out hoping to catch him in the balls. I missed, flew off my feet, and landed on my ass.

Carol picked up the knife and stuck it into the forearm behind the fist he had aimed at me.

He swung at Carol and the knife flew to the ground next to my hand.

I picked it up as I scrambled to my feet and lunged at the black body.

He ducked.

The plunging knife caught him in the neck. He grabbed my hand, twisting the knife from my grasp.

Then the dark figure, and his knife, lurched out of the bushes, and ran across the lawn.

Carol and I found our bags and stumbled in the opposite direction, out of the bushes, and onto the sidewalk where we collapsed to our knees.

"You okay?" I asked. My heart raced pounding in an effort to jump out of my chest.

"Fucker." Carol sat down hard and pulled her purse to her chest. "Fucking asshole."

We stayed on the ground in the pool of light from the streetlight, breathing hard for several minutes before Carol started laughing hysterical hoots.

My chuckles were soon followed by me rolling on the ground in hysterics. Tears and snot poured down my face; I tried to catch my breath.

"You . . . guffaw . . . picked up . . . the knife. I couldn't believe it," Carol snorted, then wiped her face. "You hate knives."

"I thought he was going to hit you," I managed to choke out.

Carol threw her arms around my shoulders. "You do care, don't you?"

She scrambled to her feet, picked up my bag, handed it to me. "He didn't even take the bag with him."

The guys weren't there when we finally got back to my place. Carol stayed with me rather than walk to her house alone.

The next afternoon, Ron called to apologize. He said Dave had gotten them involved in some kind of bar brawl, and they had spent the night in a hospital emergency room getting patched up. None of the three of them had nerve enough to show up at our house for weeks. By then any evidence of their excuses had healed.

"Only those assholes could find a brawl in the middle of the center for peace and love," Carol said when I relayed the apology.

I bit my tongue rather than remind her that we managed to find a knife-wielding mugger midst the same celebration.

18

BERKELEY, ALTA BATES HOSPITAL, MARCH 2008

The footsteps Steven heard in the hall outside his sister's hospital room didn't sound like the crepe soled shoes worn by the medicos. He watched the door open as a man he had yet to meet entered the room.

"You must be Steven. I'm Detective Schmidt." He extended his hand to Steven.

"Detective Schmidt . . . Hello." Steven got up from the chair he'd pulled to his sister's bedside and shook the detective's hand.

Steven checked his watch. Well after midnight, and the detective was still working. "Thank you sir."

The policeman nodded in response staring at the girl whose color barely contrasted with the white bedding.

"Any word about—" Steven asked.

Steven was interrupted by a shake of the detective's head. Schmidt continued to stare at Al for several minutes. Even though the detective was silent, the emotion on his face and in his silence communicated his regret at not having prevented her from being shot.

"Whadda they tell ya?" the detective asked.

"Not a lot," Steven answered.

19

BERKELEY, FALL 1968

"Lexi, you're late." Jeff pounced on me before I closed the entry door to our house. "Carol's in Cowell Hospital. I'll drive you over."

"Wha-at?" I dropped my bag of art supplies and books.

"What happened?" I asked.

"I'll explain in the car." Keys in hand, he raced down the front walk to the driveway.

"Is it bad?" I ran after him.

"Don't know. She was conscious. That's a good sign."

Better than the last time she was hospitalized. It took days for her to come out of the coma when she fell down the cliff.

I jumped into the passenger seat of Jeff's VW bug. "What happened?"

He looked over his shoulder, backed out of the drive, shifted into second gear, and drove around the corner towards the student hospital. "She got burned in some kind of explosion."

"Oh my God." My beautiful friend Carol, please don't let her perfect face be burned. "Where?"

"I'm not certain, at her house maybe?"

Carol lived with two of our girl friends in the second floor apartment in a brown shingle craftsman, on Southside several blocks from the campus.

"When?"

"They called an hour ago. I know she's conscious because she had them call you. You aren't listed as her next of kin, or anything. Right?" Jeff smiled to show he was teasing.

His effort barely registered. My mind raced with what-ifs and horrible mental pictures of Carol scarred for life. I took a deep breath trying to calm down.

Jeff scanned the small parking lot for a space.

I hopped out. "See ya inside."

I ran to the first door I saw. It was locked. I ran around to the lobby entrance and across the worn linoleum. At the curved reception desk, I shoved aside two other students. "Where's Carol Huntington?"

"Just a minute. Let me finish with the people in front of you." An overweight bitch with attitude, Carol would've given her—oh God, Carol.

"Please, my friend's been burned. The hospital called an hour ago, I was in class—"

"Go ahead," Both students stepped back waving me in front of them.

"Thanks." I looked the receptionist in the eye. "Carol Huntington."

The bitch stared at me without moving.

"Please, you don't understand, she wouldn't have had them call me unless it was serious."

Bitch ran her long red fingernail down a clipboard and dialed a phone, "Carol Huntington?" She listened then hung up the receiver.

"You can't see her now."

"What? Why not?" I wanted to reach across the desk and throttle her. "Where is she?"

Jeff's hand on my arm pulled me back from the counter. He smiled at the bitch and asked, "What can you tell us?"

She returned the smile. "The doctor's with her now. She's been moved from the emergency area to the second floor. You can wait in the lounge just outside the elevator."

"Thank you." Jeff continued to hold my upper arm as he moved me to the elevator. "Calm down. You aren't going to be much help to her if you're freaking out."

I don't usually freak out. In fact, I'm calm in emergencies. I took several more deep breaths.

At the nurse's station near the elevator, I flashed a quick smile before I asked about Carol. "Do you know how bad it is?"

All the smiles in the world weren't going to get me an answer to that question. I'd phrased the question all wrong.

"The doctor is with her now. He'll talk to you if she wants him to do so."

"Do you know what happened?"

"There was a gas explosion in her apartment."

"Her roommates?"

The nurse shook her head in a quiet way that scared the hell out of me.

"Are they alright?"

"One person was transported to the burn unit at UCSF."

I sucked in my breath. Oh, this was bad. UCSF, University of California in San Francisco, was the university's medical school and one of the best hospitals in the state. It was better equipped than Cowell, the Cal student hospital, to handle serious injuries.

It took a few seconds to realize it was a good sign that Carol was still at Cowell. It meant she wasn't that seriously hurt.

Or it could mean she was hopeless.

I paced between the elevator and the vinyl sofas in the waiting area and the nurse's station. Jeff sat reading a textbook he'd thought to bring with him, looking up to smile at me periodically in a manner that I imagine was meant to be reassuring.

Finally a white clad nurse walked from a room down the hall to the nurse's station. She asked something I didn't hear but I saw the seated nurse nod in my direction.

"Your friend, Carol, asked me to check for you out here. Would you like to come with me?"

Carol sat on an examining table; her forearms were wrapped in white gauze. The only marks on her face were the tracks of tears, a few of which still flowed. She turned up the corners of her mouth to smile at me, but it was a sad smile.

A doctor scribbled on a prescription pad, ripped off the top sheet, and looked at me briefly before handing the paper to Carol.

"You'll need to come in tomorrow to have those bandages changed." He nodded at her forearms. "That prescription is for pain. Don't mix it with anything else, no alcohol . . . or anything else."

He looked at the grin of relief on my face. "You here to take her home?"

I nodded.

"I'd like to keep her here for observation. But she refuses. Her burns aren't life threatening, but I'd like her watched for signs of shock. She's had a traumatic experience. She shouldn't be alone."

"She won't be. What do I watch for?"

"Pallor, clammy skin, agitation, dizzy, lightheadedness, confusion, shallow breathing. If she faints or has any of those symptoms, get her in here immediately."

I nodded my agreement, "Yes, of course."

"She is going to have some pain. If she gets too uncomfortable, bring her back so we can give her stronger pain medications."

Carol slid off the table. Cut open, the singed sleeves of her sweater dangled over the white gauze. "Thank you," she said to the doctor and nurse.

"Let's get the hell out of here," she said to me.

She gave Jeff the same sad smile and followed him to the car without a word. Once she was settled into the passenger seat, and Jeff and I were in, Jeff closed his door and she let out a loud, "FUCK!"

I waited for an explanation while Carol sobbed incoherently. Jeff turned to gesture to me for instructions as to where to go.

"Let's go home," I said thinking it best not to take her back to the scene of whatever the hell had happened. And

God knows what condition her house might be in. I pointed to the north. "To our house."

Was this sobbing what the doctor meant by agitation? Crying was not something I'd seen Carol do very often in the twenty years we'd been close friends.

We walked her up the drive and steps and into the living room. I made her a cup of tea, found a box of tissues, and then Jeff excused himself to give us privacy. I sat with my arm around her shoulders until the shaking subsided and the convulsive breathes stopped.

I moved to the ottoman in front of her chair. "What happened?"

"Karen and I came home at the same time. When we walked into the apartment, we smelled gas. She went into the kitchen." Carol sighed and blew her nose. "I was just about to say, let's get out of here, when I heard her say the gas is on in the oven, and then the sound of a match striking. And boom. I was knocked onto my ass. And little patches of flames popped up everywhere. In the curtains, on the sofa. Karen was on the kitchen floor, unconscious." This brought a fresh flood of tears.

"I . . . I slapped at flames on her clothes . . . grabbed a kitchen towel and beat at spots of fire, but it just kept spreading." She sobbed a few more times.

"Karen's hair, I got it to stop burning. Smothered it with a towel." She wiped her nose with the tissue. "Then firemen grabbed her. And me. And then when we got outside, they took Karen away in an ambulance. My ambulance was following the ambulance to Cowell. I went inside, but they never brought her in."

"They took her to UCSF. That's what the nurse told me." I explained.

Carol looked at me with relief.

"Oh, I was afraid they didn't come in because she was dead." Carol sniffled.

Jeff came into the room. "I've been on the phone with UCSF. Karen's parents are there. She's listed as critical, but stable."

"What does that mean?" I asked.

"She's seriously hurt, but she should be okay."

The apartment was toast, but Karen was eventually okay. She went home for a long recuperation and lots of plastic surgery. Denise, the third roommate, moved in with her boyfriend, and Carol moved in with us.

20

"Doctor, she's been flailing around." Steven stood up from the chair he'd pulled up to his sister's bed. He was glad to see the doctor had finally arrived on his morning rounds. "Do people in coma's usually move around like that?"

The doctor glanced at Steven, but he didn't answer. Instead he walked to the bedside and lifted Al's eyelids one at a time, shining a flashlight into each eye. Without turning to face Steven, the doctor muttered, "The coma patient sometimes awakes in a profound state of confusion."

"Is she waking up?"

Again Steven's question went unanswered.

"Occasionally, a patient will suffer from dysphasia," the doctor said.

"What's dysphasia?" Steven asked. When a minute passed without the doctor speaking, Steven repeated his question. "Dysphasia, what is it?"

"The inability to articulate any speech."

"She's been talking," Steven said. "Well, sorta muttering."

The doctor looked up from his patient to Steven. "A coma-tose patient does not regain consciousness instantly. They are awake for a few minutes, and then the time gradually increases. She may be speaking during the moments she is awake.

"She said she was worried about Carol. Maybe because Carol was with her when she was shot. Maybe she thinks something happened to Carol. But that's probably a good sign, right?"

The doctor nodded.

"Is she aware of me being here?" Steven asked.

A shrug from the doctor, "We don't know all we could about comas. But patients recovering from comas have said they heard people speaking to them."

"I think she's dreaming, but once it seemed like she was trying to tell me something."

"Often patients wake and don't know where they are or how they got there." The doctor continued to examine Alexa, tapping parts of her body, placing his stethoscope on her chest. "It's almost as though they've been some place else." The doctor listened to her chest. "Perhaps reliving a memory."

21

After months of dating, Ted's blue green eyes, beneath his sun-bleached hair still got me every time. It was important to know more about him by meeting his family. I was in love, truly so for the first time. And with this invitation it seemed, one I had pestered him about for months, perhaps he felt the same way.

I tried on everything in my closet, and then started in on Carol's clothes. Nothing was right. Not a thing looked acceptably uptight to wear to meet Ted's parents. If only I hadn't thrown away all the things that I had recently adjudicated as too boring, too stuffy, too un-hip to be seen in. My black velvet dress with a white collar, or even one of the dinner suits my mother dictated every college woman should have several of would have been perfect for dinner with the parents.

I'd read between the lines of our conversations enough to know that Ted's parent's Seacliff address in the city was synonymous with old money and a butler at the door. Dinner would *not* be served family style, and denim would not be seen on anyone. I tossed the jean skirt on the teetering reject pile on the bed.

"What am I going to do?" I asked Carol.

"Stop your whining!" Carol pulled a pair of black velvet bellbottoms that had survived the purge from the back of my closet and tossed them at me. "Put these on."

She slid open the bottom dresser drawer, lifted a white cloth envelope that I knew contained one of her most precious possessions, a black cashmere sweater. "You'll wear this."

She dug in my jewelry box and pulled out the other thing my mother said every college woman must have is strand of pearls. Everything else I owned were strands of hippie beads.

I looked at my feet. I no longer owned high-heeled pumps of any kind, those having gone out with the velvet dress and dinner suits.

"Wear the boots," Carol sighed. "They won't show under the bell bottoms—if you remember not to cross your legs." She gave me that look meant to remind me that ladies do not cross their legs at the knees, only at the ankles, after which a lady tucks her feet back under the chair.

"Take off the dangling earrings, pearl studs only," Carol ordered as she hurried off to answer the doorbell.

I glanced at the clock. "Shit." That would be Ted.

I pulled on the clothes, found a black velvet ribbon to tie back my long hair, jammed the studs into my earlobes, and struggled to fasten the pearls with trembling fingers.

Damn, I hated being so nervous, hated caring so much about what his family thought of me. I should put on makeup, if only I knew how. I swiped Carol's mascara onto my lashes, swore when I smeared black under my eye. I cleaned it off and applied some lipstick.

I was right about the butler. In the wood paneled entry hall, Jones took our coats including my very hip sheepskin, which had left deposits all over the black cashmere. Jones discreetly picked wool hairs off my sweater, and ushered us into the living room. Ted's father, predictably dressed in blazer and khakis, rose to shake my hand. His mother and sister set down their cocktails, nodded and smiled ever so politely. Ted, knowing my inability to handle hard liquor, asked Jones to bring us both a white wine, and joined me on the loveseat near the majestic fireplace.

Ted's father sipped and smiled indulgently while his wife and daughter prattled on about a wedding they had attended the afternoon before. I recognized a few names from Carol having read aloud, in her most affected voice, an account in that morning's society pages. I blushed thinking of the fun we had made of the picture of Ted's sister and her stick-up-the-ass husband. But how were we to know it was Ted's sister that looked so much like a horse. Now that I compared the two faces, the same features on Ted made for a handsome man, and his sister looked okay in person. She was perfectly groomed, every hair on her head including her eyebrows in place.

I wondered when was the last time I'd plucked my eyebrows.

The stick-up-his-ass husband arrived with his sister and her girl friend in tow. The two girls fell all over themselves fawning over Ted while ignoring my presence. I forced a smile and drank the wine a little too fast.

Fortunately, Jones announced, "Dinner is served,"

I was seated next to Ted's father, the quietest man ever, and Ted sat between the two giggling girls across the table. The girls had attended the same wedding and the pre-dinner conversation about the occasion and attendees of the reception continued at the table.

"Lexi is a very talented painter," Ted said in an attempt to bring me into the conversation.

"Oh. Where would I have seen your work?" the sister asked.

"Only on campus," I answered.

She turned to her mother. "Oh. Mother, what did you think of Bart's girl?"

I attempted to converse with Ted's father who was polite, but, I soon realized, shy. The girls competed in flirting with Ted, who, to my disappointment, flirted right back.

It was the longest meal of my life. I suppressed a sigh of relief when Ted excused us soon after dessert was served, saying that I had classes early the next morning.

"I'm sorry. You wanted to meet them," he said helping me up into his jeep. "I told you, you wouldn't like them, but I forget how rude they can be."

I nodded, refrained from mentioning the flirting. I pulled the sheepskin collar up tight around my neck and pretended to enjoy the scenery on the drive back to Berkeley.

"Stop for a drink?" Ted asked as he turned onto Alcatraz. "Sure."

Ted ordered us Irish coffees to take the chill off both the drive in the open vehicle and the evening's mood.

"I was actually planning to make an announcement at dinner tonight, but . . . I didn't know who all would be there, and . . ." Ted said when our drinks arrived, "I'd like to drink a toast."

I held my breath. What was this about? We'd been seeing each other for a few months, sleeping together since a week after Carol fell down the cliff. He made it up from Big Sur and his grandfather's place once a week on days when the restaurant wasn't busy. Were we going to the next level with this relationship? Would I ever fit in his life?

"I've been accepted at Harvard Law."

I tapped my glass mug against the rim of his. "Congrats."

Ted knew I would graduate at the end of the term. Would he ask me to go with him?

"I was hoping you would maybe visit, but it is a long way away. And, well, the more I thought about it, I realized it wouldn't be fair to you, or to me, to expect either of us to be, well, faithful. Considering the distance, and all."

Holy shit. He's breaking up with me.

I downed the coffee, burned my mouth and throat, and then struggled back into my coat. "I'd better get home. I do have a class."

Goddamnit, shit. Tears sprang to my eyes. Fuck. I refused, refused to cry in front of this prick. I stood up turning around so he couldn't see my face.

I ran into my room as soon as I hit the house. I didn't want to see anyone. Didn't want to answer, "how it went". I was relieved that Carol wasn't in our room, I pulled the pearls over my head, and carefully folded the sweater back into its cloth sleeve.

I found my flannel nightie under the pile on my bed and shoved everything onto the floor, planning to crawl into my bed and pull the covers over my head before anyone knew I was home.

I hadn't burrowed all the way in when the sound of violent retching in the bathroom pulled me out of my snit. Who was that? Carol?

■ ■ ■

I helped a pale, shaking Carol into Jeff's car and he rushed us back to the student hospital.

"Food poisoning" was the doctor's verdict.

Carol wrapped her arms around her knees holding herself in a fetal ball. Whatever it was that her stomach had reacted to now attacked her intestines.

"Abdominal cramping," the doctor said. "A common symptom of food poisoning."

"This seems pretty bad. Are you sure that's all it is?" I asked.

"Food poisoning can be lethal. I'm going to put her on intravenous fluids to prevent dehydration." He nodded at the nurse who left to get the IV. "Anybody else eat whatever it was that she ate?"

I shrugged and shook my head. "Apparently not. No one else in the house is sick."

"Hmm." He walked out of the room and I heard him speaking to the nurse in the hall.

The nurse returned with a rolling IV stand from which a plastic bag hung. I looked away as she stuck a needle in Carol's arm and inserted a plastic tube into the back of it. "That'll handle any chance of dehydration." She attached two small bags to the larger bag. "Just a little something to handle the pain and settle down your digestive system."

I sat down in the chair. Carol's poisoning had pulled me out of my funk without a word. How could I feel bad for myself when my friend was enduring such pain?

22

BERKELEY, ALTA BATES HOSPITAL, MARCH 2008

The swish of the door to Al's hospital room swinging shut aroused Steven from his dazed state. He had dozed off after the doctor left only to be awoken by a phone call from his grandfather. It was good to know that his grandfather had hired additional investigators to look for Lauren. Despite his exhaustion, he'd been trying to think through the events of the last couple days, searching for something helpful he could have his grandfather tell the PIs.

"Aunt Carol," Steven stood, "I'm glad you're here. She was asking about you. Like she's worried about you being okay."

Carol waved Steven back into his chair and walked to the opposite side of the bed. She picked up Al's hand. "My poor child, darling girl."

Steven rubbed his forehead. He rose from his chair, walked to the window and stared through the glass not really seeing anything of the view. "I've been trying to figure out what the hell is going on. Who could possibly hate my family enough to do this? How could someone be so evil as to harm someone as good as my mother? Or my sister?"

Carol pulled a chair to the bedside. "When I was younger I saw the world in black and white. Now it's clear to me that it's all shades of gray . . ." Carol stroked Al's hand. "You see, sometimes I'd realize that thoughts and impulses of mine were bad, even the ones I would try to rationalize. You know, by saying the person deserved me being mean to them."

This is how she comes to make me feel better he thought, but Steven waited while Carol hesitated. She sighed then continued. "Because I knew evil lurked in me, I thought I was bad . . . I was much older before I realized that we all have some bad in us, of course not serial killer bad, but it's a matter of the good outweighing the bad."

"Or can the good keep the bad in check?" Steven offered. "So most people aren't bad enough to be serial killers?"

"I don't think it's the same thing," Carol said. "Serial killers are a whole different thing. I think other people are not quite real to a serial killer. He doesn't recognize in others the same capacity for feeling or caring. Or maybe he's shut off from feelings and doesn't realize that others do feel. He doesn't see what he is doing as evil. He's satisfying a craving, seeking a thrill . . . like a guilty pleasure. He knows others don't approve, but he's convinced they are just being some kind of prudes."

"You seem to know something about serial killers," Steven said.

"My best friend was murdered, supposedly by a serial killer," Carol frowned, breathed deeply. "Yeah, I was obsessed with the subject."

"Was?" Steven asked.

"It was so long ago." Carol turned up the corners of her mouth in a weak attempt at a smile.

"Maybe not long enough," Steven said.

"Steven, long enough that it was a different world." Carol sighed. "Actually the world was just starting to change. Or at least that's how it seemed to us, the generation of children who roamed free from dawn to dusk riding our bikes through safe California towns. We had no idea how dangerous the world could be. As young adults we did terribly foolish things; picked up hitchhikers, swallowed pills that could have been anything—" Carol was interrupted by Jeff opening the hospital room door and coming into the room.

23

BERKELEY, MAY 1969

In my dream, I heard Carol's voice. Was she talking about serial killers? Or dangerous cars?

"Are you sure about this?" Carol looked over the rusted nineteen fifty-three Chevy. "This thing doesn't seem reliable, let alone safe."

"It'll be fine." I wiped dust off the windshield and threw two sleeping bags in the trunk. "Trust me."

"Yeah, cause trusting you has proven to be such a smart thing to do in the past," Carol said.

"Are you gonna guilt trip me about Big Sur for the rest of our lives?" I ignored the creak the driver's side door made. "You recovered without any permanent damage, didn't ya?"

"By some miracle." Carol stood glaring at me making no move to get into the car. "Fat lot you cared. You got to hang out at the Pebble Beach Lodge while I lay there with tubes in every orifice."

"I didn't hang out at the Lodge. I went there to get cleaned up, but I slept on the bench in the waiting room until they decided you were okay and kicked you and us out." I slid onto the car's bench seat. "Get in the damn car, will ya?"

Carol gave me "the" look, but climbed into the car. She flung two duffel bags over the seat to the floor behind us as she said, "I don't see why we don't just wait for the mechanic to finish with your car."

"I'll tell you why, cause that guy said it would be ready two days ago, but today there were still parts on the garage floor, and he said *maybe* by tomorrow. I really want to go to the beach *today.*" I turned the ignition key listening for the engine to catch. On the third try, the motor started. "I, personally, was thrilled when Tom offered us this car."

"Yeah, real generous of 'im." Carol was not fond of any of my other best friend Jeff's circle of male friends.

"C'mon, it was. Just 'cause nobody uses it right now, and his brother happened to leave it in our driveway."

"Funny, I was under the impression that it broke down in *our* driveway."

The car was moving along with just an occasional sputter on the way down University Avenue. In the block before the freeway, a row of hitchhikers held out thumbs and signs. I pulled over.

"What're you doing?" Carol asked.

"Didn't you see that guy's sign? It said *Point Reyes.*"

Carol sighed. A crowd of hikers swarmed her side of the car. "Let me see your signs." She pointed to the guy with the *Point Reyes* sign. "You, get in."

Carol turned around to watch the shaggy haired guy move the duffel bags out of the way and slide onto the back seat.

"Thanks chicks. Thanks for stopping."

"We are not chicks." Carol turned back, stared straight ahead.

I fumbled with the radio dial until I found a station playing local music, Dan Hicks and the Hotlicks sang, *"How can I miss you, when you won't go away?"* I put the car in gear, and hit the road.

We made it over the San Rafael Bridge and to the highway leading to the beach. On the off ramp, I hit the brake pedal.

Nothing.

I pumped.

Still nothing.

A four way stop intersection loomed dead ahead.

"Hold on." I leaned down and pulled the emergency brake. I came up with it in my hand, wires dangling free off the end. "Shit."

Carol looked at the item in my hand and braced her leg and arm against the dash. Her other hand was on the door handle. "Shit."

From the backseat a yelp, and a "Holy shit" preceded a loud wail.

We whizzed through the intersection.

But the next intersection was a two way. And we were supposed to stop.

An eighteen-wheeler barreled down the road to our right, timed perfectly to meet us at the intersection.

I hit the gas and zoomed through with inches to spare. We sped on down the road that would soon turn into a twisting nightmare.

I engaged the clutch, down shifted the gears. A horrible grinding screech was heard over the scream of my passengers.

I tried again. More noise, but no slowing.

On the left was the steep side of an oak studded hill.

On our right, a wood fence guarded a pasture.

"Brace yourselves. We're goin in." I twisted the wheel, hit the fence dead on.

The car flew over a hump. We were airborne, then we landed with a thud that rattled my back teeth, but we didn't stop.

We were still moving.

My passengers were still screaming.

And I was out of ideas of how to stop the damn car.

A second fence in a wide ditch loomed ahead.

The nose of the car flew into the ditch.

Wham. My head hit something. Maybe the steering wheel.

Blackness closed in.

■ ■ ■

"Carol, please stop slapping me," I came to sitting in the dirt, uncertain how I had gotten out of the car. "I'm okay, I'm awake."

Carol looked like she was unharmed, but as pissed off as I'd ever seen her. "Now what, Miss-Trust-Me? My God, when am I gonna learn?"

Wailing from the other side of the car scared us both onto our feet. Our hitchhiker lay shaking on the ground, screaming, his limbs thrashing.

Carol switched her gaze from him to me, "Is he having a seizure? You can get those from hitting your head, can't you?"

"No cuts, what could he have hit?" I leaned down to examine his head, at which point he jumped up, knocked me over, grabbed his backpack from the open back door of the car and ran screaming across the field to the road.

"I guess I scared him," I said.

"You could've said you had no brakes." Carol stood next to me watching the figure grow smaller until he disappeared around a bend in the road. "He must not've been seriously hurt if he can run like that."

"Wasn't it obvious, about the brakes, I mean?"

Carol gave me the I-am-not-amused-look before she pried open the trunk to retrieve our sleeping bags. I removed the two duffel bags from the back floor.

"What do we do about the car?" Carol asked as she slung her purse and duffel bag over one shoulder and hefted her sleeping bag under the opposite arm.

"When we get to a phone, I'll call Tom." I checked the glove compartment for valuables and picked up my things.

A VW bug rounded the corner at the same moment we exited the field onto the shoulder of the road. As the mustached driver pulled over, his bearded passenger asked, "Where ya headed?"

Carol and I looked at each other and shrugged.

"Point Reyes?" I said.

"Far out. So are we." The passenger got out of the vehicle, extended his hand to me. "I'm Dick, that's Andy."

"I'm Lexi. She's Carol."

Dick opened the door. He threw in Carol's things, and waved her into the back seat.

Then he held open the passenger door for me, and I climbed in holding a duffel and sleeping bag on my lap.

"How did you end up out here?" Andy asked.

I explained what had happened with the car.

"Far out," Andy said.

In the back seat, Dick lit up a joint and offered it to Carol.

"No thanks," she said.

"What, are you two straight?" Dick passed the grass to Andy.

"Not in the mood," Carol responded.

"That's the point, to get you in the mood." Dick chuckled, took the grass back from Andy and offered it to me.

"No thanks," I said, following Carol's lead.

Dick took an enormous toke and held his breath while he handed off to Andy.

"You always smoke while you drive?" Carol asked.

"Sure." Andy giggled. "Why not?"

Carol raised an eyebrow. "You don't think it might impair your judgment?"

Dick finally blew out smoke and took a breath. "Aah, his judgment is permanently impaired anyway."

"Hey, cut that out," Carol yelped. "Get your hands off me."

I turned to look in the backseat.

"Aah, come on baby." Dick rubbed Carol's thigh with one hand, placed his other hand on her neck.

Carol swatted his hand off her thigh. With all the bags in the seat with them. she didn't have room to really wind up a punch, but she gave her best and slugged him in the jaw. Before he could recover, she jammed her elbow into his lap.

"Pull over," I said to Andy in the shocked silence that preceded Dick's scream.

"Hey, I thought you girls were hip. What's the matter?" Andy actually looked hurt, as though we had insulted *him*.

He stopped the car at the side of the road. Carol and I unloaded our things and ourselves.

Dick flipped us off with both hands as they drove away.

We sat on our bags, and contemplated our dilemma.

"I'm not getting into another car with a stranger," Carol said.

I looked around. We were quite literally in the middle of nowhere. All I could see was winding road, oak trees, dry grass, and a few cows. "We could camp right here," I offered.

Carol did not say a word, gave me "the" look again. Her eyes glaring, the set of her mouth said without uttering a word, "I am not amused."

"We could walk to the beach," I said.

Carol looked away.

"I could walk to a phone?" I stood up. "I'll leave you and our stuff here. I'll come back for you."

"Not a fucking chance in hell am I staying out here in the middle of nowhere by myself." Carol picked up her things. "I hate nature, hate camping. I only agreed to this stupid outing 'cause I felt sorry for you and your goddamn broken heart. But

I'm not gonna get raped or killed to cure your lovesickness."
She stomped off in the opposite direction of the beach.

I hurried after her.

We walked in silence for miles. I admitted to myself that I had perhaps over dramatized my heartbreak over Ted's betrayal. If I'd been as hip as I was supposed to be, I would have shrugged off his interest in other women.

But he was too damn attractive. Women were constantly throwing themselves at him. There was always some chickie flirting with him, making goo-goo eyes at him, rubbing her breasts against him, throwing her arms around his neck.

Maybe I asked too much, expecting him to be faithful. Faithful was an old fashioned concept.

Oh well, too late now. I'd burned that bridge, told him to hit the road. No way I was sleeping with him up until the day he left for Harvard.

It was for the best really. I was too young, had too many plans to fall for the love of my life at this time of my life. The events of the day had scared me back into touch with the real importances in my life. Like how lucky I was to have good friends.

"I'm sorry Carol," I called out to her.

She ignored my apology, walked faster.

I called after her, "I'm sorry. I really do appreciate your coming with me. When we get to a phone, I'll call Jeff to come get us. We'll go back to Berkeley, back to civilization."

"Good." Carol walked even faster.

I looked up a dirt road and thought I saw a small house tucked in the trees. I pointed in that direction. " Hey look! Maybe they would let us use their phone."

"You think that shack has a phone?" Carol backed up to consider the dirt road. "Looks pretty creepy. Bad vibes. With our luck, probably a crazy person, a serial killer lives there." She looked down the blacktop. No other sign of a possible phone was in sight. She exhaled a deep sigh and walked up the dirt road.

■ ■ ■

The people who lived in the small house hidden in a circle of eucalyptus trees didn't appear to be serial killers, and initially, seemed only slightly crazy. Three skinny, shaggy young men, clad only in boxer shorts, stood in a half circle at the door to greet us. Apparently visitors to their habitat were rare. Our arrival was a major deal. Soon another two men and two girls joined the curious group surrounding us in the dark entry hall.

"May we please use your phone?" I asked the assembly.

"Sure. Of course. Yes," answered the chorus.

A slender, bearded young man, with tangled hair trailing down his bareback, ushered me into a room furnished primarily with mattresses and floor pillows. He waved at a phone in the far corner on the floor. I sat down and picked up the receiver.

No dial tone.

I looked up at the young man. "Uhm, this phone doesn't seem to be working."

"Oh, yeah, it doesn't work." He smiled a crooked, goofy grin.

"Do you have a phone that does work?" I asked.

"Not really." He continued to grin.

I returned to where Carol stood in the entry hall. "The phone doesn't work."

"What?" Her look was becoming more of a glare. "Where is your phone that does work?" Carol asked with ineffectively forced politeness.

"We don't got one," said a young girl who looked pretty close to normal. That is, she was fully clothed, but in what looked like pajamas.

Carol sank onto her pile of belongings.

"Do you have a car we could borrow?" I figured it was worth a shot.

"Yes, we do." All of the inhabitants nodded their heads in agreement. "Sure."

"Great." I nudged Carol and picked up my things before they changed their minds.

Carol stayed where she sat. "Does it work?"

"Oh, yeah, sure."

"It runs?" Carol asked.

"Yeah, it runs."

Pajama girl spoke up, "But it's not here right now."

I addressed my next question to her. "Will it be back some time soon?"

"Yeah," She nodded. "Yuri took it to the city. He'll most likely try to be back before dark 'cause the lights don't work too well sometimes."

"Hey, wanna see something real cool." The guy who had shown me the phone waved his arm back to the mattress room. A large, hot, potbelly stove stood a few feet off the far wall.

Carol stayed put, I politely followed the group into the room with the stove.

Three of the men took turns feeding wood pieces into the opening to the firebox. In minutes the metal chimney glowed orange and the circle of crazy people jumped in a frenzy of excitement.

"Fucking great, huh?" one asked.

"Oh, yeah, great." I looked up to where the glowing metal flue pierced the wood paneled ceiling and wondered when the wood would burst into flames. "A little dangerous, don't you think?"

"Nah, we do this all the time."

Eight people danced around the circle of heat and I realized why they were half-dressed. I tried not to think what would happen if one of them were to fall against the red hot glowing metal. I couldn't look.

I returned to Carol's side.

"From the frying pan to the fire," she said. "We gotta get outa here before they burn the place down."

"You want to wait for Yuri to come back?" I asked.

"What day might that be?" She stood, picked up her belongings.

We had gotten as far as the front porch when an ancient pick up truck drove up the driveway.

"You, Yuri?" Carol asked.

"Yep." It was hard to tell the age of the driver. A heavy, black beard and waves of equally dark hair hid his face.

"Will you give us a ride to a phone?"

"Hop in. I think I have enough gas to get there."

■ ■ ■

"Jeff is just leaving for work," I relayed to Carol who stood in the door of the phone booth.

She rolled her eyes. "Wonderful!"

I thanked Jeff for helping us out, hung up the receiver. "Jamie's farm is close to here. Jeff's gonna have Jamie pick us up and take us to the farmhouse outside Novato. Jeff will either come out there tonight, or first thing in the morning."

Carol   shrugged   with   uncharacteristic   apathy. "Whatever."

We walked to the nearest intersection and sat down on our bags. Half an hour later, Carol said, "How far away is this farm?"

"Jeff said, as best he could tell from my description, we're maybe ten, fifteen miles from there."

"It's taking awhile." Carol sighed. She stood, rearranged her bag seat, and plopped back down.

"Maybe he couldn't leave right away. It's not like he was expecting us." I waited for Carol to once again tell me I was always making excuses for people, but she was silent.

Another half hour went by. "Can you call him?" She glared at me.

"I don't know the number. And it's unlisted," I said.

"Call Jeff back." Carol stood and paced three feet to the street tree.

"He left for work."

"Maybe Jamie can't find us. What did Jeff tell him?" Carol walked as far as the stop sign on the other side of our bags.

"Carol, chill out."

I breathed a sigh of relief when the VW bus with Elliott and Ron inside pulled up to the curb in front of us.

Ron rolled down the passenger side window. He flashed his imp grin. "Hey, girls, need a ride?"

"Fuck you" Carol opened the door to the back seat of the VW bus and threw in her bags.

"Thanks guys. Thanks for rescuing us." I slid onto the seat next to Carol and leaned between the front seats. "Jeff said Jamie—"

"Jamie's a bit tied up." Ron grinned at Elliott, "Well, maybe even literally."

Both men chuckled.

Carol shook her head at me sending the "don't-ask" message. I settled back in the seat and relaxed for the first time since the brakes went out.

■ ■ ■

The fragrance of something wonderful wafted out of the kitchen as we entered the back door of the Victorian farmhouse. We dropped our bags as we passed through the utility room and followed the aroma.

The housekeeper, Mrs. Mac, had allowed Tom into her kitchen.

I walked to where Tom stood in front of the huge, old-fashion stove, stirring a kettle of aromatic stew. He said hello without his usual warm smile. I gave him a hug, wondered, but didn't ask what he was upset about. I'd noticed that Tom handled every crisis by cooking up a pot of soup; comfort food, meant to make his clan of friends feel better.

"Are you upset about the car?" I asked.

Tom shook his head, "No, just glad you two are okay." He didn't look happy.

Mrs. Mac stood at the sink and drain board peeling apples. "Glad to see you girls, I need some help with these apple pies." She wiped her hands on her apron and pushed her glasses into her graying hair.

I hugged her hello, introduced her to Carol, and washed my hands in the sink. "How many pies're we making?"

Mrs. Mac had never asked for help before. The first time I'd visited, I'd been informed that Mrs. Mac didn't like anyone in her realm of the kitchen and utility room. Later, when she allowed me in after I had volunteered to pick apples off the gnarly old tree, I realized it was the young men she was keeping out of the one area she could keep orderly. The rest of the ramshackle house she kept clean, but with slobs around, neat lasted only until they entered the room.

That day, it seemed that Mrs. Mac was keeping us out of the other rooms of the house. She even suggested that Carol use the previously-unknown-to-me, bathroom off the utility room.

Elliott and Ron had disappeared through the swinging door that led to the dining room and adjoining living room.

We soon heard the sounds of Beatles music cranked up to full volume.

"They're gonna blow out the speakers again," Tom said.

Carol pushed the door open a crack to peek into the rest of the house.

"Carol, come here and core these apples for me please." Mrs. Mac motioned to Carol to join her at the kitchen counter. "Here, let me show you how that coring thing works."

I slid over to where Tom stirred his soup.

"What's going on?" I whispered.

Tom shrugged.

Mrs. Mac glanced in my direction. "Here're some more apples to peel."

I returned to my peeling station. On the table behind me were two large bushel baskets of red and green apples. "Wow, how many pies are we making?"

Mrs. Mac saw me studying the baskets and smiled. "Oh, some of them apples are gonna be for apple butter. The red ones are for juice. I was thinking a couple pies, but now I got some help, maybe we should make a half dozen. Then you can take some home with ya."

Carol failed to suppress a sigh, but Mrs. Mac didn't let on she'd heard any protest.

With the occasional eye roll from Carol, we peeled and cut in silence until all the green apples were sliced. Mrs. Mac rolled out shells, then showed Carol how to fold the dough to lift it into the pie dish.

Ron came in to take a beer out of the fridge without commenting on the novelty of seeing Carol cooking. In fact, he didn't say anything: no jokes, no wise cracks, nothing. That really made me wonder what the hell was going on.

Mrs. Mac went into the utility room to get the apple juicer.

"Okay, Tom, what gives?" I asked.

Tom scowled at me, gave me a look that implied that he had no idea what I meant.

"C'mon, you guys are acting strange."

Tom shrugged.

"I'm not imagining things. Mrs. Mac usually doesn't want anyone in her kitchen—now she won't let us out." I said, "And Ron hasn't made one crack about—well, about anything. You've been standing in front of that pot like something was going to jump out of it. Mister-proper-polite-host, Jamie hasn't even come to say hello."

Mrs. Mac returned and placed the juicer on the table. "Lexi, you can show Carol how that juicer works."

"Okay, that's it." I pushed open the swinging door, walked through the dining room and entered the living room at the same time Jamie came through the hall door. Ron put down his empty beer bottle and headed down the hall. I heard a girl's voice from the room at the end of the hall.

"Lexi." Jamie stopped and looked at me with surprise. "I didn't know you were here."

"Carol and I have been trapped in the kitchen, helping with pies."

Jamie looked momentarily puzzled. "Oh. Carol's here?"

"Yeah, I thought Jeff spoke with you," I said.

"Yeah, right, yeah." Jamie walked behind the sofa and the over stuffed armchairs headed toward the kitchen. "Want a beer?" he called out from the dining room as he headed into the kitchen.

"No. Thanks." I sat down on the ottoman in front of the brick fireplace.

I wondered who the girl was, and why they didn't want us to know a girl was there. Did we know her? Was the girl why Mrs. Mac had welcomed a stranger into her kitchen?

Jamie stuck his head out the kitchen door. "Lex, are you hungry? We're going to eat in here tonight. Please join us."

Eat in the kitchen? What the hell was going on?

Jamie and Tom were clearing the apples and the juicer off the table. Mrs. Mac wiped off the wood top. Carol, unaware that eating in the kitchen was unusual, carried a stack of plates, setting one in front of each chair. "How many of us are there?" she asked.

"Yeah, how many?" I asked with an eyebrow raised. "And who's the girl?"

Jamie ignored our questions. "I thought after we ate, I would drive you two into Berkeley."

"Jeff said he could come for us after work," I said.

"I need to do some stuff in town. Might as well take you."

"Thanks." I guess whatever was going on here, the guys, and even Mrs. Mac, didn't want us to know. Tom, Elliott and Jamie ate with us. Ron never made a re-appearance.

"Isn't Ron going to eat?" Carol asked.

I noticed the exchange of glances before Jamie answered, "I think he had something he had to take care of."

Elliott looked down at his plate in an attempt to hide a grin. Mrs. Mac slammed the utility room door as she left the house.

My friends did not welcome our unexpected arrival at the farm. And that seemed the strangest, most upsetting part of what had been a strange, scary day.

24

BERKELEY, ALTA BATES HOSPITAL, MARCH 2008

The chime of his cell phone woke Steven.

OMG, he was stiff from sleeping in that chair. He looked at his phone. It was Aunt Carol calling.

"Hey," Steven answered.

"How is she?" Carol asked.

"She's muttering occasionally. It still sounds like asking about you. And some guy named Ted. Do you know anyone named Ted?"

"Hmm." Carol was silent for a moment. "No, not anyone she would know anyway."

Jeff pushed open the door, walked to Steven's chair, and patted his shoulder. "Any change?"

Steven said goodbye to Carol. "Hi Dad. She's been talking, muttering actually. About some guy named Ted."

Jeff scowled. "Does she have a friend named Ted?" He walked to the bedside, took his daughter's hand in his.

Steven shook his head. "Not that I know. Any word about Mom?"

"I'm sorry, nothing new."

25

BERKELEY, MAY 1969

"Aren't those two guys Jeff's friends?" Carol nodded at the far end of the bar. We had ended our study night at the library with a quick trip to the Monk, our favorite student dive bar. Officially it was the Monkey Inn, but everybody called it the Monk. The beer was cheap, cheaper than bars close to campus, but the main attraction after a long night of studying, was a savory filled pastry called a pierogi.

Hoping to avoid dealing with men on the make, we'd chosen a small table in a dark corner to await the arrival of our midnight snack.

I strained my neck to see the faces of the two she meant. The pudgy body closest to us resembled Elliott, and both men were short enough to be Dave and Elliott. Subtleties of hair color were lost in the dark bar. The swing of a door flooded their location with light long enough for me to recognize Dave's face. Ron came through the open door and joined the other two.

"Yeah, that's Dave. And the guy with him is probably Elliott." I lifted a mug of cold beer, clinked Carol's, and chugged. "And Ron just walked in."

Carol licked suds off her upper lip. "What do you think of those three?" she asked.

I shrugged, more interested in my beer.

"They're a little creepy," she said.

I frowned at her.

"Come on, you've noticed how different they are from the rest of that group. " She nudged my arm. When I failed to respond, she continued. "Dave and Elliott. They're both so uncomfortable . . . self-conscious. The others are confident, good looking, well spoken—"

I had to admit she had a point, but, so what?

"Why are they part of the group?"

"I think Elliott and Jamie went to prep school together."

"That doesn't explain it."

"They're fraternity brothers."

"And how did that happen?" Carol asked.

I drank my beer, considering her point.

"You know, why did they let those two in?" Carol said.

"They liked them?"

Carol rolled her eyes and gave me the look that said, "How stupid do you think I am?"

"Maybe they were legacies," I said. "Dave's okay looking."

"Yeah, he'd actually be good-looking—if he weren't so creepy."

"Define creepy," I asked.

"There's something weird going on with him."

"He's just uncomfortable because he grew up poor."

Carol shook her head. "It's way more than that."

The bartender waved at us to come for our pierogi sandwiches. I jumped up, grabbed the two paper wrapped snacks and hoped that Carol would be distracted from her subject by the food.

She nibbled an exploratory bite. "Oh! Real hot." She put the filled dough aside. "It's something more than the poor thing with that guy Dave."

I raised an eyebrow at her without giving up on the steaming hot sandwich. I took little bites around the edge of the crisp crust letting some of the heat from the center filling escape.

"When Dave tries to smile, he leers. And he's really condescending."

"That's a cover for his lack of confidence," I explained.

She squinted one eye at me. "Maybe. But it's like—like a hollowness. Like he's just a shell with nothing inside, no heart or emotion, except occasionally he's annoyed. But he tries to hide it."

I burned my mouth on the pierogi, took a gulp of beer, and gave up on the pastry until it cooled. The word hollow did fit Dave's character.

"What's your thing about Elliott?" I asked.

"Well, he's funny looking." Carol bit into her now cooled beef and onion filled pierogi.

"Not funny looking in a bulldog cute way?"

"No." No hesitation in her voice. "He's pear shaped . . . and . . . puffy. With bad skin. I don't trust ugly people. Ugly on the outside, ugly on the inside. " She chewed and thought. "Decidedly not athletic, definitely dorky. I have never met a rich person who doesn't play tennis . . . or golf . . . or ski . . . or ride . . . or sail—I mean, what *does* he do?"

"That doesn't make him creepy." I'd heard this ugly theory of Carol's before without reacting. Not this time. "This ugly thing of yours, I mean, easy for someone as gorgeous as you to be critical of ugly. But some people can't help it. They were born that way."

"Bullshit. Ever seen an ugly baby? They're all cute, even if it's in a cute, ugly way." Carol washed down the last bite of her pierogi with a gulp of beer. "We should've ordered more than one—lots more." She finished off her beer. "Look, here's the thing; as rich as Elliott is, there's no reason for him to look ugly. Hasn't he ever heard of a dermatologist? And why can't he get some exercise? It's not like he has to work to support himself. He just sloths around."

"What about people who are born with weird shit, like huge noses, or major Adam's apples?" I asked.

"There are plenty of very attractive people around who do not have perfect features, but they make themselves look good anyway."

"Are you okay with Ron? He's not ugly."

"Your right. He's not ugly, but terribly phony."

I lifted an eyebrow.

"He pretends to be just like the rich guys, but I know the Compton neighborhood in LA he grew up in and believe me, he had to have been dirt poor." She stood up. "Let's see if we can't get out of here without having to talk to the creeps."

26

Steven looked up from his book, saw his father enter the room. "Dad, she's been mumbling stuff again."

"About Carol?" Jeff ran his hand across his daughter's cheek before he sat in a chair on the opposite side of her bed.

"Some, but mostly about Ted again."

"Who?" Jeff asked.

"No clue. Not anyone I know. How's your investigator doing?"

Jeff shook his head. He looked like shit, even worse than Steven thought possible.

"What about this Ted? Didn't you know someone with that name? Have you seen him lately?"

Jeff shook his head again. "He was just a guy my friend Lexi dated."

"Did he know Mom?"

Jeff shrugged. "They might've met." He thought about it for a moment. "No, Lexi broke up with him before I met your mother."

"I think you should get your PI to find him."

"What for?"

"I don't know, it's something. Al has clearly said the name Ted more than once," Steven said. "Please do it. Or should I ask grandfather to talk to his PIs about this Ted guy? What was his last name?"

"Steven, there's no way that that Ted could have anything to do with any of this. But I have no problem with you giving your grandfather any ideas you might have. God knows nothing else seems to be working. Tom's investigators haven't been much use, so I asked for help from investigators in my office. And Detective Schmidt has been following up on anything and everything any of us have suggested. He's a good cop," Jeff said, forcing a weak smile. "He'll find your mother, I'm sure he will."

Steven tried not to notice that his father sucked at being reassuring. Thirty-two hours. His mother had been missing for thirty-two hours.

27

BERKELEY, MAY 1969

Finally, I'd finished my paper, and turned in the preliminary version of my thesis. I'd studied all I was going to until time for exams.

Now it was time for my real love—in the studio, painting. I cranked up the music, shutting out the sounds of the city and my housemates. I was lost in the flow of the paint off my brush, the battle to get just the right shade of blue.

A tap on my shoulder made me jump. I hadn't even noticed the door open.

"Lexi, can we talk for a few?" Carol faked a smile as though she hoped I would allow the interruption without anger. She turned down my stereo.

I sighed and placed the tube of blue acrylic next to the black one. "Of course. What's up?"

"Something's bothering me." She sat in the wreck of a wicker chair in the sunny corner of the light filled greenhouse I called a studio. "You could paint while we talk."

"Just tell me." I swirled a brush in a jar, cleaned it on a rag.

"I know you think someone has it out for me—so I've been thinking, there's really only one thing that could've been on purpose. What worries me is that guy could have been after you as well as me." Carol stood up then walked over to look at my canvas before returning to the chair. "I keep thinking that the guy who attacked us, well, tried to attack us, after the concert was somebody we know."

"Yeah, I know what you mean." I had trouble getting him out of my mind too.

"You do?"

"Yeah, because he didn't say anything, like he was afraid we'd recognize his voice."

Carol jumped forward in the chair. "Exactly. Got any ideas?"

I shook my head.

"It could've been one of Jeff's short friends. The guy was short, but in the dark, hard to tell if he was pudgy."

"You think it was Elliott, or Dave?" I failed to keep the surprise from my voice. "Really?"

"Do you know anybody else that short?"

"Good point." I twirled the palette knife through the black swirls in the blue paint. "But why in the world would either one do such a thing?"

"For kicks. The thrill," Carol said.

"You think one of them is crazy?"

"Maybe he hates us." Carol pulled her knees up to her chest and rested her feet on the front edge of the chair.

"Why?"

"Because we're beautiful and he's ugly?" She hugged her knees.

"You think it was Elliott?" I asked her.

"I don't know. Maybe it's a crazy idea." Carol jumped from the chair. She strode to the window behind me "Did you hear someone out there? Can people hear us in here?"

"Probably. I can hear when people talk out there."

She moved close to me and whispered. "My point is, it could just as easy be you that someone has it in for. Think about that."

I turned to look at her. She raised an eyebrow at me before she walked out of the greenhouse.

I didn't want to think about Carol's theory. As soon as she left, I turned the music back up and painted through the night. The sunrise glow greeting the new day behind the Berkeley Hills surprised me.

I'd finally gotten the blue the shade I'd had in my mind's eye. Even the yellow looked pretty close to right. So seldom was I able to capture the colors, get the light and shadow just the way I had imagined it. It was a thrill, a tremendous sense of satisfaction when I was able to get a painting to look right. I hoped I would feel the same way after some sleep.

Carol pushed the door open with her foot, a steaming mug in each of her hands. She handed me one.

The steam off the tea smelled wonderful "Thanks," I said.

"You been out here all night?" Carol asked.

"Yeah." I stood back to admire my work, suppressing my smile of satisfaction.

"Wow." Carol whistled.

I blushed, sipped the hot tea.

"That is so-o fuck-ing beautiful. The colors, I love it."
Carol grinned. "You are damn good, aren't you?"

I sank into the creaky, wicker chair. The tea soothed the
rough edges, mellowed the bite of exhaustion that hit once I'd
gotten the color right.

"Even though it's abstract," Carol said, "looking at it
makes me feel like I could walk right in between giant red-
woods and smell the fresh scent of a forest." She stared while
she drank her morning cuppa before she spoke again. "Lexi, I
didn't sleep much myself."

I looked at her with surprise. "I thought you'd finished
your thesis."

"Yeah, I did," she hesitated. "It was our conversation, what
we talked about last night. Here's what's bothering me. In Big
Sur, Elliott *and* Dave were both with me coming down that
cliff."

"I thought you just, tripped," I said.

"Yeah, I did."

"So?"

"I don't know how I tripped. What I mean is . . . someone
could've tripped me."

28

"Dad, why don't we have a policeman, or any security here?" Steven said. "Don't they usually post someone outside the door?"

"There is a man out there." Jeff looked at his son. "Haven't you noticed him?"

"It seems pretty obvious, she's in danger as soon as whoever shot her learns that she's still alive. They sure didn't give up after the first time they shot at her. And the last couple times I went out to get food, the guy wasn't there."

"I'll take care of it," Jeff said.

"Dad, could this possibly have to do with the case you are trying?"

Jeff shook his head. "I did consider the possibility but I don't see how."

"Has anyone threatened you?"

Jeff continued to shake his head. "No. No threats, no demands."

"Al had a letter—"

Jeff interrupted, "That letter had nothing whatsoever to do with this. Did either of you happen to look at the date? It was years old, just happened to be on my desk as I'd been cleaning out file drawers. Your sister must've scooped it up along with the Zodiac file."

"What is the case?" Steven asked.

"What?" Jeff looked at his daughter, his attention on her. He picked up her hand, rubbed her fingers.

"The case you're trying? What is it?" Steven asked again.

"It's a homicide. No possibility of a connection. A man killed his wife. Pretty straight forward except he's well enough off to hire the best defense. That's always a challenge to the prosecution, but no possible connection to our problem."

"I don't believe you. This has to be connected to you Dad. Maybe the defendant hopes to distract you."

"That has definitely been accomplished, but doesn't this seem extreme?" Jeff shook his head. "No, I don't think so."

"What else would it be?"

29

BERKELEY, MAY 1969

Crisp, fresh, pine scented air; a view, bracketed by evergreens, of the Golden Gate Bridge across the bay; clear, deep blue skies; and the anticipation of hot coffee; these all put a bounce in my step as I strode down the hill to Euclid on the way to campus and my first class of the day.

I turned onto the concrete, art moderne Leroy Steps, a mid-block detour that provided more of an aesthetic inspiration than a short cut. Having reached the bottom of the steps, I didn't bother with the sidewalk but strode down the center of the empty, half block long dead end street.

The roar of an engine behind me gave the few seconds of warning I needed to jump clear of a car exiting the dead front lawn of a frat house.

My heart jumped as dramatically as my body. I yelled, "Hey, watch it!" after the disappearing car flew by me. The style of that '53 Chevy, the same model as Tom's brother's car, niggled some thought, some recollection that my caffeine deprived brain couldn't catch.

I hurried down the sloping street to coffee on Euclid.

I sipped steaming hot coffee from a paper cup, until I noticed the time on the wall of the coffee shop, and then hurried onto campus.

In my seat in the auditorium, I enjoyed the coffee while waiting for the laggard prof. I tried to grasp the elusive concept triggered by seeing that '53 Chevy. I decided to let it go until it came to me.

When the thought returned, while I was scribbling lecture notes, I wrote it down. "Chevy, not that old, why lost brakes?" The idea that maybe someone had tampered with the brakes had me shaking my head in denial. Couldn't be. Why would anyone want to hurt Carol and me?

I thought about all the strange, dangerous things that had happened to Carol in the last year and a half.

Falling down the cliff in Big Sur—did someone trip her?

The knife-wielding attacker in the park. What would've happened if we hadn't fought him off?

The gas explosion in Carol's house. Was it an accident that the oven was left on? Or did someone turn it on without lighting it, knowing what would happen? The firemen explained to Carol later that flipping a switch to turn on a light could've sparked the gas explosion.

Then there was the nearly lethal food poisoning. Had someone purposely added a toxic substance to her food? No one else in the household was sick with nausea and diarrhea.

When Carol recovered, after a few days in the hospital, I quizzed her as to what she'd eaten that day. Salad, yogurt, canned soup, tea, noodles—nothing suspicious like mayo or beans or old meat. We'd thrown out all the food in the fridge as a precaution.

I never imagined at the time that someone could possibly have slipped something into her food. Lots of people had access to the kitchen and the fridge. Certainly not Jeff, or Jamie, Dave, Tom, Elliott . . . the usual guys, but what about somebody they'd invited into the house.

They were all so casual about bringing strangers into our house, people they met at bars, at a football game, "Hey, yeah no problem, use the bathroom here." Like it was their house.

Losing the brakes on the car. What if that had occurred at a worse spot on the road? Like on the winding, cliff roads closer to the beach?

I'd known Carol since nursery school. She'd never been a magnet for trouble. In fact, quite the opposite . . . until recently.

My heart fluttered with a sudden panic. I had to find Carol. She *was* in danger.

I climbed over the row of legs hindering my exit of the auditorium, and dug a dime out of my jeans pocket. There was a pay phone in the vestibule. I called the house. No one picked up. I tried to remember what class she had this morning.

She had complained about having to face the tear gas first thing in the morning, so her first class must be on the south side of campus closer to where the National Guard and the People's Park demonstrators fought over a vacant half block of land.

Shit, I'd have to take my chances on getting gassed.

Carol's favorite spot in the library was empty.

Dwinelle Hall was my next guess. I poked my nose in the auditorium and scanned for Carol's black hair. Plenty of dark heads, but none with her sheen and soft waves.

I fought the panic that threatened to keep me from thinking straight. I couldn't try every classroom in the building. From the benches in the plaza outside the entrance, I could watch all three exits.

The Campanile struck eleven, and students poured from the building. I spotted Carol flirting with tall-dark-and-handsome just outside the north entrance of Dwinelle Hall.

"Carol," I yelled as I ran. "Carol."

"What's the matter?" The annoyance on her face sent a loud and clear message, I-like-this-guy, back off.

I ignored her look, and dragged her to the wood bench surrounding the raised planter and a Loquat tree. "Carol, I don't know why we've been so stupid."

She scowled. "Hey, I was just about to give that cute guy my number. What is your problem?"

"Someone *is* trying to kill you."

"Look, I'm sorry I started this. I was overtired, reading too much Kafka. My imagination ran away with me."

I grabbed her arm, and held tight when she tried to stand.

"Oh, for Christ's sake." She shook off my hand, stood up. "I've got a class in Kroeber." She walked between the trees in their giant planters.

I rushed after her. "Really, think about it. All the weird, possibly fatal, so called accidents you've had in the last ten months."

"Lexi, now *your* imagination is running away with you."

"No. Really, the fall—"

"I tripped."

"Or someone tripped you."

"I tripped."

"The explosion."

"Someone left the oven on. The pilot light blew out. Accident." She turned left and hurried across the wood bridge leading into faculty glade.

I pushed between her and green foliage, "Carol, you are in danger. Poisoning. Remember that? You almost died."

"Bad food. It happens. Get over it."

"The brakes."

She stopped walking, then turned to look me in the eye with one brow raised. "I told you that car was dangerous. You said, 'Trust me.' Remember that?"

"Carol, I'm afraid."

"I'll tell you what, I won't eat. I won't get in a car, or turn on any ovens, or climb any cliffs." She strode off.

I followed, but she ignored me until we reached the door to her class. I grabbed her arm. "Why'd you change your mind? Yesterday you thought maybe all those things weren't accidents, you said maybe some one had tripped you. Now you're in denial."

"Lexi, I love you. I stopped freaking out, got over my paranoia. I appreciate your concern, but why would anyone want to kill me? After all, I'm such a nice person." She slammed the door in my face.

"Bitch," I yelled after her.

30

"Al, can you hear me?" Steven asked as he brushed a wisp of blonde hair off his sister's forehead. The orderly and nurse had just wheeled her back into the room. Her head was no longer fully swathed in bandages, just a relatively small patch on the right side where a razor had cut a swath through her thick tresses.

"What did the MRI show?" he asked them.

"The doctor will be up soon to speak with you," the orderly said.

Steven didn't like the way that sounded. Oh shit. Please don't let her have brain damage.

An eternity later the physician showed up. "Well, the MRI still looks pretty good. The inflammation is going down. Looks as though she should recover just fine."

"It's almost been two days. How long will she be unconscious?" Steven asked after breathing a sigh of relief.

"Hard to say." The doctor smiled at Steven. "I think your sister is going to be okay, although it is a puzzle. We don't know everything we could about comas. Sometimes patients regain consciousness in minutes, sometimes months, even years . . . and anything in between. But you say she has been speaking which indicates she is waking up. Her GCS is good."

"Her what"

"Her Glasgow Coma Scale.

"What's that?

"GCS measures the depth of the coma. The deeper the coma, the lower the score."

"So how deep is her coma?" Steven asked. "Please, I just want to know if my sister is going to be ok."

The neurologist looked at Steven with sympathy. "Here's the deal. Coma is a response to injury that allows the body to pause activity in order to concentrate on healing immediate injuries before waking up." The doctor looked at Steven as if to see that he was following. "Your sister's wound in the cerebral cortex was away from any critical structures in her brain. She is in a mild coma and appears to be waking up. Likely the worst after effect she will experience will be PTA."

"PTA?" Steven asked.

"Post-traumatic amnesia. And before you ask, the length of the amnesia correlates to the length of unconsciousness. And she may not experience much at all. Unlikely she would experience total amnesia. Usually it's just some details. Or names. Bottom line, there is every reason to believe your sister is going to be just fine."

31

BERKELEY, MAY 1969

"Where're ya headed?" He stuck close to my side as I rushed across the street before the light turned red.

Aw, for chrissakes. Yeah, he rescued me, but did that mean I had to be nice to him? Why couldn't I be a bitch without guilt tripping myself? He was exactly the excessively handsome kind of guy I wanted to avoid.

"Thanks again. I do appreciate you helping me." I forced a smile and waved. "Ciao."

I lengthened my stride; maybe he'd give up. I glanced to my left; he was hanging in there. His legs were even longer than mine. I wouldn't lose him easily.

He caught my eye and smiled that charming crooked grin. Oh man, those crystal blue eyes. And dimples.

I couldn't help myself. I returned the smile.

He grinned. "Groovy." He waved at the tables and chairs on the wide patio of the Euclid Café. "Coffee?"

I nodded and followed him to a table.

"Sit, please. Cream?"

I nodded.

"Sugar?"

I nodded again, dropped my book bag next to one of the chairs, and sat down.

He walked to the line of students and faculty waiting to order.

A newspaper left on the table headlined another Zodiac killing. A photo of his latest victim led the front-page story; a copy of a letter purportedly from the Zodiac was next to the photo.

I couldn't handle any more evidence of our fucked up world that day. I moved the newspaper to a nearby table.

Derek returned with two steaming mugs of coffee before I had a chance to reconsider befriending a stranger. Especially a handsome one. He placed both cups on the table and passed me a handful of sugar packets.

"So—where do you live?" he asked.

At least he didn't ask me "what's your sign?" Or "what's your major?" But then the smears of acrylic paint on my bell-bottom jeans might have given my art major away.

"Up the hill." I waved up toward the top of the Berkeley hills.

"Headed home?"

"Yeah. I've got a lot of work to do." I rubbed dried paint off my finger.

"What're you painting?"

"Kinda abstract nudes in landscapes."

He raised an eyebrow. "Like cubist nudes descending staircases?"

"I'm not Picasso or Braque. Landscapes, not interiors."

He flashed that damn smile revealing dimples again. "I'd love to see them."

That I ignored. "What's your thing?"

"Architecture."

"And you escaped the Environmental Design building?" I asked with a smile. "Don't they keep would-be architects chained to their drafting tables? I see people working in there twenty-four hours a day."

"True, too true." He sipped his coffee, and then grinned. "Couldn't hack it, had to get out and find a pretty girl to rescue."

I drank the last of my coffee. "Thank you." I forced a smile.

I wasn't going to violate my new agreements with myself. No more handsome and charming men. Too dangerous for my bruised heart. Women throw themselves at men like this one.

"I really do have to get to work."

He drained his cup and stood up. "May I walk with you?"

I shrugged an "if you want to" and picked up my bag.

The small talk continued as we headed up the hill to the house I shared with a group of close friends plus an assortment of guys who did not officially live there but hung around a lot.

My roommate Carol was about to graduate and already job-hunting. She was beautiful and talented so she would land a position in a fashion house quickly.

Jeff was a law student and my best friend since childhood when we had spent summers at the same camp, playing the same sports.

Dave, a Cal grad, commuted to a job in the city.

All three of them led busy, productive lives.

The others, the hang-arounders, needed to get a life. They used our place as their Berkeley base. All were graduates, and either trust fund babies or wannabes who managed to kill every day fucking around, tripping to the beach, hanging out in the Haight, going to Janis Joplin & Big Brother & the Holding Company concerts in Golden Gate Park or the Grateful Dead at The Fillmore.

Some days I was envious of their freedom. But once I started painting, I forgot everything but the music and the flow of my brush.

Two of the hang-arounders, preppie looking Jamie and Ron, lounged on the front porch swing smoking. Jamie had actually attended prep school and was one of the trust fund beneficiaries. Wannabe Ron imitated Jamie's mannerisms, dress, and accent, but his rugged face and his engaging smile charmed both men and women. Jamie's relaxed manner was equally appealing. Both lit up with curiosity when we came up the front walk and climbed the stairs of the entry.

"Yo, Lex," Ron said. "Who's your friend?"

Shit. I'd planned to say good-bye and close the door in his face if I had to, but these two guys were going to make it awkward.

"Can I see your paintings?" Derek asked.

"Ah, shit man, you gotta see her work. It's far-out." Ron jumped up from the porch swing, opened the door, grinned in answer to the scowl I shot his direction, and invited Derek into *my* house before I could think of how to get out of this one.

One of my recent canvasses, a colorful abstract landscape hung above the fireplace in the living room. I followed the three guys into the entry hall and groaned as I watched Ron point out the painting.

"Wow. Cool." Derek directed a nod of appreciation to me.

"I really gotta get some stuff done. Thanks again." I ducked down the hall toward my room as I heard the men introducing themselves. Jeff was exiting his room.

"Hi," I said to him. "If you see Carol, please tell her I need to talk to her."

Jeff nodded his strawberry blonde head. "Sure."

In my room, I dumped my bag on my bed, grabbed a new brush from my desk and headed out to the garden shack I had converted to my studio.

Through open green house windows, I could hear Derek, Ron, Jamie, and my housemate Jeff in the living room, yukking it up and talking in those low, guttural voices that told me they were passing a joint. Any minute now they'd start discussing the relative merits of Acapulco Gold versus whatever they were smoking.

I loved those guys, but that dope story was getting old.

I closed the rusted, metal-framed windows, slid a Beatles record out of the album cover and set it on the turntable. "*In Penny Lane there is a barber—*" The sweet sounds took the edge off my tension.

Carol cracked the door enough to poke her dark head in. "Jeff said you wanted to talk to me."

"I went to the library after I saw you on campus." I motioned for her to come in. "Know what the symptoms of arsenic poisoning are?"

She shrugged, pulled her long black hair back from her pale face. Seeing how white her face was made my heart ache with concern for my best girlfriend. Carol did her best to hide her soft heart and anxious nature, but I saw through her tough shell.

"Vomiting," I said, "diarrhea, abdominal cramps."

"You're still on that subject!" She walked out; the crooked hinges thwarted her attempt at a door slam.

32

BERKELEY, ALTA BATES HOSPITAL, MARCH 2008

"Ste-ven," a hoarse whisper.

He looked up from his reading to see his sister struggling to speak.

"Wa-ter," she whispered.

Tears sprang to his eyes. "Oh my God, Ali, thank God."

He held a water cup and straw to her mouth. She sipped and worked to swallow.

Steven gave his sister a weak smile.

Her eyes looked toward the water cup.

"More?" he asked.

She gave a tiny nod and took a larger swallow this time.

"Steven." Al smiled at him. "I've had the strangest . . . most vivid dreams. It was like I was reliving . . . a memory."

"I'm so glad you're back." He squeezed her hand; afraid to touch more of her for fear he'd hurt her. "I've been so scared."

She squeezed back and seemed to doze off.

He called his father. "She's awake. She spoke to me."

Steven hung up the phone. "Dad's on his way over."

Al groaned, muttered something. It sounded like she said, "Steven, it's so real, maybe I've been reliving—it was like I was there." She nodded off.

33

Definitely strange, but the dreams were so real. *Had* I been reliving Lexi's life?

I had a lot to think about as I lay in my hospital bed. My imaginings were so realistic. Was it real? Had I really chosen my best friend and his wife for parents? Or was it all another bad dream?

I tried to remember the thoughts I'd had just prior to being shot in front of Kroeber Hall. I was onto something, but the concept kept slipping from my grasp.

"Steven?" I said.

My brother looked up from his book. "Yes?"

"How bad is it?"

"Your injury?"

"Uh-huh."

"The doctor says there's no reason you won't recover completely. And the second MRI they did this morning showed the inflammation has gone down a lot."

"How soon can I get up?"

"I think we better ask the doctor that, but I imagine as soon as you feel like it."

I attempted to lift my head, but it felt impossibly heavy. A wave of nausea hit me.

Steven looked alarmed. "Hey. Wait until we talk to the doctor, will ya?"

"Yeah, I think I better." I rested for a few minutes before I asked him the next question.

"Steven . . . what do you think about . . . the idea . . . of reincarnation?"

He shrugged. "Seems logical. Could explain a lot of things. Feeling like you've been somewhere before. That immediate connection you feel towards some people. Even love at first sight. There are more people on this planet who believe in it than don't. But . . . it's a little . . . um . . . freaky. Why?"

I didn't want to answer his why. I decided to drop the subject until I'd had a chance to think about it with a clearer head. "I thought I heard Dad's voice."

"He's been in and out," Steven answered.

"What about Mom?"

Steven got a pained look on his face. "Hmm . . . mm . . . uh." He looked at me. "Al, we haven't found Mom yet."

"WHAT?" Waves of panic shot through my body, my limbs began to tremble.

"Chill!" Steven said. "Shit, I shouldn't've told you. But she called Dad and said she was okay."

I looked at the tubes and cords hooked up to my hand and chest. "What is all this shit anyway? What are they putting into me?"

"There's the heart monitor." He pointed to the machine. My heart felt strong to me; in fact it was racing with panic.

"Tell them to get it off me."

"The nurses said they were planning to unhook it today."

"I want it off now." I looked around the bed trying to find the call button. Steven handed it to me from where it was wrapped around the bed rails. I held my thumb on the button thinking I'd get some immediate response. Nothing happened.

"Steven, what about drugs? What's in this thing?" I touched the tube running into my hand and looked at the clear plastic bag that had countless little baggies hanging off it.

"Sugar water to keep you hydrated and fed and medicine to take down the inflammation and I don't know what else."

"How long've I been out?"

"Two days."

That was all. It seemed like a lifetime.

Oh God, Mom had been missing for two days! "What's Dad doing about Mom?"

"The police, of course, and his investigators. And grandpa hired private investigators too."

"And?"

"Nothing. Ab-so-fucking-lutely nothing."

I ripped the round heart monitor tape things off my chest. Ow, that stinging hurt as much as my head. "Are there more of these damn things on my back or something?" I sat up, turned my back to my brother and opened the back of my gown.

"Al, what the hell? We agreed to wait for the doctor."

"Uh, no, you suggested we wait for the doctor. I didn't agree to anything."

Steven drew his phone out of his pocket, punched some numbers and spoke to the doctor's office.

It must have been the heart monitor flat lining because all of a sudden we had a room full of nurses and medical personnel.

"The doctor's office says he's in the building somewhere. Can you get him?" Steven asked one of the nurses.

"He's already been alerted." The male nurse walked to my bed. "Well, you look pretty good," he said.

"I need to get outa here," I answered.

"I strongly recommend you take it easy for a bit. Lie back down. You don't want to get up too fast or you'll have one hell of a headache," the nurse said.

Like I didn't already.

A doctor I'd never met before came into the room, ordered people around and everyone but Steven fled the room.

"Alexandra, I'm Doctor Worthy. My partners and I have been taking care of you."

"What about Dr. Fleiss? He's always been my doctor."

"Well, apart from the fact that he's a pediatrician, and you're hardly a child anymore, he's also only a GP and you've suffered a fairly serious head wound."

"Are you a neurosurgeon then?" I asked.

He had removed the bandage from the side of my head and was inspecting the wound. "Yes."

I did my best not to react to the pain he was causing. "I want to go home."

"Maybe tomorrow morning we can discuss that. You need some rest before you're ready for going anywhere."

"You don't understand. I have to get out of here."

"No, you don't understand young lady. You have been in a coma for forty-eight hours. You aren't going anywhere. In the morning, a physical therapist will see you. We need to assess how much damage has been done with this wound and how to address it." He scribbled on a chart while he lectured me, then he turned to my brother to make sure that Steven had been paying attention to what he said. "Do you both understand? You may be past the most acute danger, and I'm certainly glad to see you alert. But we are not out of the woods yet."

What's with this *we* business? *You* were never in the damn woods. But what came out of my mouth was, "What time will you be here in the morning?"

"I can't be specific. I make my rounds after the surgeries I have scheduled for tomorrow morning. But I'll make sure the physical therapist comes by here first thing so that by the time I get here we'll know where we stand."

There's that *we* again.

He walked out, I heard him talking in the hall. A nurse rushed in and put something in the IV bag.

As soon as the nurse cleared the door, I turned to Steven. "Are you gonna help me?"

"Help you do what?"

"Get outa here."

"Al, did you hear anything that doc said?"

"Steven, Mom is—well, fuck." A sudden urge to sleep overcame me. I shoulda ripped out that damn IV. Drugged sleep, again.

"Al, in the morning, I'll help you all you want. We can't do anything tonight. Besides, what can we do better than the police? Or Dad's investigators? You need to get well. Please just get well. Sleep."

It appeared I had no choice. Waves of dozing slid in and out even as I listened to his assurances.

But it wasn't a restful, peaceful sleep I was pulled into. Faces flashed in and out of view, mad faces, bloody faces, grinning faces, Derek's light blue eyes set in an equally handsome face, Ted's friendly smile, an ugly leer through a black hood, a very young beautiful Carol, Dave's stoned expression, Lauren's ladylike appearance that few knew hid a free spirit. The last convinced me that Mom was still alive.

But the experiences of the last few days had brought home to me the fragility of human life, and how quickly, in a flash, life changed. Or ended.

34

The next morning I wasn't taking any chances on getting drugged again.

"Are you gonna take this thing off? Or am I?" I said to the nurse who was fooling with the IV bag.

"I don't have any orders from the doctor," she answered.

A tall, skinny dark guy entered my room and pointed to the IV stand. "You might want to use that as a support while we walk you around," he said.

"I want it off," I said. "Are you the physical therapist?"

"Yep." He nodded at the nurse who slid the needle out of my hand and applied a bandage. "I'll be back when the nurse is finished."

Next out came the catheter.

The physical therapist returned and introduced himself, told me what we were going to do, put slipper socks with sticky stripes on my feet, and offered his arm to help me out of the bed. We walked very slowly to the door and a short way down the hall. I felt unsure of each step and woosy as hell, but I did my best to tough it out.

Steven and Dad arrived as we made our way back to the door of my room.

"Ah, Al, I'm so glad to see you up." Dad carefully, tenderly kissed my cheek and smiled into my eyes. "I hear you're anxious to go home. I'll arrange whatever nursing and security is needed, but of course, by home, you mean to the city, not Berkeley. Right?"

"Sure Dad." Wherever. Just get me outa here. This was all so confusing. Dad *was* Jeff!

Dad went out to the nurses' station.

"Steven, any word?"

He knew that I meant about Mom. He shook his head.

"I'm glad I don't have to break out of here," I said.

"You're not the only one." Steven grinned. "I wasn't looking forward to that drama."

My doctor arrived. Dad and he discussed what I might need at home, when and where I would have physical therapy while I took my bloody clothes into the bathroom and changed.

Dad paled when he saw the blood on my sweater and jeans. "Oh, Al, sweetheart. We didn't think to bring you clean clothes."

"I don't care Dad." Standing in the bathroom door, I was suddenly dizzy and still confused. "I'm having trouble remembering what was happening right before, uh, before . . . I think I had some things that were important in my pocket. Yes. What happened to the papers I had with me when I was shot?"

The nurse stared at me, Dad shrugged his lack of knowledge but Steven spoke up. "I have'em." Steven pulled a handful of papers and the 8 x 10 photo, all of which he'd folded in half, out of the back of his book. "Sorry about the crease."

"Just get me out of here." I started to the door when a wave of lightheadedness swept over me.

"Hold it young lady," the nurse said. "Sit down in that chair while I get a wheelchair."

"A wheelchair? I can walk." I didn't want Dad or Steven to know that I wasn't feeling all that strong.

"Hospital policy." She walked out the door and I sank into the chair holding my hand toward my brother for the papers and especially for the photograph. I studied the photo of my father and his friends, and started my mental list of what needed to be done.

35

The ride across the Bay Bridge and through the city was long and painful. Every bump in the road hurt like hell.

I was exhausted by the time Dad got me to my room in Sea Cliff. The turned down bed was tempting, but I changed into clean sweats and sat down at my computer instead.

The two security guards Dad had arranged sat on each end of the side terrace watching the front and rear of the house.

Search engine time. I worked my way down the list of names of the men in the photo. I had managed to know these men for two lifetimes, yet I knew little about their business lives.

Bits and pieces, comments made by my parents and their friends had told me that Jamie was well respected for his crime fighting legal work and prosecutions.

I knew that Dave was enormously wealthy from furniture manufacturing in Southeast Asia and retailing in the US, UK, and EU.

Elliott had some sort of title company. All, but Dave, practiced some form of law. Maybe research as to what the world in general—well, at least the internet world—thought of each of them and the particulars of their businesses would give a hint as to which of them could possibly be involved in murder and kidnapping.

I tried to ignore the pains in my head and the mental images of a dark figure in a black hood that threatened to distract me from my task. Mom, I reminded myself, Mom has been missing for three days.

Rather than read each article or blog I found, I printed them off. I was halfway through my list when Steven knocked on my half open door.

"I thought you'd be in bed," he said.

I scribbled the rest of the names on a pad of paper, the names of Dad's friends from college. Come to think of it, they may have been my friends too. "If you do this search or go through Dad's address book, I'll lie down and read." I picked up my papers from the printer.

"Sure." He googled the next name.

I climbed into bed and started reading.

36

I tried to remember Derek's last name. Did I ever know it? Damn, how would I find him? Was he alive? Why had his body never been found? If he hadn't been killed, he might be able to help.

"Steven, please google the Zodiac killer and print off a list of his victims. Also, see if Lexi's date the night of her murder is mentioned, get his name, and google that. His first name was Derek."

I continued to read, Steven searched. Twenty minutes later he said, "Got it. Shi-it, I'm good. There are several possibilities, but based on age and education, here's the most likely." Steven showed me a phone number and an address.

He lived in San Francisco. In the same city I grew-up in. I could have run into him at any point in my life. "Let's go."

"Are you fucking kidding me?"

Steven, dramatic? Wow.

"You're not going anywhere."

"Okay, hand me the phone." I took the phone, dialed the first number on the list of possibilities. Straight to voicemail:

"You've reached Derek and Lynn. We aren't available at the moment. Please leave your name and number, and we'll get back to you."

Whoa, he's married. Why was I surprised? Did I actually think that ever since our one-night stand he'd been pining away for me? "My name is Alexandra Nichols. Derek, please give me a call." I left my number and hung up. Why would he call me back? I wouldn't call me back, or somebody I didn't know from Adam. I needed to go see him.

"Steven, I'm going to give you a note. You're gonna drop it off at his house." I thought for a minute. "If he's not there, see if anyone knows when he will be."

"Whatever you say." Steven went to get a jacket, returned to take my note, and closed my bedroom door behind him.

I tried to read the printouts. We had a number of addresses and a few phones numbers. I tried a second phone number for Derek, another voicemail. I didn't leave a message.

We would have to go to the addresses. I didn't see how we could possibly do any good other than in person. I would have to see him to know if it was the right Derek. When Steven got back, I would have him drive me.

It was only midday, but I already felt so tired. I dozed.

I awoke with a start. It was dark in the room. The sky outside my window was black. Damn. I had only meant to nap.

Oh shit, was Steven okay? Why the hell had I sent him off by himself? I fumbled for the phone, punched numbers with a shaking hand.

"Where are you?" I asked without preamble.

"Right here," Steven said as he walked through the doorway of my room, his phone at his ear. "Just waiting for you to wake up and give me my next instructions."

"Why'd you let me sleep?"

"You needed to rest?" He twisted his head, raising an eyebrow at me.

"What happened at Derek's?"

"Nice place." Steven flashed a thumbs-up.

"I don't need an *Architectural Digest* report." God, I had to stop being a douche.

"He wasn't there. His neighbor says he usually comes home around five or six."

"What time is it now?" I hopped up from my bed and immediately regretted it. I reached for a bedpost to steady myself.

"Hey, you okay?" Steven caught my arm.

"I'm fine." I shook off his hold. "Time?"

"Almost Six."

I grabbed clean clothes as I went through my closet to the bathroom. "Be ready to leave in five."

"I don't think you should be going anywhere," he said. "Let's have the investigators check it out."

I splashed a lot of cold water on my face, tied a scarf around my head, hippie style, covering the bandage and missing hair, and threw on jeans, a turtleneck, and boots.

"Let's go." I stepped into the bedroom where Steven sat in front of the computer.

"I don't think—"

"Don't think! Let's go." I walked to the doorway. "Or should I drive myself?"

Steven groaned, but stood and grabbed a jacket from the entry hall on the way out to his jeep.

I waved to the startled security guards as I walked to Steven's car. One of them pulled Steven aside and they spoke briefly.

"I told them to follow us." Steven said to me as he climbed into the driver's seat.

37

Derek's house *was* a nice place. Built in the 1960's version of modernistic International Style, it was tucked into the traditional Pacific Heights neighborhood. Lots of steel and glass faced the bay with an entrance courtyard surrounded by a low concrete wall.

We rang the bell. A thin slit of glass beside the door showed a slender figure walking to answer.

"Yes?" Derek stood in the doorway impatiently waiting for us to speak.

I stared, speechless.

Seeing him, decades later, with touches of gray at the temples of his dark hair, blue eyes still startling in his tan face, still as attractive, no—more attractive. And he wasn't a figment of my imagination. My dreams, my nightmares in the hospital were based on actual occurrences. He was living proof that my dreams had been real. Holy shit!

But wait, he had no idea who I was. And in my rush to get here, I'd given absolutely no thought to what I was going to say to the man.

I looked into those amazing blue eyes. "Hi." I smiled.

He stared at the young woman on his doorstep. No sign of recognition. Duh.

Steven spoke, "Sorry to disturb you sir. We think you know our parents from Cal."

"Who are your parents?"

"Jeff and Lauren Nichols."

Derek knit his brow, shook his head, and moved the door towards closing.

"Lexi," I said. "You do remember her, right?"

Alarm spread across his face. "What do you want?" The door moved closer to the frame.

"Look, we're desperately trying to find our mother. She's disappeared. We think you might be able to help," I said.

"What makes you think that?" He looked each of us in the eye. "I know nothing about your mother."

"Please, please talk to us. We won't take much of your time." I wanted to put my foot in the door, but thought better of it. Wrong message. "If you could just tell us what happened the night Lexi was murdered."

"I've talked to the police about this. Ask them." The door inched closer to shut.

"But their reports say you disappeared that night. Where did you go?"

"What?" Derek stared, shook his head. "Who are you again?"

"My . . . our parents were friends of Lexi's. I was named for her. My name is Alexandra Nichols. This is my brother Steven."

Derek searched my face, hesitated. Did he feel it too? The attraction like some giant magnetic force stretched between us. After several moments, he opened the door and waved us in to the entry hall. "We can talk in here."

We followed him into a dramatic high ceilinged living room two walls of which were glass overlooking the city and the bay. He motioned to a sofa.

We sat. He took a chair from nearby and pulled it closer to us.

"You're Jeff's kids?"

We nodded.

"And Lauren's," I said. "Remember her?"

A shadow of sad crossed his face, turning his eyes a deeper shade of blue. He nodded, turned his head away to look out at the bay. He stood and walked to the wall of window. Brushing his hand over a life-sized sculpture, he began to speak in a soft monotone.

"I was kidnapped the night Lexi was murdered. Held captive for a matter of weeks. I was drugged and woke up to find myself in Florence."

"Italy?" Steven asked.

Derek gave him nod, turned back to the window and continued. "I found a note that said if I ever wanted to see my father again to keep my mouth shut and stay away from the police. In the end, I went to the polizia, but my Italian sucked and so did their English. I think they thought I was some crazy American student with a scheme to have some one else pay for a trip back home."

"How did you get home?" I asked.

Derek studied my face for a few moments as if deciding how much to tell us. Or maybe something about me reminded him of someone else. "I didn't for years. I went to the American embassy. They also thought I was up to no good, but did eventually help me get a passport. It took several months just to get papers. Meanwhile, I lived and worked at a restaurant washing dishes, sleeping in the basement. I even wrote to the Berkeley PD with no response."

"What about your father? Couldn't he help you?"

"I tried to call him, collect of course, but he didn't accept the charges. I figured at the time that he thought it was a prank call or something. I mean why would he think his son would be calling him from Italy?"

Steven and I nodded our understanding.

"What about your mother?" I asked, realizing I knew next to nothing about this man with whom I, that is Lexi, had shared an intimate moment. And he still awakened my lustful urges.

"She left us many years before this happened, and as far as I know, she's dead."

"What about your father? Did he ever come through for you?" Steven asked.

"I wrote him, and my daily routine was to visit the American Express office looking for either a letter or money from him. Never happened."

"What was his reaction when you turned up again?" Steven asked.

"He died before I got back."

"Oh . . . sorry," I said.

Derek shrugged.

"How long were you gone?" I asked.

"Three years."

"Wow!"

"I met an artist who took me under his wing. He taught me to sculpt. Turned out I liked it. A lot. So I stayed to work with him."

That explained the unusual sculptures of metal and plaster that lined two walls of the room. I thought I recognized one or two of them as having been exhibited and featured on art book covers. Looking at the house, I'd guess sculpture worked out well.

"I finally came back to the Bay Area to find my father. I intended to confront him, to find out why he didn't respond to my letters. But he'd died in a car accident three months earlier."

"So you never found out why he didn't answer your letters?"

"Well. Yeah, I did. Sorta."

We waited.

"I found my letters in his safe when I had a locksmith open it."

"But why didn't he answer them?" Steven asked.

"Why lock them up?" I asked.

"It was the other items I found in the safe that gave me the answer." He stood. "Here, come with me, I'll show you." We followed him up floating curved staircase to a duplicate window walled room above the living room. He walked to a large writing table and opened a drawer. He pulled out a wooden box and set it on the table.

Inside the box were locks of hair of many different colors, blonde, brunette, auburn, platinum, light brown, strawberry blonde, some quite faded. At the bottom of the hair and a few aged pieces of paper, was a black hood with two holes cut out for eyes.

I sucked in a deep breath and held a hand to my head. I stared at the contents before I spoke. "Your father . . . was the Zodiac?"

"That's what I think. And that's what I told the police. But they weren't interested."

"Why?" Steven asked.

"They were convinced the Zodiac was this Allen guy. Didn't care about a box of hair . . . even though they did admit that the Zodiac had taken hair from some of his victims. DNA wasn't really a thing then or they would probably've been more interested."

"How very strange." I studied Derek's face.

Could this be true? I wondered. Aloud, I said, "That's why you weren't in the file I saw. Because you turned up three years later, and they didn't believe you."

"And the Zodiac had been inactive for awhile. I gathered the press on the killer had whipped public opinion into such a fevered pitch that the police were being pressured beyond belief, yet they couldn't come up with enough evidence to indict their best suspect. Bottom line, the police did not want to get the whole thing heated up again. They hoped the bad publicity and the killer would just quietly fade away and out of the public eye."

"I don't get it," Steven said. "Why didn't your father answer your letters if he got them and he wasn't dead yet?"

I got it. "Because his father was the one who kidnapped him," I said.

Derek returned my look and nodded. "That's what I figured."

"That's why you were one of the two people he moved. Because he didn't want to kill you, but he needed you out of the way. As your father he could take you on an airplane in a semi-drugged state. He probably made up some story about taking you to a medical specialist or something."

Derek continued to nod.

"There was one woman, a Jane Doe, whose body turned up around the same time, and maybe was a Zodiac victim. Her body had been moved after she died. Did you know her?"

"No," Derek said, "and there's no evidence that she was definitely one of his victims. He didn't usually move their bodies. In fact, from the research I've done, she's the only body that was moved."

"Aside from you, that is." I pointed at the creepy box of hair. "Would you be willing to give these to the San Francisco PD now?"

"Sure . . . if they were interested."

"Let's ask them." I punched numbers on my cell. "If they're not, I'll have the DNA tests done."

"We'll need to have evidence samples for comparison." Derek pointed out.

"We'll get them. Some evidence from bodies of victims must've been saved." I frowned while I listened to Dad's voicemail. "There's one big problem with this theory."

Derek and Steven both looked at me.

"If your father was the Zodiac, and he's dead, who wanted the papers in Dad's file? Who the hell shot at me? And who has our mother?"

38

"Good question." Derek answered while he rubbed his hand over his chin. "I'm afraid I may not be that much help to you."

Steven looked at me. "Did you call Dad?"

"Voicemail," I answered.

Steven took his phone out of his pocket. "I'll call the SFPD detective who's looking for Mom. Schmidt should want to help us." Steven wandered into the hall at the top of the stairs, speaking into his phone.

"So Derek, were you your father's only heir?"

"As a matter of fact, no," he shook his head. "My cousin Harold, that is Harry, occasionally stayed in my Dad's house in Vallejo while I was gone."

"Where's your cousin now?"

"Maybe traveling?" He sat down in the desk chair. "I don't know. We aren't close. After we sold Dad's house and divvied up the estate, we haven't really seen much of each other."

"Shit." I plopped in the guest chair across the writing table. "Well, the police ought to be able to track him down."

"What for?" Derek asked.

Steven came back into the room and sat in the other guest chair. "The detective's on his way over here."

"I guess he was interested?" I said.

"Oh, yeah," Steven answered, "very."

"Where did we meet before?" Derek asked me.

I shrugged my shoulders, I really didn't feel up to explaining that the last time we met, we'd fucked, and then his father killed me.

I wasn't too sure of the reaction I would get. From him, or Steven. I decided keeping some of what I knew, or how I knew it, to myself, had advantages . . . like people wouldn't decide I was nuts.

"When does your wife get home?" I asked.

Derek gave me a puzzled look. "My wife?"

"Lynn?" I answered. "On your voicemail, it says you and Lynn are not available."

"Lian is my son. My wife died ten years ago."

"I'm sorry," I hesitated. I seemed to have developed a knack for putting my foot in it. "Where's your son?"

"At school. Basketball practice." Derek pressed his palms against the desktop. "He'll be home soon."

A glance at his hands stirred feelings I didn't want. I fought the urge to reach across the desk, to place my palm on his.

The doorbell rang. Derek and Steven went downstairs to answer it. I took advantage of the opportunity to look through the writing desk drawers. I was curious about the newspaper clippings I saw when Derek pulled out the box of hair. I found a thick file of newspaper articles. I recognized some of the same ones I'd seen in Dad's file. And a whole bunch more from various newspapers around the country.

Everything else looked like the usual desk shit. I heard the three men on the stairs, replaced the file, closed the drawer, and sat back down in the chair.

"Al, you know Detective Schmidt."

I stood and shook his outstretched hand.

"You look a little better than the last time I saw you, miss." Detective Schmidt looked to be somewhere in his fifties, with close-cut gray hair, a clean-shaven face, and twenty extra pounds.

"I guess that must've been in the hospital." I smiled at him.

Derek pointed out the box of hair. The detective called for lab technicians to deal with it and then asked Derek enough questions to get him talking. Derek told the detective pretty much the same story he'd told us.

I waited for him to mention the file of newspaper clippings, but he didn't.

So I did. It was pretty much an admission that I'd been digging in his desk, but nobody seemed to notice, or at least to comment.

Derek looked startled. Perhaps he'd forgotten the clippings were in the desk.

Detective Schmidt and Derek re-hashed the whole story. I figured the detective was listening for discrepancies in Derek's explanations, but I knew any differences found would be meaningless. Derek had not shot Lexi.

When the detective continued to ask Derek questions that I failed to see would help with finding Mom. I wandered down the hall that ran the length of the oval stairwell. A master suite was straight ahead. To the right was a room lined with shelves full of video games, shiny unused sports helmets, candles, a few books about vampires, CD's, a couple of basketball trophies, a photo or two, and a few wood boxes. Black curtains that matched a black comforter on the bed covered the window wall.

I opened one wood box. Trinkets. String. A ring. A harmonica.

I looked at the drawers under the bed and nudged one open.

A voice from the bottom of the stairs called out, "Hey Dad, wassup here?"

I shoved the drawer closed and hurried to step into the hall.

A familiar looking, tall, dark-haired, skinny young man with teenage acne and Derek's light blue eyes ran up the stairs, and threw a backpack on the sofa.

"This is my son, Lian." Derek introduced Steven, Detective Schmidt, and me. And then explained to Lian that we were interested in the evidence of his grandfather being the Zodiac killer. Lian shrugged it off as though it was an old story, history of little interest to him.

But his eyes hovered on the news clipping in Schmidt's hand for a few extra seconds.

"Gotta meet a dude at the library." Lian headed to the kitchen. "Gonna grab a sandwich."

I wondered if going to the library was still code for "I'm gonna hang with friends tonight." It sure had been in each teen hood I could recall. The vacant look in Lian's eyes indicated a stronger interest in drugs than libraries.

I stared after Lian, trying to catch the thought the sight of him had sparked. He was a skinnier version of young Derek. Lian. Was he the kid on the bike? Yes. The kid from last summer, the one in Pacific Heights. No wonder my heart fluttered at the sight of him, my déjà vu recognition triggering nightmares.

Derek caught me staring after Lian. "He's had a rough time since my wife died."

I nodded, wondering how many pharmaceuticals Lian was on. They might explain his nobody-home-look.

I followed Lian down the curved stairs where a skateboard rested against the frosted glass window in the entry hall. I stepped into the kitchen where he was spreading peanut butter on bread.

"I've seen you riding a bike around the neighborhood. My aunt lives nearby here," I explained. My attempts to start up a conversation were met with grunts.

"That was awhile back. Guess you're into skateboarding now?"

He nodded while he crammed the sandwich into his mouth. Before the last morsel disappeared, he picked up his board and hurried out the front door.

The lab guys showed up to bag the hair, the box, the hood, and the articles. Then Detective Schmidt asked Derek what else he had.

He opened a sliding door to a large compartment in the paneled wall. A wall mounted gun rack held two rifles and two pistols. "Those were my Dad's. My cousin Harry has the other half of his collection."

Detective Schmidt looked very interested. I couldn't help but wonder why the Berkeley police had been so uninterested years ago.

39

It was almost midnight before Steven and I started home. "Are you going to stay here tonight?" I asked my brother.

"Who else is going to keep an eye on you?" He smiled and pulled into the driveway. "Besides getting a good night's rest, what are we going to do next?"

"I don't know. But I'll think of something."

"Why were you asking about heirs?" Steven asked.

"I was wondering if anybody else had access to the guns and the hood."

"Oh, yeah. Sure." Steven gave me a quizzical look. "So you think Derek has taken his father's place?"

"Or Harold." I hadn't been thinking Derek but why didn't he tell the detective about the newspaper clippings? Did the collection of clippings belong to Lian?

"So what are we going to do next?" Steven asked.

"There's that whole list of people to question."

"Why didn't you give the list to the police? To Schmidt?"

"I don't know how to explain the list, or why to question them. Not to mention, all of them being pillars of the community, the police are not likely to see them as suspects. I just have a feeling that at least one of them knows something," I paused. "Maybe all of them. Crooks stick together, right?"

"What? The old birds-of-a-feather theory of crime?"

"Yeah, I guess so." I yawned and waved goodnight as I watched him close my door. I peeled off my clothes and fell into bed.

Sleep came easier than I expected, considering the way my heart raced every time I thought of my missing mother.

40

I woke up with the sun, feeling guilty for sleeping while Mom was still missing. I hurried into my clothes, woke up Steven, and crammed down toast as I located the list of addresses map questing a couple.

"We can use the GPS," Steven said over the top of his coffee mug.

"Yeah, yeah, I just want to be efficient, not zigzagging from one end of the Bay Area to the next."

We caught Dad's oldest friend, Uncle Dave, at breakfast in his Victorian paneled dining room. I recognized the dining table as one mother and I had bought for him at a London auction on Lots Road. We sipped the coffee his housekeeper Maria served.

Steven managed to eat a second breakfast, filching bacon and muffins off our "Uncle's" neglected plate while I distracted him with questions.

"Remember the night that Lexi was killed?" I asked.

"Sure, one of those moments you never forget." He gave me a glance then drank from his porcelain coffee cup.

"Moments?"

"Yeah, you know like where you were when you heard Kennedy was killed? Well actually you wouldn't remember that, but . . ."

You might be surprised Uncle. I kept that to myself.

He tried again. "Like the moment you first heard about September 11."

"We get it." I nodded. "So?"

"I woke up in the middle of the night to the doorbell ringing. I heard Carol screaming, 'No-o-o,' and crying. Commotion, lots of people in the hall." He put the cup down in its saucer and fiddled with a piece of toast. His eyes studied his plate.

Was he hiding emotions? I tried to remember if I'd ever seen Dave truly emotional.

My Uncle Dave had a pervasive hollowness to his character. Like he had a shell that on the surface looked good, but on the inside he was missing a heart. He seemed to have no ability to sympathize. Or empathize. Like other people were not quite real to him. He said and did all the right things in a practiced manner, but his act never came off as quite real to me.

I wondered if other people felt the same way about him. My sympathetic mom, of course, said he was hiding a soft heart and a lack of self-esteem behind that hard shell.

"What then?" If he had more feeling than showed, I was torturing him.

"Police got us all up, herded us into the living room, and questioned us. We were all in shock. I don't think we were much use." He stared out the window, searching the blue sky for memories.

"Who was there?"

"Your mom and dad, of course Carol, Ron, Suzy, Tom, Jamie, Elliott." Uncle Dave fiddled with his monogrammed cuff, checked the distance the shirtsleeve stuck out past his jacket. Was he looking everywhere but my eyes hoping I wouldn't see his pain? Or what was he hiding?

He must have a thing about his neck because he always wore either a turtleneck or a cravat. Did I mention Uncle Dave is known among his friends for his fastidious, obsessive compulsions?

"No wait, I don't know that he was there, in fact we wondered where Elliott was." Dave said after some hesitation.

"Anyone else?"

"No. I don't think so." He looked maybe actually sad now. "No."

"Who was usually at the house?"

"Well, Jeff, Lexi, and I lived there officially. Our names were on the lease." Uncle Dave hesitated. "Carol had moved in a few weeks before. She shared a room with Lexi. And Jamie, Tom, and Elliott hung out there a lot. Ron too, but he actually spent most of his time at Jamie's ranch."

"Did they usually sleep there?"

"Only if they were too stoned or drunk to get home." His smile was actually sad.

"Where did they live?"

"On a ranch in Novato that Jamie's family owned."

"With Jamie's parents?"

"No-o . . . the parents didn't live there. They were separated or something. The mom lived in New York. I don't remember the dad." He seemed to have recovered some of his appetite. He readjusted the napkin in his collar and took a bite of his egg white omelette.

"Why did the guys live there?"

He swallowed. "They were kinda taking a gap year between undergrad and law school."

"What about you?"

"I couldn't afford a gap year, or grad school, I worked here, in the city, but I was mostly around on the weekends. I commuted from Berkeley." He wiped his mouth with his napkin and pushed back his chair.

"What did they do with themselves?" I wasn't through.

"Drugs, sex and rock'n roll—all in an upper middle class verging on intellectual sort of way."

"And what way would that be?" Steven asked.

"They tried to be considerate of the caretaking couple at the ranch. The housekeeper saw to it that they were cleaned up after, especially after one of their cook-a-thons. Hell, they were among the original foodies, now that I think of it. Drugs were mild, just marijuana and some hallucinogens. Sex was definitely all heterosexual, mostly monogamous if serial. And private. Orgies were not part of the scene."

"Is the caretaking couple still there?"

"I doubt it. That land has to have been sold off and developed years ago." He stood, rearranged his slacks, straightened the crease, and plucked off a piece of lint.

"Do you know their names?"

"Na. Hell, I wasn't there that much. I worked, remember."

"How would we find this place?" Steven asked.

Dave's cell chirped an incoming text. He picked it up, studied the screen. "Damn. Fucking idiots." He looked at the sideboard. "Maria" he screamed, "I want a damn piece of paper." He stomped his foot. "Maria. Goddamn! Where the fuck are you?"

My theory of Dave was that he thought of other humans as worthless annoyances. He made no pretense otherwise with his servants.

A pale Maria scurried through the swinging kitchen door, pen and tablet in hand. She placed the items on the table and shook while awaiting further instructions.

"Get outa here," Dave snapped at her.

Steven frowned as though he were about to chastise Dave.

With a look I reminded my brother about Uncle Dave's hypersensitivity to anything that he could construe as criticism. I remembered Dave bitching to Dad that he thought Mother had insinuated that he was nouveau riche when he complained about a scratch on the dining table. In fact, my mother never criticized anyone. But I knew from her reaction to being told about Dave's complaint that she does not, in fact, think too highly of him, and his new money has nothing to do with her low opinion.

Steven got the message. We wouldn't get anything out of him if we pissed him off.

Dave scribbled on the paper. "I don't have a clue as to the address, but I can draw you a map of how to get there." He tossed the scribbles at us as he stood up.

"Were you home when Lexi left that night?" I wasn't through with my questions.

"No. I was at work." Dave turned his back to me and walked toward the entry hall.

I knew he wasn't at work, unless he'd gone back to the city after being home in the early afternoon. I followed him into the hall. "What was the name of that place, the bar on San Pablo?"

Dave picked up his briefcase. He didn't answer, but I saw red creep up his neck past the cravat.

"Was it something like the Monk?" I pressed.

"The Monkey Inn." Dave turned to glare at me, then softened the look. "I really gotta get to the office." He forced a smile. "I am sorry I can't help you kids, if I think of anything that might be . . . useful, I will definitely be in touch."

"Did you stop there on the way home from the city?"

"Sometimes," Dave threw a Burberry trench over his arm.

"That night?"

He shook his head.

"The day before?"

"I don't remember." He walked out the door.

One of those events you never forget, he had said. Did you forget what you were doing right before it happened?

Steven and I exchanged shrugs as we got in the car. He turned to look at me as he pushed the power button. "Wow. Dave has serious money. That was a Jasper John in the entry hall, a Renoir on the staircase wall. Did his . . . hmm . . . *intensity* earn a fortune?"

"You know Steven, he always was weird."

Dave was intense even when we were still in school. Intense just wasn't cool then. Laid-back, like Jamie's insouciance. That was the way to hang.

Maybe it was because he grew up poor. Many in that generation grew up with enough financial security to give more attention to saving the world, or creating great art, or changing the social structure, or bringing peace to earth, something other than making money. Not Dave. He'd parlayed a waterbed company into a chain of waterbed stores, then into furniture stores, and then into an enormous import company that brought in furniture from all over the Orient. When the China market opened up, he became a billionaire. But all that success, all that money sure hadn't made him happy.

41

The drive to Marin would have been beautiful, had we been in the mood to enjoy the Golden Gate Bridge, the rich yellow, rolling hills dotted with dark coast oaks. Not this time. After we got off the freeway in Novato and passed the usual new shopping centers that look the same everywhere these days, we drove on a two-lane road that wound among giant oaks and golden pastures.

We found the farmhouse set in the midst of an apple orchard. It looked just as I had imagined it—or, rather, as I remembered it. I had been there before; that is Lexi had.

White clapboard siding, covered front porch—style elements known among architectural historians as farmhouse Victorian. The decorations are much simpler and more functional than on the fancy painted ladies of San Francisco.

The house, barn, and some orchard were still intact, but instead of being set in fifty acres, a single acre was surrounded by a housing development of McMansions. A sedan and an old Land Rover were parked in front of the barn. We found the front door and knocked.

No one answered. We peeked in windows, pounded on another door. There was no sign of anyone yet the house was furnished and a bowl of fruit was visible in the kitchen.

Steven checked out the barn. I walked through elderly, gnarled apple trees. I saw Birkenstock clad feet and worn denim-covered legs at the top of a wood ladder.

"Hello, hi." I stood near the bottom of the ladder. There was no response to my greeting. "Hello," I repeated. "Hi."

"I hear ya. Wadda want?" asked a gruff voice.

"Can we talk?" I still couldn't see a head and didn't know if I was addressing a man or a woman.

"We're talkin', aren't we?"

"My name is Alexandra Nichols. I'm looking for some people who used to live here. A couple, the caretakers, and some friends of my father's."

"Can't help ya."

"Do you live here?" I asked.

"Sometimes."

"How long have you lived here?"

"Why is that any of your business?"

"I would very much appreciate your help," I said.

"I'm busy."

"Could I come back later?" I figured he or she would have to come down that ladder eventually. Maybe I'd just wait.

"No."

"Are you the owner?"

"Get the hell out of here."

Steven joined me. "Who are you talking to?"

I shrugged, pointed up to the legs.

"Hello," Steven said to the legs. "Sorry to bother you. Could we just ask a few questions?"

"Oh for godsakes." The feet started down the ladder and a head swathed in netting over a hat emerged from the branches. "Are you friends of my son?"

"Who's your son?" I asked.

Steven gave me a look that said 'you are going about this all wrong'. "Our father used to visit here some decades back when he was in college. His friend Jamie's parents owned the place then. We're trying to locate the couple who acted as caretakers at that time."

Hands covered in leather work gloves unwrapped the netting and removed the hat uncovering the attractive, wrinkled face of an older woman. "You have any idea how long it took me to get all this crap on and finally do something about trimming these damn trees?" She walked toward the house. We followed. "Wait here," she said when we got to the front porch. A few minutes later she emerged from the house, handed us a piece of paper, and walked back to the orchard.

I looked at the paper. At the top it said, "Caretakers" followed by "Susan and Mac McAller" and an address in Novato. Now it came back to me. We had called them Mr. and Mrs. Mac.

"Who was that?" I asked Steven.

He shrugged.

42

The address turned out to be a rest home. Mac and Mrs. Mac sat in wheelchairs in the sun of the atrium. I was determined to do a better job of interviewing these two.

"Hello, Mr. and Mrs. McAller. I'm Alexandra Nichols. This is my brother Steven. Our father, Jeff, used to stay at the Gregg's farmhouse back in the late '60's and early '70's. Would it be alright if we asked you a few questions?" I pulled the photo of the gang out of my pocket thinking I could use it to jog their memories.

"What's she saying? Can't hear her," Mr. McAller yelled at his wife.

Mrs. Mac reached over to readjust her husband's hearing aid, smiled at us, and said, "Please have a seat. Presumably Mrs. Gregg told you where to find us. I'm Mrs. Mac, that's what the young people like you always called me." She offered her hand, pulling her housecoat closed on her legs.

I shook her hand. So that was Mrs. Gregg at the farmhouse, Jamie's mother.

"We'd be happy ta talk. What would ya like ta know?" Mrs. Mac continued.

"When you took care of the place, who all lived there?"

"There was just one year, 1969, when anyone actually lived at the farm. Rest'a the time, it was just weekends when they'd come. 'Course we never knew when they was comin'. They'd just show up which made shoppin' complicated, but Mr. Gregg insisted we always be prepared for company, and he footed the bills, so who were we ta complain?"

"Who lived there in 1969?"

"Jamie Gregg and three of his friends mostly. Others would show up. Most we ever had at once was about thirty, I'd say. Lord. Had bodies everywhere. Every bed, every sofa—even the hammocks and chaises on the porch. Some even slept in the orchard. They helped with the cookin', wanted me ta teach 'em how to cook everything, apple pies, apple butter, stews. They was a real nice bunch ya know. Good kids."

"What did they do besides cook?" Steven asked.

"Played a lot of cards. Liked ta play with maybe ten people, lots of decks. Mostly hearts."

"Cooked, ate, played cards, slept. Does that cover it?" I asked.

"Oh, no! They used ta crank up the sound on the hi-fi so loud it 'bout shook the house down. Could hear it all through the orchard. They'd dance through the trees, even on the roof." In a sweet but cracking voice she sang, *"All ya need is love, love, love: love is all ya need."* Those songs and the like. Of course they'd be smokin' that mary-juana all the time. And drank up the good wine from the cellar, Mr. Gregg wasn't too happy bout that but he didn't care about the maryjane."

"The three friends, male?" Steven asked.

"Oh yes. Course they had girls around, too. Sister of one of the boys come pretty often and she'd bring her friends." Mrs. Mac leaned over to whisper, "We'd always find it interestin' ta see who would end up in what beds. Plenty of that going on too, ya know."

I returned her smile and nodded. "What names do you remember?"

"Jamie, of course."

"What girls did he have around?"

"Not many, really. Which was surprisin' 'cuz even as a young man, he was a charmer. Very much a gentleman."

Mrs. Mac hesitated in thought for only a second. "One girl named Nancy that came with Elliott's sister the first time and then he'd go pick her up sometimes. I'm pretty sure she ended up with Elliott, ya know in the end when they was all grown ups and started gettin' married."

"Who else?" I asked.

"Tom. Now he was a handsome Irish boy. Liked ta cook. Had a different girl every week until that Linda come along. Then it was just her. They're still married ya know, I read about them in the papers, society pages."

"Elliott came there?" I asked "Before Nancy?"

"Yeah, he were one of 'em. That poor boy got his heart broke so often. He would go for the kinda plain ones, too. But they never lasted more than a week or so. Now that Ron. He practically had ta beat'em off with a stick. Weren't just 'cuz of his looks either, he was kinda a rugged blonde. 'Course he was so much fun. Always laughin', smilin', jokin' around. Sure did enjoy him. Smile that lit up the room."

"Those were the three that lived there with Jamie in 1969?" I asked. "Elliott . . . Tom . . . Ron."

Mrs. Mac nodded after each name.

I continued, "and then Linda, Nancy, and what was Elliott's sister's name?"

"Lucy," she said.

"Boy, what a memory. Do you remember any other names, Mrs. Mac?" I asked.

"There was Lexi that come sometimes. She brought her friend Carol once when they'd had some car trouble. Lexi would go ta the orchard and paint the most lovely landscapes. She gave me one. Still have it. Hung it in our suite here." She smiled at me. "And your father. He and Lexi were close, but just friends I think. Later he'd bring Lauren with him. She was such a nice girl, so polite and helpful. Your mother right?"

I nodded. "Anyone else?'

She looked away for a moment, then shook her head. "No, not that I recall, not regular like."

"How wild would it get? When the music was cranked up. Did the parties ever turn violent?" I asked.

"Oh heaven's no."

"No fist fights or brawls?"

"They was all good friends. Nothing bad like that. They had the right idea."

I looked at her questioningly.

"All peace and love, ya know."

"Was there ever any yelling? Did the couples fight?" I persisted.

"A little bickering, but no yelling ever. Not when they was at the farm. Or when we was there, anyways. We did take off every Wednesday, but they wouldn'ta been different then, I don't guess."

"So no violence, no fighting, nothing ever like that?"

"Definitely not." She smiled, patted her quiet husband's hand. "I sure did love all those kids."

"They loved you too, Mrs. Mac," I said as I gave her a gentle hug.

43

We climbed back into the car. "Sounds pretty idyllic, huh?" Steven said.

"Can you imagine Mom and Dad never yelled?" I said.

My brother and I laughed. Our parents famously talked—that is, fought out all of their differences of opinions until they agreed or agreed to disagree. It was never a quiet process after Dad taught Mom to yell.

"Regardless of what Mrs. Mac said, I still think that farm and what went on there in 1969 has something to do with this whole thing." I said.

Should I mention to Steven the memory that came to me while Mrs. Mac spoke? An overheard conversation that made no sense to me at the time. Would he think I was nuts if I said the conversation took place in 1969?

Instead I said, "Let's work our way down the list. Who's closest to here?"

"Tom's law office is in Napa." Steven answered.

Tom's address went into the GPS and off we went, grabbing sandwiches to eat in the car on the way. We arrived at a Craftsman bungalow an hour later.

"We need to see Mr. O'Connor." I told the receptionist.

"Appointment?"

"No." I shook my head. "We'll just take a few minutes of his time." I gave her our names confident that he would see us. We'd spent time with him on several occasions.

She asked us to have a seat and went through a door. A few minutes late she returned. "Mr. O'Connor would be happy to see you now. He has a few minutes before his next appointment."

"Good to see you kids." Tom turned to me. His grin brought twinkles to his eyes. "Especially good to see you lookin' healthy. What's up?"

We shook hands over his oak desk. The oak paneling, sisal carpet, and leather chairs went well with his jeans, cashmere V-neck over a polo shirt, and beat up cowboy boots. Other than deep lines around his mouth and warm brown eyes, and the shorter graying hair, he looked much like he had in Carol's photo.

"Have a seat." Tom gestured at the Stickley oak chairs.

"We're trying to get information about the summer and fall of 1969 that you spent at the Gregg's farmhouse." I was surprised to see Tom's face pale under his sailing tan, but I continued. "We just came from seeing Mrs. Mac. She told us who, including you, lived there; Uncle Dave said it was a year of drugs, sex and rock'n roll. Our parents, just so you don't worry about what you say to us, have always been honest about their wild youth."

"Why do you ask?" Tom asked with a forced smile. "Are you writin' a thesis?"

I really did need to prepare a speech for these guys. What do I say? I'm trying to figure if one of you kidnapped my mother? Or shot at me?

"Our mother's missing. I was shot."

"Well, I know about you bein' shot. And your Dad called me to recommend a PI firm." Tom frowned. "But what the hell does this have to do with the farm in 1969?"

"I don't know, maybe nothing. But we feel like we have to look into every possibility and this is such a long shot, well, the police aren't gonna . . ."

"What kind of possibilities are you thinkin'?" Tom asked.

"Mrs. Mac said you had house parties with like thirty people. Any of them connected to like, I don't know, Weathermen? Or Black Panthers, or . . .? Well—it was Berkeley in the sixties."

"That was the whole point of the ranch; it wasn't Berkeley, no tear gas, no National Guard; just peace and quiet, music and love. We weren't political—other than avoidin' the draft, but hell, that was more self-preservation. No radical groups. We weren't into that shit. Every one of us went to law school. We expected bright futures. Sure didn't want to fuck them up."

"What about the drugs?" Steven asked.

"We avoided any that would really get us into trouble, and certainly didn't deal. It was also part of the reason why we kept pretty much to our own group of friends. Never wide open parties."

"Ever any strangers come around there?" I asked.

"Chicks, not men. No one threatenin'."

"What chicks?"

"I don't know." He grinned. "They were strangers. Seriously, *I* never got involved with any strangers."

"Did anybody have anything against Lexi?"

"We had nothin' to do with her murder. That was the Zodiac guy," he snapped at me, then caught himself and smiled. "Sorry kids, but my one o'clock appointment." He pointed at his watch.

"Just one more thing. What did you think of Lexi?" I couldn't help myself, I mean how many times do you get the chance to hear the truth of what others think of you? I know I'm not Lexi now, but I was.

"Oh hell, hate to speak ill of the dead. But. She was a selfish bitch. Terribly talented, but a typical artist. Only cared about her work."

"Did she shut you down?"

His face went red. "No."

Liar.

44

We headed to Oakland.

I called Carol as we drove south across the Carquinez Bridge.

"Hi Carol." Would I ever be able to tell her just how long we'd known each other?

"Al, you sound good. Thank God. I was freaked. Any word from Lauren?"

"No."

"O-oh," Carol sighed. "I'm glad you're okay. I stopped by your parent's house to check on you today. I was surprised you weren't there."

"We're looking for Mom."

"Let the police and Jeff's investigators do that, please," Carol said.

"I can't do that. No way I'm going to lie in bed waiting to hear," I said.

"Please be careful. You should be resting. I'm amazed Steven let you—"

"His choices were to come with or stay behind."

"I see." Carol sighed again. "Well, I left food in the fridge and on the kitchen counter. Goodies from Citizen Cake."

My favorite bakery. The thought reminded me we hadn't eaten much since breakfast, but I was too anxious to have an appetite. My stomach flip-flopped every time I thought of Mom.

"Thanks. Your thoughtfulness is much appreciated." I paused for a second between subjects. "You said you've done some research about serial killers?"

"Ye-a-h," Carol said guardedly.

"So, what do you think is going on here?"

"I don't . . . why do you think this has anything to do with serial killers?"

"It seems like this all started when I got interested in Jeff's, uh, Dad's file on Lexi's murder. Do you think she was killed by the Zodiac?"

"That's what we were told by the police. I didn't have any real evidence otherwise."

"What about Lexi's concern that someone was trying to harm, maybe kill *you*?"

"Whaaat? How did you—? I'd forgotten about that." She let out a deep sigh. "Who the hell brought that up?"

"Is there a connection?" I asked.

"No. That had to 've been nonsense. After all, I'm still here. I haven't had a serious accident since . . . hmm, 1969."

"So not since Lexi died?"

"Yeah. What's your point?" Carol's annoyance came through the phone line loud and clear. "Lexi had nothing to do with my accident-prone days."

"I don't know. Is it possible that Lexi was the intended victim all along?" As soon as I said it I realized that that theory didn't really fit all the facts.

"There was one time. A car Lexi and I were both in lost its brakes. But that was the only time that any of the accidents I had could've threatened Lexi," Carol said. "No, it makes no sense. It was just Lexi's imagination running away with her sense."

"What about the mugger?" I asked.

"How the hell—? Who have you been talking to?"

"Unless the killer was just working his way up to a more overt kill, and the two of you were convenient targets," I theorized aloud.

"What are you saying? That the killer was someone Lexi and I knew?"

"What do you think?"

"Look, from what I know of serial killers, it's true that sometimes they work their way up to actual killing with lesser acts of violence like torturing animals, roughing people up. So-called accidentally hurting other children . . . stuff like that. So it's not entirely out of the question that the accidents I had were some how connected. But—and this is a big *but* in my head—that would have to mean that Lexi was killed by someone we knew. Or at least, that's what I think you're saying?"

"And?"

"That doesn't make sense. Think about it Al. We still know all the same people who were Lexi's friends then, and as far as I can tell, no one has been killing anyone in the last few decades."

"As far as you can tell," I emphasized.

Carol was silent so long I thought I'd lost the connection.

"Where are you now?" she finally asked

"On our way to Elliott's office, or maybe his and Nancy's house in Piedmont."

"Stay there. Let Nancy take care of you. Or head home. You really should get a good night's rest," Carol said. "God, I can't believe you left the hospital. Let me speak with your brother. He needs to take you home."

"Bye, Carol. Thanks for the info." I hung up.

"Do you think we can catch Elliott in his office?" I asked Steven just as his phone rang. He answered via the Bluetooth in the car, so I heard Carol insisting he take me straight back to our parents' and put me back to bed.

"Got it Aunt Carol," he said.

Steven indicated the line of slow moving, stop-and-go traffic ahead of us.

"I'm taking you home." His face was set in that stubborn look that I knew well.

45

We stood at the kitchen counter so ravenous that we bolted down the food Carol had left for us without sitting.

The drive through rush hour traffic had kept us on the road well past dark. I felt lightheaded, my pain only slightly relieved by the pills Steven had handed me.

"Go to bed, Al," Steven ordered.

"Can we get started early tomorrow?"

"Elliott probably doesn't get into his office much before nine. Do you want to show up at their house for breakfast?" Steven asked. He was sweeping the take out containers into the trash, washing out the recyclables.

"I'm thinking maybe he won't be as forthcoming with his wife there." I lifted an eyebrow at my brother. "Tom lied about a couple things, BTW."

"Like what?"

"Mrs. Mac said he had a different girl there every week until he hooked up with Linda. Some of them had to 've been strangers." I thought about Tom. Not only had he definitely come on to me when I was Lexi, he also was infamous for his pickup lines and his promiscuity. "He took every advantage of that free love shit."

Steven glanced away from the sink and gave me a look. "You gonna explain anything to me sometime soon?"

"What do ya mean?"

"You seem to have a train of thought that I'm not following."

"Humph." Maybe I would have to at least talk to Steven about my new understanding of life . . . and death, but I wasn't ready for that yet. "I'm gonna head to bed."

"Good." Steven nodded. "Good night."

I drifted off as soon as my head hit the pillow. Those pain pills really knocked me out every time. When I came to, the bedside clock said ten twenty. I lay still, hoping to fall back asleep. When that proved futile, I listened to hear if Steven, or Dad were still up, if they were in the house.

I opened my bedroom door, thinking I would hear the ten o'clock news on the television in the den. But the house was quiet except for the breezes off the ocean rattling a window or two. I pulled on sweats, a jacket, and sneakers, and quietly let myself out of the side door slipping past the security guards. I needed fresh air, a walk to shake the restlessness.

Lights were starting to go off in the surrounding houses. There was something liberating about being out in the night by myself, with no destination, free to wander.

I planned to walk until I felt relaxed, tired enough to go back to sleep. My feet carried me through the Presidio and up into the hills of Pacific Heights. I realized I had walked a very long way when I found myself in Derek's neighborhood. I decided to walk by his house.

I was across the street, trying not to look like a stalker when a small SUV pulled into his driveway. Lian got out of the driver's door. He walked around to the back of the house and disappeared from view. He returned, opened the rear door, and loaded a long, narrow case.

I had walked another five feet when he reappeared with a bicycle, mounted the bike to a rack on the rear of the SUV, and climbed into the driver's seat. I continued to walk, hoping he wouldn't notice me. He backed out of the drive and zoomed down the street away from me.

The porch lights came on, front door opened and Derek stepped out. He stood in the courtyard, and looked after the car. He shook his head. The way his shoulders fell in a dejected stance rushed sympathy to my heart.

Without thinking, I crossed the street and called his name.

His surprise at the sight of me was obvious in his voice. "Miss Nichols, is that you?"

I reached out to touch his hand and felt the sparks when my fingers grazed his. What was I doing? I jammed my hands into my sweatshirt pockets. "Yes, I'm sorry, I was having trouble sleeping, so I'm trying to walk off my restlessness. I don't know how I ended up here . . ." OMG, now I was compounding my idiocy by blabbering like a nervous teenager. And to top it off, I shivered.

"Are you okay?" Derek asked. "Didn't you just get out of the hospital?" He looked at the bandage on my head.

"I'm fine." I turned away, anxious to get out of this awkward moment. I stumbled.

Derek's arm shot across the gate and grabbed my elbow. "I think you should come in. Have some warm milk, and then I'll drive you home. It's a bad idea to wander around the city late at night by yourself."

"I guess I'm not thinking too clearly yet," I said.

"Probably the pain pills," he said opening the gate, pulling me inside and through the front door. "Kitchen's this way."

I was sorry when he released my arm, but I followed him down the hall and into the modern yet warm room. A book lay open on a wood table in front of a wing chair.

"Sit." Derek waved at the other wing chair.

I sat while he poured milk, sugar, and cinnamon into a mug. The microwave bell rang and he placed the steaming mug on the table in front of me.

I watched him over the top of the cup. The strength of the attraction I felt for him amazed me. The "what-ifs" rushed into my mind: what if I hadn't died the night we met? What if I'd been Lian's mother—? Oh for god's sake Al. Cut it out.

He poured milk into a mug and repeated the microwaving. When the bell rang, he sat down in the opposite wing chair and gazed at me through the steam rising from his cup.

"I can't shake the idea that we've met before. I . . . you feel like, I don't know, as though I've known you for a long time. Comfortable," Derek said. "And yet there's a . . . tension." He shook himself. "Hell, you are very young, I'm going to shut up before I say something inappropriate."

"I feel it too." I raised my eyes to his. "And I'm not that young."

He stood. "I'll get you a jacket. I'm taking you home." He went into the hall and returned with a down parka. "Here, put this on."

Derek motioned me to follow him into the elevator and down to the garage where he opened the door to a Triumph roadster.

"Where did Lian go?" I asked after I had explained where my parent's house was.

"I wish I knew." Derek shook his head. "I don't really know what to do with that kid. Nothing seems to work."

"Is it drugs?"

"He has all kinds of problems. Probably all my fault. I wasn't paying close enough attention when my wife was alive. She was from Florence. Maybe she didn't understand what was going on well enough. She agreed to the Ritalin, and that proved to be impossible to get him off of without putting him on still another so-called medication. Ah, it's been a nightmare." Derek sighed. "I'm sorry. Sorry to go on about my familial problems."

"It's okay, I don't mind." I wanted to hug him, to comfort him. "Does he use street drugs too?"

"God, I hope not. The combination could be lethal. He doesn't confide in me no matter how hard I try to be understanding." Derek looked at me as he turned down the street to my parent's house. "I'm a shit dad."

"At least you try," I said. We were both silent for a moment. "Can I ask you a question about the Zodiac?"

Derek nodded.

"Why do you have the newspaper clippings?"

"I took them out of Lian's room. Planned to ask him that question, but haven't found the right moment. You know, a time when he'll talk to me rather than just running in and out of the house."

"Why would Lian have them? Where did he get them?"

"I don't know." Derek pulled the car to the curb in front of my parent's house. "It seems unhealthy that he's so interested."

"I can understand why he might be curious, especially if he knows you think his grandfather was the Zodiac," I said. "My father had clippings and files about Lexi's murder around when I was a kid. My parents were careful not to talk about it around my brother and me. But we were aware of more than they realized. The way Mom and Dad shut up when we came around made me curious. I wanted to be let in on the grown up secret."

"I hope that's all it is." Derek reached for the door handle. "Because it scares me."

46

Once I got back to bed in the middle of the night, I'd slept much later than I intended. And since no one woke me up, we'd gotten a late start hitting the road.

"You know, Nancy would be happy to have us for lunch," Steven said.

I nodded my agreement. "I'll give Elliott's office a call and see what his afternoon schedule looks like."

I called 411 and was connected to Elliott's office. "Mr. Burns is in court today."

"Thanks." I hung up the phone. "He's in court."

"I thought he didn't litigate. Isn't he president of a title company?" Steven took his eyes off the highway long enough to see how I was doing.

"Yeah, must be a lawsuit. I'll call Nancy," I said and gave him a reassuring smile.

"Good. She'll feed us while we wait for him. And who knows? She might help us to get him to talk," Steven said as he corrected course to Piedmont instead of Oakland.

Nancy fed Steven chili while we waited for Elliott to get home. Chili was more spice than my nervous stomach could handle. She made me a cup of tea generously laced with milk.

"To be honest, I'm glad you'll be here when he gets home. You'll force him to be sociable. This case has got him really upset. His company is being sued so it is understandable, but he's no fun lately. Always worried," Nancy said as she poured cups of tea.

I wondered if Elliott was ever fun. If so, it wasn't any time I was around him. I looked at the Thomas Hill painting of Yosemite Valley that hung above the mantle.

Nancy caught my gaze at the painting. "It's a copy, a reproduction, the original is in the Bancroft Library. All of our Hill's are reproductions. The real ones are all donated to museums now. Elliott loves those paintings, because he says they remind him of Lexi's work. Honestly, I never saw it that way."

Nancy directed my attention to a colorful abstract painting on the opposite wall.

I gave the painting a quick glance but it evoked too strong of emotions. My heart fell before I looked away. I couldn't get sidetracked.

Nancy chattered on, "Lexi's work was quite an advancement over Hill's. Captured the feeling of the valley without his realism. And that is a lot harder to accomplish." Nancy sighed. "She was damn good for a kid. Just imagine what a fantastic artist she could have become." Nancy looked at my face. "I'm sorry Alexandra. Hardly the time for an art lesson."

I gave Nancy a hug; gently, because she's so thin I always worry I'll break her. Mom told me that Nancy was actually on the chubby side in college, and instead of blonde, she was a brunette.

Now I remembered exactly what she used to look like. Now she has a new nose, and a new chin. She's had more work done than anyone else in Mom and Dad's circle, but she is sweet—if insecure.

"I'm sorry Elliott's got troubles," I said. "Thank you for inviting us."

"I had no idea Lauren was missing," Nancy said and hugged me back. "I'll do whatever I can to help you."

"You were at the Gregg farm back then, right? Did strangers ever come there?"

"There were girls. I guess you would call them strangers."

"Who brought them?"

"I imagine every one of the guys did on occasion. Well, maybe not Elliott. He was looking for a wife and enough of a snob to want to be *introduced* to the right girl." Nancy gave me a soft, sad smile. "That turned out to be me."

"Were there ever open parties?" I asked.

"Not that I know of. Not when I was there."

"Anything suspicious ever happen?"

Nancy looked at me for several seconds before she answered. "There was one strange thing that happened that I've never gotten Elliott to explain to my satisfaction. He always says it has nothing to do with us, but it's a secret he swore to keep."

"What?" This sounded promising.

"One Wednesday, Carol and I drove up after class. We didn't have classes on Tuesdays and Thursdays, and Carol needed to get away. It was soon after Lexi..." Her voice trailed off, she took a deep breath and then continued. "When we got to the farm, Elliott and, I think it was Jamie, were standing near the front gate, on the cattle crossing. They looked quite serious. Elliott told us that Mrs. Mac and Tom were sick with some terrible flu, and they didn't think we should expose ourselves to it."

"Thoughtful of them," I said.

"Yes, but it was weird too. Elliott leaned in the car, planted a big kiss on me. Surprised me because Elliott wasn't normally that affectionate." Nancy smiled. "He always wants to avoid a public display you know. And it was before we were really a couple. He was nervous, and looking kind of pale, but he insisted he felt okay. I think Carol was particularly crushed because she had been invited there to escape from reminders of Lexi. This rejection reinforced her feelings that all those guys didn't care for her."

"Yeah?"

"When we drove away, Carol said it was strange that Mrs. Mac's car wasn't there, nor was Mr. Mac's. We both thought something funny was going on that day. And Elliott as much as admitted it years later, but he wouldn't tell me what."

That was the best info we got from that visit. Elliott was damn grouchy, even with us there. In fact, it seemed as though seeing us there upset him more. Nancy tried to coax him into helping us, but he insisted he didn't know anything, excused himself without eating, and said he was going to his study. He must not have been skipping a lot of meals; he was bigger than he looked in Carol's photo. He had been stocky, but now he was also bloated. And his nose and cheeks were stained with a heavy drinker's broken blood vessels instead of acne.

He pulled Nancy aside and whispered to her for a minute. She nodded and he stripped off the jacket and vest of his three-piece suit as he walked up the stairs.

"You'll have to go to Tahoe to see the other two. Jamie is just outside Sonora. Ron lives in Tahoe City. I could drive you up," Nancy said. "We could stay in our place tonight because I think your folk's place is still shut down for the winter."

Elliott and Nancy's place was newer, bigger and fancier than ours. Our place had been in Mom's family for generations. It was a great location on a beautiful piece of lakefront property, but it was old and hadn't had much updating. Opening it up was a big deal. Not something you wanted to do late at night, while you were tired and freezing. Nights are always cold in the Sierras, but especially so in March.

"What do you think, Steven?" I asked.

"I'd prefer to take you home to your own bed. You need rest." He frowned at me. "If you insist on going tonight, it's not a bad plan."

"Let's make a bed for her in the back of my Lexus. It'll be comfortable. She can sleep. I can turn the heat on up at the lake by phone so it'll be toasty when we arrive."

"Sounds good to me," I said.

Nancy found warm jackets for each of us and we loaded into the car. I had a feeling she wanted to escape that house and Elliott's bad mood.

Steven called Dad from the car, "We're headed to the lake. Nancy's driving us, we'll stay with her."

Steven hung up. "Dad said be careful."

47

The sun sparkled and flashed off ripples of water. Snow covered mountain peaks surrounded the deep sapphire Lake Tahoe with its tranquility in the cold of March undisturbed by boat traffic. I opened the French door, and stepped onto the balcony facing the quiet lake. The cold air, fresh with the fragrance of evergreens, cleared the cobwebs from my brain. It wasn't right that this beauty would exist with Mom missing. The lake should be shrouded in fog.

I'd been half asleep when Nancy ushered me into this bedroom late last night. I vaguely remembered the kitchen was towards the front of the house. The sound of a car on the otherwise quiet road beyond the entry gates gave me a hint where that was. The smell of coffee clued me in that I wasn't the first one up. I followed my nose.

"Good morning," Nancy greeted me, handing over a mug of coffee and nodding at the sugar and cream on the marble island.

"Thank you for doing this for us Nancy," I said. "It's very kind of you."

"Your mom is one of my oldest, dearest friends," Nancy responded. "She has always been very good to me."

I looked at her, hesitated before speaking and in the end, just nodded.

"I know," Nancy smiled at me. "We aren't all that close. Because we met through our husbands when we first started dating. The men always came first, and we didn't share secrets knowing whatever we said might well get back to our husbands. But I love your mother. And I know she would be there for me in similar circumstances."

I hugged her. She was so tiny, she felt like a bird in my arms. That social skeleton thing had shrunk her over the years.

"Is Steven still asleep?"

"No, he's in the exercise room."

I'd never been in that wing of Nancy's cabin. Could you call fifty-five hundred square feet a cabin?

She pointed to a door off the breakfast room. I stepped into a wide hall lined with books, DVDs, and CDs. A cupboard door was open to a sound system that must have held thousands more CDs. I kept walking past a sauna, a steam room, a huge shower room, and into a high- ceilinged exercise room with three elliptical machines, two treadmills, two StairMasters, a Gravitron, a stationery bike, a weight rack, two flat screens, four speakers, a shelving unit filled with yoga mats, wrist bands, bottles of water, and headphones. Steven was on one of the ellipticals.

"Wow!" I said.

"Yeah," he answered and stepped off the machine. "How are you doing?"

"I'm okay. I guess I slept a long time, huh?" I was okay too, just a slight headache. The itch of my dirty hair was bothering me more than the wound. "You really have to stop letting me sleep so long. I'll get washed up and we'll borrow a car from Nancy."

"Yeah, I mapquested both addresses. Meet you in the main entry hall?" Steven said.

"Yeah, I think I can find it."

We shared an insincere chuckle as neither of us actually felt like laughing.

I passed back through the breakfast room. Nancy looked up from her laptop. "Alexandra, there's lots of winter clothes in the closet of your room. And extra jackets in the mudroom."

I thanked her and got ready to take off with Steven. Nancy handed Steven keys to a Range Rover and waved us in the direction of the hall that connected to the garage. She gave me a plate of bagels with cream cheese and insulated travel mugs filled with hot coffee.

We headed over Fanny Bridge into Tahoe City. Fanny Bridge got it's nickname because lines of tourists bend over the railing to watch fish ride the Truckee river out of the lake. The result looks as though the railing is composed of butts in the air. I have no idea what its actual name is.

We found Ron's condo in a planned community in Tahoe City.

"Do you think he's still home? Maybe we should've gone to his office?" I asked.

"According to Nancy, his second divorce, together with the falling housing market has pretty much wiped him out.

He's not at his office much these days. She's not even sure he still has one."

When I was little, Dad took me to a place with what I thought were dollhouses. The models of planned communities scattered through a two-story lobby were just at eye level for me. My imagination wandered through them. But it wasn't a plaything; it was Ron's development company.

That development company was a partnership with his first father-in-law that ended with Ron's first divorce. His second wife came with her father's mega construction company and more development projects.

"There he is." Steven pointed to a tall, wiry man clad in bike riding gear, a helmet, spandex leggings, and a windbreaker. Ron was walking a bike down a meandering path to the street.

"Hey, Ron," Steven yelled. We trotted toward him.

Ron stood still, looked at us seemingly without recognition, but he grinned a lopsided smile, as we got close.

"Yo, kids. What do we have here? What are you two up to?"

"Hi," Steven and I said in unison. Seeing him again, remembering his fun loving, amiable personality, it was hard to imagine that he would be involved in anything evil. What were we thinking?

But then wasn't the capacity for evil in all of us?

I hugged him.

"We're trying to find Mom," I blurted out.

"What do you mean? Did you lose her?" he joked. Then he noticed my serious expression. "What's up, guys?"

"Mom went missing," Steven said.

"Then someone shot at me," I said.

Ron pulled back his head and studied us for a moment before he spoke, "Did you think I might know something or someone who could help find her?"

"We hoped you could help us," I said. "I don't know what we thought. I've had this idea that this whole thing had something to do with the farm you guys lived on in 1969."

Ron stared at me.

"I can't explain why. It's just a feeling." And a memory of an overheard conversation, but I wasn't about to get into that.

"I've no idea how to help, but I'll do whatever I can. Just excuse me for a minute. I need to call my riding partner. The one I was just leaving to meet."

He punched a number in a cell, turned his back to us, and walked away six feet before he spoke to someone.

He turned back to us. "Okay, I'm all yours. Come inside. I think I have some coffee or tea or juice or something."

We followed him back down the winding path, through a patio gate where he parked his bike, and in through a garage door where he removed his helmet exposing thinning blonde hair touched with gray. He led the way upstairs to an open and cozy living, dining, and kitchen room.

He opened a refrigerator. "Juice? I've got orange or apple."

"I'm fine thanks," I said.

Steven accepted the orange juice.

We sat on the love seat and two armchairs that furnished the living area.

"So? How can I help?" Ron asked.

"Tell us about life on the farm."

"That could take awhile. We lived there over a year, from May of '68 to August of '69."

"How often did Tom bring new girls around?"

He laughed, reddening. "About as often as I did. I'm embarrassed to admit it was a contest."

"So there were a lot of strange girls around?"

'Not a lot, but some."

"What about around the time that Lexi was killed?"

He blanched, but that could have been at the bad memory. They, make that we, had been good friends at one point, until Lexi, that is I, had spurned his attentions.

"Ya know, we didn't have anybody around then. We weren't in a partying mood."

"And what was Mrs. Mac sick with?"

"Huh?" He looked at me with a blank stare.

"Nancy said that she and Carol came to the farm a day or so after the murder, but were told to leave because Mrs. Mac and Tom had a bad flu."

"I guess I'd forgotten that. Ya know, I don't remember all the details."

"Were you at the Berkeley house the night Lexi was killed?"

"Yeah. I had been around earlier that day, and I stuck around after to see if I could be of any help."

"When did you return to the farm?" I asked.

"Let's see. I went home—that is back to the farm—right after rush hour at the end of the week. Ya know, we used to have what we called rush hour, then it became rush hours. Now it's all the time down there, isn't it?" Ron was still selling the benefits of mountain living, in denial, forgetting the summer traffic jams around the lake.

"What girls had been around right before that? Over that weekend?"

"You really think I can remember that? No way, Jose."

"Did you have a girl there then?"

"I'd been in town for a couple days. Suzy was my Berkeley girl."

I wondered if she knew that was her classification, but then, it wasn't cool to fuss over things like that in those days.

"What about over the weekend?" I asked.

"It's possible, I don't remember. That was a long time ago, ya know."

"I'll call Mrs. Mac." She had the best memory of them all. She hadn't lost brain cells with drugs. Those hallucinogens were killer.

Ron looked startled, perhaps uncomfortable that I was going to talk to Mrs. Mac.

"Did Tom have someone there?"

"Tom was in Berkeley." Ron studied my face as though trying to understand where I was going with these questions.

"Do you recall if he went back to the farm with you that Friday evening?"

"No, I distinctly remember driving back by myself."

"Who was there when you arrived?" I asked.

"No one. Well, the Macs were probably in their place, but of course I didn't go in there, I just went to bed. I think I had a hangover. *Maybe I* had the flu." He grinned, it was that lopsided, flirty grin, the one where he kinda dropped one side of his head and his blue green eyes twinkled at you.

I couldn't help but return the smile, but I continued, "When did the others show up?"

"I really don't remember. Boy, you should be an interrogator. Hey. That could be a career." Another grin. "Maybe the guys were in their bedrooms. Nobody was in much of a mood to socialize, ya know?"

"Do you remember when you heard about Lexi?"

"Of course." His smile disappeared. "Police pulled us all out of bed the night it happened." He rubbed his eyes, blinked a few times. "That was a hell of a time. For everyone, ya know. Back at the farm, Mrs. Mac was crying in the kitchen the next afternoon when I got up."

"Who was there then?"

He thought for a moment, looked out the window at the lake. "Pretty much everybody who lived there: Jamie, Tom, Elliott," he hesitated. "I don't think anyone else."

"Got any idea where my mother might be?"

He shook his head very slowly with a sad smile on his face.

"Al, maybe we should go over to our place, here at the lake," Steven said.

"What for?" Ron asked.

Was that alarm fleeting across Ron's face?

Steven shrugged.

"Want me to go to see Jamie with you?" Ron asked. "I know how to get there, it's a bit tricky."

"If you want," I answered.

"Sure," Steven said. "That would be great."

"Give me a minute to change." He hurried down the hall.

"Steven, what was the name of that place where the Macs are?"

He ran fingers through his blonde hair. "Happy Valley, I think."

"I'll be back in a minute." I stepped outside onto a deck and called information. When I was connected to Happy Valley Retirement Home, I asked for Mrs. Mac, and was informed she had her own number. I called her private line.

"Mrs. Mac? Hi. It's Alexandra. Remember me?"

"Yes, of course, dear. Can't decide if it's your mother you remind me of, or for some reason, you make me think of Lexi."

This woman was the most perceptive of them all.

"Did you get sick a couple days after Lexi was killed? Or maybe right after?" I asked.

"Lord girl, I've never been sick a day in my life." She chuckled.

"Didn't you come down with a bad flu? Weren't you and Tom both sick?"

"No. I was heartsick, but I didn't have no flu."

I took a deep breathe of the clean mountain air before I asked the next question. "What about Tom?"

"One time he and the other boys all got real bad food poisonin', not from my cookin' mind you—but now, that wasn't around when Lexi died. That was months later."

"Who was at the farm the weekend before Lexi's murder?" I leaned against the railing, stared at the lake without really seeing it. Below me, a cyclist got off his bike, walked it off the cycling path and cut through the evergreens.

"Let me think: the four boys, not the usual girls. As I recall, it was gettin' close ta finals, or midterms, or somethin' where the girls all had studies. Girls that were usually around were all at school that weekend. 'Course, your mother didn't come around until much later." She was quiet for a moment. "No, I think there was just the one girl that weekend."

"What girl was that?"

"Oh, a very not nice girl," she answered. "Honestly, a bad girl."

"Bad?" I held my breath awaiting her answer.

"A slut, a real slut. Even in those days of that free love stuff, she was a sick one."

Wow. Mrs. Mac was usually so permissive. "Why do you say that?"

"Cause she was. She was a . . . I gotta think of the word . . . I know, a nymphomaniac."

"What did she do that made you think that?"

"Cause she made the rounds of the bedrooms. She seduced every one of those boys, one right after another, and maybe even more than one at a time," Mrs. Mac said with a tsk, tsk.

Yeah, like that would be real hard. "What did she look like?"

"That was just it. She didn't look like a whore, she didn't wear much make up, she was only a little pretty, not like the other girls. Real curly, frizzy hair, dark auburn, kind of freckles, a pug nose."

"What was her name?"

"I never knew her last name. Her first name was Jennifer."

"Where did she come from?"

"One of the boys picked her up hitchhikin'. She needed a place ta stay, so he brought her home."

"How long was she there?"

"Come ta think of it, she was the one that got sick," Mrs. Mac said. "Then she got well and left all a sudden like."

"Please tell me what happened." I watched a domestic cat stalk a bird in the grass peeking through the snow. The cyclist continued to walk between the trees, heading toward a neighboring condo. Something about his walk and physique was familiar, but his helmet hid his head and face.

"She was there for 'bout three—no four days—then the boys left ta go into the city, but told me that Jennifer was sick and ta leave her alone. They didn't want me ta catch anythin' from her. I thought that was funny, I made a joke about I wouldn't be the one catchin' something from her. You know in those days people were maybe less worried 'bout social diseases, I mean the ones that the young people knew 'bout then were easily treated with a shot of penicillin." She sighed. "She locked herself in the master suite. I knocked on the door, asked if she needed anythin', but she didn't answer, and since one of the boys had already taken a tray inta her, well, I just left her be."

"When and how did she leave?"

"I don't know the how, 'cause I went on my day off. When Mr. Mac and I got home, she was gone."

"What day of the week were you off?"

"Wednesday. Always Wednesdays, so as I could get stuff ready for the weekend, and clean up after."

"Who brought her home?"

"I don't know as I ever knew that, she just was there in the livin' room, and when I saw her behavior . . . well, I asked Elliott where she'd come from."

"Thank you, Mrs. Mac, you've been a big help, as usual."

I looked around for the cyclist but he had disappeared.

When I turned to go back into the condo, I ran into Ron who had been right behind me.

"Talking to Mrs. Mac?"

I nodded.

"How is she?"

"Well."

"Hey, I loved that old dame. She still sharp?" he asked without his usual jovial attitude.

"As a tack."

Did my answer make him nervous? I didn't see any obvious change in his demeanor.

"Ready to go?"

"Sure."

He opened the door. We went inside and down the stairs to the garage.

"I'll drive," Ron said pushing the remote lock and opening the door to his Highlander. "It'll be easier since I know the way."

Steven looked at me. "We could follow you?"

"Whatever for?"

I knew Steven felt the same bad vibe I did, and was not so much a fan of getting in a car with this man. On the other hand, we had known him all our lives, and he was looking uncomfortable. I mean, he'd offered to help us. How awkward was this?

"Okay, Steven, let's go with Ron." I climbed into the back seat behind Ron, leaving Steven to go around to the front seat.

"Hey, what did you find out from Mrs. Mac?" Ron asked while Steven circled the car.

"She has an amazing memory," I said.

"Yeah, she kept those old brain cells intact," Ron answered. "Never could talk her into dropping acid." He went on with a long story about an LSD trip, all of which was pretty unbelievable, filled with unlikely occurrences and a story I'd heard many times both in the sixties and in this century.

I nodded and pretended to listen; glad I had distracted him from the subject of Mrs. Mac and her revelations. I didn't know how much of our conversation I wanted to share with him.

48

Jamie wasn't home.

He worked in the Tuolumne County Court house, a masonry building with a distinctive clock tower that actually made it easy to find. Sonora hadn't grown as dramatically as many other California towns.

"Wow, he's official. Is he really the district attorney?" Steven said.

"Something like that, yeah," Ron answered with his usual carelessness.

Ron took us in a back entrance. Jamie's secretary sat in a rotunda in front of a private office. "Mr. Gregg is not in the office today," she said and refused to answer any further questions regarding Jamie's schedule.

Ron pulled a phone out of his pocket. "Yo, Jamie, I've got some people with me that'd like to see you. Sometime today man, or if you're doing a deposition or somethin', maybe this evening." He winked at us. "Voicemail. Wanna grab lunch?"

He called Jamie back and told him where we would be. Then he showed us around the corner to a wine and bistro place that looked like Tuscany on the inside. I ordered crab-cakes on salad. I looked longingly at the wine list, but I was still taking pain meds.

"What do you want to ask Jamie?"

"Same stuff I asked you." I toyed with the breadbasket, picked up a piece of focaccia bread.

"Al's got this idea—a theory I guess you'd call it—that for some reason somebody shooting her and Mom's disappearance has something to do with Lexi's murder," Steven said. "But it seems likely that the guy who killed Lexi is dead. Then again, we can't figure out why someone would steal a file Dad had on Lexi's murder. Or why they'd try to kill Al. So we are talking to Dad's friends. Lexi's friends."

Ron seemed to think over what Steven said before he asked, "Who have you talked to?"

"Dave, the Macs, and Tom," Steven said.

"We tried to talk to Elliott, but ended up just talking with Nancy," I said.

"What about Carol? She was Lexi's closest friend."

"We did talk to her, and definitely plan to do more of that. We'll head back to the city when we finish here."

"Ya know, I could talk with Jamie." Ron said. " Tell me what you want to ask him."

"Thanks for the offer, but I'd rather do it myself. I don't really know exactly what to ask until I see how he answers," I said.

"Don't suppose you considered doing this by phone?" Ron asked.

Totally not workable, I thought, facial expressions and body language were important in these situations. I had learned a few things in my criminal anthro class, like signs that a person was lying. But I didn't voice any of those thoughts, merely shook my head.

I remembered that Ron had been quite the drinker in college. I wondered if he still was. Maybe beerboarding would work. You know, when you get someone drunk to get answers. "Steven," I said, "Don't you want a cocktail before lunch?"

Steven gave me a blank look. He didn't get it.

"Maybe a martini?" I looked at Ron. "You like martinis Ron?"

"Sure, but I gotta drive." He shrugged. "Well, maybe one." He grinned and waved down the waiter.

We ordered three martinis with Steven glaring at me until I slid my untouched glass in front of Ron. By then Ron was chattering his way through college hero stories, more than half of which were bullshit. I let him rant on until he finished the second drink without seeming to notice it had miraculously appeared in front of him.

"Ron, around the time that Lexi was killed, who was the girl staying at the farm?" I asked.

His eyes widened. His mouth opened, then shut without a sound. He cleared his throat and said, "What the hell?"

"The girl at the farm. Who was she?" I repeated the question.

"No idea what you're talking about." He waved at a waiter and motioned at his empty glasses. In need of more alcohol, it seemed.

"The guy that Tom met in the bar, at the Monk. Did you guys suspect he was the Zodiac?"

Ron jerked his arm at the bartender. He stared at me for a quick minute, then got up and rushed to the bar.

When he returned with a fresh martini, I pounced with a new question. "Did Tom worry that he might have led the Zodiac to Lexi?"

"Look, Missy, I don't know where you're coming up with these wild ideas, but you'd better watch it."

"Watch what?"

"Saying stuff you might regret." No sign of his usual grin now.

"Like Tom regretted getting the Zodiac involved in our— your lives?"

Ron's face glowed red. Was it anger? Embarrassment? Or both? He glared at me, looked away, then glanced back. His eyes glistened with tears. He downed the cocktail. "When awful shit happens to your friends, like when Lexi was killed, I'm sure we each and every one of us worried about what we might've done to . . ." he cleared his throat. "You can't help but wonder if you could've done something to prevent what happened. We were so fucking careless in those days."

Over Ron's shoulder, I saw Jamie walking toward us in his usual Armani suit. He ran a hand through longish hair, still thick, but gray at the temples. For a small town lawyer, he was quite the dresser and had lost none of the elegance in the photo I carried with me—or in my memories of him.

Jamie had carried through on his professed dedication to building a better civilization. Carol had stolen a line from a song from *Hair* when she talked about Jamie, he "*cares about strangers, evil and social injustice, more concerned about the bleeding crowd, than a needing friend."* That was before he accompanied her unconscious body to the Pebble Beach hospital. He could seem oblivious of his wealth, or his friend's lack thereof until the occasion called for generosity.

He didn't seem all that surprised to see us even though Ron had described us as "some people." Perhaps word had gotten around to expect us to show up. We exchanged hellos.

"Well, to what do I owe this unexpected pleasure—to see my niece and nephew?" He emphasized the niece and nephew bit although of all our "aunts" and "uncles" he was the least involved in our lives.

"We're looking for Mom."

"For Lauren?" He frowned as he pulled up a chair. From the hovering waiter, he ordered a merlot and a salad. "Is she missing?"

"Yes."

"How may I help you?"

"Tell us about the weekend before Lexi was killed. Who was Jennifer, the girl who was at the ranch? What happened to her?"

"I am surprised you are interested in her." He didn't look surprised. His red face looked more like embarrassed. "What does she have to do with now, with your mother?"

"I'm not entirely sure, but I think there's a connection to what has been happening recently and what happened then." I said.

"Jennifer got some kind of flu. When the rest of us went back to Berkeley, she stayed behind." He studied the napkin on his lap like it was the key to the world's greatest mysteries, flipping it over, checking out the seams. "When we got back, she was gone."

"Did Tom catch the flu?"

"Yes, I believe he did." Still looking at the napkin.

"And Mrs. Mac? Did she have the flu that week?"

"Perhaps. Yes, as I recall she may have." He squirmed in his chair, but didn't look up from the napkin. His fingers went to his nose.

Shit, they were all lying, well at least Tom, Ron and Jamie, all in this together. In my criminal anthro class I'd learned that when a person lies, a rush of adrenaline to the capillaries in the nose causes it to itch. Thus Jamie touched his nose when he lied about Mrs. Mac having the flu.

I asked him more questions, about Lexi, about my mother, about the year spent on the farm, but I already knew what I was disappointed to learn.

We ate; Jamie threw some money on the table without waiting for the bill, and excused himself. "I have to be in court." He gave me a quick peck on the cheek, shook Steven's hand and dashed out of the restaurant.

"Busy man," Ron said. "Well, shall we head back?"

"Sure," Steven said standing up. "Can I drive?"

Ron shrugged. "Why not?"

49

Steven pulled up next to Nancy's car and we said good-bye to Ron.

My brother and I were relieved to get out of his car, as relieved as I think he was to be rid of us. We couldn't miss the effort he put into being his usual jovial self, acting as though he were sober enough to drive into his carport.

I watched for the cyclist as we drove down the private road. I thought I caught a glimpse of his bike leaning against a tree halfway down the hill to the lake.

"What do you think, bro?" I shook my head at Steven as soon as we cleared the front drive of Ron's condo development.

"Do *you* know what they are hiding?" he asked.

"I'm pretty sure it has something to do with that girl who spent the weekend at the farm right before Lexi was killed. Maybe she turned out to be a high-class whore, like the Hollywood Madam, and they don't want the world to know their connection to her, or something happened to her. Or . . . what do you think?"

"Yeah, could be her. Or maybe they really did deal drugs, and don't want that known. After all, they're respectable professionals now."

I shrugged. "Carol's next?"

"Let's call her. She won't be hiding anything from us, and we're taking a long time to do this. Every time I think of Mom, my heart skips a beat."

"Mine too." I scrolled to Carol's number on my cell. "Hey Carol, it's Al."

"Oh sweetie, how are you?"

"My head's doing okay. I'm freaked about Mom." I tried to calm down by watching the dark green trees lining the roadway.

"I know what you mean. I wish I knew what we could do, that there was something I could do."

"Steven and I are trying. Look, I have this idea. Back in 1969—what do you know about a girl named Jennifer who stayed at the farm the week before Lexi was killed?"

Carol was quiet for no longer than an instant.

"That name doesn't ring any bells. I was only at the farm one time before Lexi was killed. Midterms, papers—it was a hell of a time. You needed a gas mask to get to class. Which was the main reason Lexi escaped to the farm some weekends."

"What about after Lexi was killed?"

Carol was quiet for a minute. "There was this one strange thing, come to think of it. Nancy tried to take me to the farm to chill after the murder, but when we got there, we were sent away. Somebody was sick, or something. I've never forgotten because, honestly, it really hurt my feelings." She sighed. "Nancy understood. She took me to the St. Francis for a few days instead. Oh, god, that was such a horrendous time. I can't stand the thought of losing another—" She didn't finish the sentence but she didn't need to. She didn't want to lose my mother.

Nor did I.

"Carol, can you think of anything, any reason why someone would kidnap or harm my mother?"

"Unfortunately, reason doesn't always have anything to do with such acts. I mean, the nut who killed Lexi had no reason, right?"

"Got it. But look, it's possible there's a reason, so what could it be?" I asked.

"To keep her from telling something. Or to keep somebody else from talking."

"Like who?"

"You. Or your dad?"

"Me? I don't know anything."

"Maybe they just think you do," she hesitated. "I mean look at it this way, either shooting you and kidnapping your mother were just random acts of violence, or . . . that's just a little unlikely as a coincidence," Carol said. "So maybe you do know something, or might know something that endangers someone. Possibly their reputation, or financial well-being."

"Hmm, gonna think about that for awhile," I answered. "Please call me back if you come up with anything at all. Please."

"Absolutely. I love you, sweetie. Take care. Ciao."

"Steven, what could I know?" Suddenly, it hit me. How could I have been so slow?

I turned to my brother and punched his shoulder. "Got it. It's the file on the Zodiac. Look at all the trouble somebody went to, to get those papers. That was Dad's file, not an official police file, but because of Dad's connection to the justice department he was able to include stuff not available to everybody."

I almost slapped my head, kicking myself figuratively. "If only I knew what it was I saw in there. There's something that someone doesn't want known." Then I remembered papers jammed into a pocket. "What'd I do with the papers that were in my jacket pocket when I was shot?"

"Papers?"

"The ones with the photo of the gang on the sofa, the one you folded in half."

Steven shook his head. "I was a little distracted concerning you at the time. I gave 'em to you at the hospital. Pretty sure you left 'em in your room at Mom and Dad's house." He smiled at me and said, "I'm hella glad you're okay."

My brother's eyes filled with tears. So had mine. He turned his head away. I figured he was as uncomfortable with the emotional moment as I was.

We arrived at Nancy's cabin without me coming up with the answer. "I'm gonna go for a walk and think about this. You go tell Nancy her car's back. See if she's ready to head home, ok?"

"A walk?" I don't think that's a good idea," Steven said.

"C'mon. Just along the lake. It's all on private land. Most of the places are empty. Nobody'll see me. You help Nancy get ready to leave." I said.

"Yeah. Ok. But be careful." He touched my shoulder. "You have your phone, right? I'm gonna see about those papers too. Maybe Dad can get a copy of the police file. I'll call his secretary."

"Good idea. I hope you do better with that secretary of his than I usually do."

Steven gave me a thumbs-up as he headed into the house.

50

I headed along the beach toward our compound. We're a mile or two past Nancy and Elliott's place. A walk would give me a chance to mull over the unanswered questions. And perhaps I could re-connect with the feelings of safety and security that our sweet cabins on the lake provided. Our lakefront property had been passed down from my maternal grandparents when they no longer wanted to use it.

Patches of snow lay in the shade. It was a nice walk; the brisk air felt good. But I still didn't get it. What could the Zodiac file possibly have to do with someone shooting at me and kidnapping Mom? The girl Jennifer: what was her connection? There must have been something in the file that still mattered to someone. But the Zodiac guy was dead. So it couldn't be him.

There had been a note on one report, in Dad's writing, "Ask Tom." What was niggling in the back of my mind? The threatening letter in legalese, yes, but what else?

I arrived at our compound. Our place was totally funky, with no pool or spa, small old cabins where the word cabin was not a misnomer. This was home. This was safe.

The windows in both the living room and the bedroom of the main house were lit from within. We'd left lights on?

Our leaving at the end of Labor Day weekend had been chaotic. Steven and I both had to be in class early the next morning, and Dad was worried about getting caught in traffic leaving the lake on a holiday. We had rushed to winterize—draining water from the pipes so that they didn't freeze and burst—and otherwise prepare the cabin for sitting vacant in the cold. We hadn't returned during the winter, skipping our normal routine of spending the Holidays there.

Had someone else used the place? Or maybe as the lights-out-in-charge, I'd screwed up the job.

I didn't have a key, but I knew where one was. I went along the side of the main house, headed for the boathouse. I caught a glimpse of a car in the parking area in front of the boathouse, not in the usual parking near the front gate, but hidden from view from the highway. Mom's car!

I took another look at the main house. A thin wisp of smoke drifted lazily from the chimney as though a small or dying fire burned on the hearth grate. Mom!

With a burst of joy, I ran to the back door.

51

Inches away from busting through the door, the thought that I should be cautious hit me. I skidded to a stop and looked through the window. The pass through from the kitchen to the living room framed the sight of my mother—tied to a wooden chair.

She was looking right at me, without any sign of seeing me. Then, just once, she rolled her eyes to the side warning me that someone was out of my line of sight.

Shit, that was close.

I crouched and rushed back to the boathouse on my tip-toes. I crept under Dad's boat and called Steven.

Damn. Voicemail, and he's sketchy about checking his messages. "Mom is tied up in the living room of our main house on the lake. I'm hiding in the boathouse. I don't think I've been seen, but maybe—cause I wasn't careful. Get help! Text me back, I'm putting my phone on vibrate," I whispered into the phone and then I texted. *"I c mom tied up lake house ck vmail get help"*

I couldn't think what to do next.

Dad would still be in court at this time of day.

I was afraid to call 911 for fear that local sheriffs won't know how to deal with the situation without Mom getting hurt, but I didn't know what else to do. I had no idea how many people were in the house or where they were.

I crawled out from under the boat. I was so scared, so nervous; it was hard to calm down enough to slow my racing thoughts, to think straight.

I decided to locate how many people were where, and then call 911 with the info. I slipped through the partially open garage doors and stole across the lawn to the bushes under the dining room window. I saw the back of a large, brawny man sitting on the sofa opposite Mom. If there was anyone else in the room, I couldn't see him.

I crawled to the bedroom window and looked in. No one in there.

If there was no one in the bathroom, there might be just one person watching Mom.

The bunkhouse, as we called the cabin that consisted of four bedrooms and a bath, had high windows. All of the curtains had been closed for the winter. There was no sign they'd been disturbed.

I would check the main house one last time, and then call. Still no sign of anyone else.

I hurried to the far side of the boathouse and dialed 911.

My heart pounded so loud it nearly drowned out the ring of the phone. "If this is an emergency please stay on the line, your call will be answered in the order received . . ."

"Name?"

"Alexandra Nichols."

"Nature of your emergency?"

"My mom is being held captive at our cabin on highway—"

Out of nowhere a hand reached from behind me, grabbed my phone, and flung it into the lake.

52

"Oh no!" I screamed and attempted to turn around, but my arms were jerked behind my back.

I was shoved around the corner of the boathouse, bounced off the front bumper of Mom's car, and manhandled toward the porch of the main house where I stumbled up the stairs.

The brawny man inside jumped up, opened the windowed door. I was pushed into the room and landed on my knees, barely missing the open fireplace.

Mom screamed.

I screamed.

Two men growled.

I rolled over and saw a three hundred pound, scary ugly man.

I cowered.

"Where'd ya get dat one? Hey, she's da one we shot. You didn't kill her?" said the brawny man who'd been watching Mom.

"Shut the fuck up. Tie'er up. I gotta make a call." The man who had thrown me on the floor slammed out the door to the front porch. I couldn't quite make out what he was saying, but he was definitely upset. Finding me here wasn't a pleasant surprise.

Mom's captor pulled another chair in from the dining room, shoved me onto it, and used a cord to fasten my hands and feet to the rungs.

The other guy, the huge fat one, came back inside. "He says just to keep'em here for another twenty-four. He's still pissed off."

Whoever "He" was, both of these men were afraid of him. I hated to imagine how awful he'd have to be in order to scare barbaric bullies like these.

The two of them went out to the porch.

"Are you okay, Mom?"

She nodded. "Don't talk," she rasped. Tears rolled down her cheeks.

She'd probably thought I was dead since the thugs thought they had killed me.

We both strained to hear what was being said on the porch, but we could only make out scattered words. Like "dumbshit," or "cocksucker" or "fuckup" or "supposed to get the papers."

Mom whispered, "Does anyone know you're here?"

"I left a voicemail for Steven."

Mom groaned. She knew the chances of Steven checking his voicemail as well as I did.

"I started to call 9-1-1."

"They said they shot you." Mom's voice cracked. She choked back a sob.

"I'm good."

"They're coming back," Mom hissed through closed teeth.

Fatty did not come inside. He hulked around the corner of the house.

Brawny came into the room, heaved himself onto the sofa. "Lady, why don't'cha have a TV here?"

Mom was silent.

We had no TV because this is where we came to get away from the world.

He fidgeted, picked up a three year old *Vanity Fair*, thumbed through a few pages, looked at the photos, threw the magazine across the room in Mom's direction, and stared at her as though his boredom were her fault.

She wasn't the reason he never learned to read. If he'd been her child, he'd have been a reader.

He pulled a pack of cigarettes out of a pocket, fingered one out, and lit it. Poor Mom, no one was allowed to smoke in the house. On the porch yes, but not in the house ever. Even in the worst storm, smokers were expected to step outside. What kind of a barbarian smoked inside these days?

Of course there were no ashtrays, but that still was no excuse for letting ashes drop to the cushions. At least, when he finished the cigarette, he flung it into the fireplace.

"Whacha lookin at, bitch?"

I dropped my eyes to my lap. No point in antagonizing the guy.

We sat in silence. Brawny's eyelids slowly closed, his head nodded, he snored like a grizzly bear.

Was it possible that my 9-1-1 call was long enough to be any use?

Did Steven get the voicemail? Or the text?

He must be wondering where I was by now. What would he do? Would he have the same hesitation I did to call authorities?

In retrospect, I realized I should've called Detective Schmidt. He could've coordinated efforts to rescue Mom.

Would Steven be smarter, calmer than me? I hoped he wouldn't come looking for me by himself.

My limbs were starting to numb. How had Mom withstood days of this? Her eyes were closed. Her head nodded forward. I hoped she was just asleep.

My mind raced with questions: I had no answers.

Who were these two goons? They worked for someone, who?

I'd heard the word "papers". Did they mean Dad's file? There was something in that file that for some reason was okay for Dad to see, but not for me to read.

There were the papers and reports from the case file. The police had those too so I eliminated them as being the problem.

There were notes from Dad, and the letter from a law firm. I tried to remember the names on the letterhead, but drew a blank.

Before I was shot at, while I raced across the campus, something about this had become clear. I mentally retraced my steps. I'd cut behind the Faculty Club to Faculty Glade, passed still another bear statue . . . Bing! A bear, what about a bear? I was afraid of bears, but so what?

I had sat down on a bench in the lawn outside Kroeber and pulled a wad of papers out of my pocket: including a letter and a note in Dad's handwriting, "Ask Tom." An overheard conversation. Could I remember a conversation that had taken place forty years ago, in another lifetime? I closed my eyes, took several deep cleansing breaths, did my best to relax. I let my mind float.

"You asshole, why did you bring that girl to the ranch? A complete stranger, for god's sake?" Was that Jamie's voice?

Yes, I took several more deep breaths and tried to forget who was in the room. Shit, could I even possibly do this. I let my mind wander to the happy times in this room. More cleansing breaths.

"You didn't mind havin' her. Besides, it's water under the bridge. That train left the station. The question now is, how the hell do we get rid of her? I found a guy who'll help us with our problem." I had been pretty sure at the time that was Tom speaking.

"What do ya mean?"

"I met this guy. He's nuts, but hell, if he gets caught, he'll get the blame."

"You told some guy you met drinking at the Monkey Inn about our problem? Are you out of your fucking mind?"

"He'll get the blame. He's a low life, a loser. We'd have complete deniability."

"What about our semen? Did you forget that?"

"So they get some blood types."

"Multiple blood types that all just happen to match the four of us!"

"She's a whore. It happens. So what?"

The big ape on the sofa grunted, snored louder, and slid down toward a more prone position.

I came out of my reverie knowing that was all I'd heard that day. Of course, back then, they didn't have DNA testing. No one could use DNA to tie criminals to their crimes.

Had they killed this Jennifer person?

More likely she'd ODed. And they didn't want to report it to the police. They wanted someone else to move the body. Was that someone else the Zodiac?

And the bear?

I'd been afraid of bears my whole life. My Dad, Jeff, had tried to get me over my freak-outs to even teddy bears. There was a bear statue in the park that had outstretched arms; he tried to get me to play on it. I screamed bloody murder when he lifted me into its arms. We were walking with one of my "uncles" at the time.

It was Tom. Tom spotted the bear statue, "Let's put her on that," he'd said. That bear seemed gigantic. I must've been six. I was so scared I couldn't breath. Dad pulled me off the outstretched arms of the bear and held me to him while I sobbed all the way back to the house. What had they been talking about?

"Remember the guy that Lexi was with that night?" Daddy asked Tom.

"Derek?"

"Yeah . . . you remembered his name?"

"Hell. Everything about that night is seared on my brain."

"He's turned up."

"Really, ok." Tom said. "That's a little scary."

"Why is that, Tom?"

"Trust me, you don't want to know."

"He says his dad was the Zodiac."

"Hmm, I thought that case was closed."

"Not exactly, there was a guy, named Arthur Allen that the police were sure was the Zodiac, but there wasn't enough evidence to indict. And you couldn't pick him out of a line up."

"So, will you re-open?"

"It's not up to me, but I'm certainly not pushing it. His father's dead, so what's the point?"

Tom nodded.

Dad continued, "It would be helpful if I knew what your problem with this case is. I've been through the file and I've never seen any links to anyone besides Lex. You couldn't ID Allen. That was for real, right? It wasn't just a matter of not wanting to get involved?

"But I was involved," Tom hesitated before continuing, "I couldn't stand the thought that I might've led the Zodiac to Lexi. It's a huge relief to hear that Derek was the link."

"What were you talking to this guy about?"

"Just shooting the shit."

"Anything to do with Jennifer?"

"What?"

"I know there was a girl named Jennifer at the ranch around the time Lexi was killed."

"Who the hell told you that?"

"A reliable source," Daddy had said, "that's not the point. Did she have something to do with the Zodiac? Did you mention her to him?"

"I may have, in only the most general way."

"What's that mean?" Daddy startled me, barking at Tom that way.

"We were talking about free love, promiscuous girls. He had a thing about them, pretty down on them, you know. Hell, if my memory serves

*me well, the guy did bear some resemblance to that Derek that Lexi was
with that night."*

"Did you tell him where Jennifer was?"

"I may have."

*Daddy moved me from his arms to his shoulders. "Tom, did you do
anything I would want to prosecute? Tell me straight." Daddy could sure
sound scary sometimes.*

*"No, I swear. None of us did anything illegal. I just happened to have
a conversation with the guy, and I was scared that he might have followed
me to your house, and that was how he saw Lexi. That's all."*

"Did he go to the farm?"

"How the hell would I know?"

"Did you tell him where the farm was?"

*"Maybe. We were drinking. Hell, I don't remember every damn
word." Uncle Tom got agitated.*

The sound of a loud grunt brought me back to the
present.

Brawny was awake. He stood up, stomped his feet. "God
damn fuckin' cold in dis fuckin' place. How come all da firewood's buried under snow? What kind of idiots store firewood
where you have ta dig through snow ta get ta it?"

The firewood wasn't actually under snow; I wondered why
he thought that, maybe the other guy had told him that so he
wouldn't have a fire, so the smoke wouldn't be seen from the
road?

"There's firewood in a box on the front porch," I said.

"Used dat up."

"There might be more in the boat house."

"That big garage lookin' thing?"

"Yeah. Want me to get you some?"

"How stupid do ya think I am, huh?" Brawny glared at me.

"There's a pile on the left when you go through the big double doors."

"Aah, I can't leave here." He settled back down on the sofa.

"I really could go get wood for you. You've got Mom. I'm not gonna leave her." I might flag someone down on the road, tell them to get help, but I wouldn't leave. "Scout's honor."

"Fuck, you do fuckin' think I'm fuckin' stupid."

"I've gotta go to the bathroom," I said. Maybe something in the bathroom would give me an idea how to get out of this. Maybe scissors or a razor stored in there could be a weapon.

He grunted. "Tough shit." He cackled. "I'm not untying ya."

He paced around the small dining and living rooms.

Fatty came in shivering, shaking himself.

"What's he want us ta do wit 'em?" Brawny asked.

"Turn'em loose."

"But they can ID us."

"He says he can take care of that."

"Bullshit! I can take care of dat—" He pulled a gun out of his pocket.

53

Fatty held up a hand in the stop signal. "Yeah, it's bull, but we won't get paid if we don't do as he says. He's still pissed that we did anythin' other than take the papers."

"But he was da one havin' fits cause we missed important papers. We was just tryin' ta do da job right. Doesn't he appreciate dat?"

"Fuck, no."

"If we do it his way, we won't get ta spend any money. We'll be in jail forever."

"I gotta think." Fatty rubbed his head as though thinking were a painful process. "Can't let'em go."

"I'm hungry, you take a turn in here." Brawny picked up a jacket and poked a thick arm into a sleeve. "I'm getting food."

"You don't think I wouldn't rather be in here instead of freezin my balls off out there."

Brawny finished putting on his coat. "Dat one," he said as he pointed to me, "has ta go ta da bathroom."

"Lock'em in the bathroom," said the big one.

"How'em I supposed to do dat? Da locks on da inside," Brawny said smugly as though proud to have pointed out a fallacy in his boss's plan.

"Oh for fuck's sake." Fatty picked up the chair I sat in, and banged through the bedroom door on into the bathroom. He returned for Mom taking no care not to run into walls and doorframes. Mom's chair was up ended into the tub.

We heard the sound of a chair being wedged under the handle and furniture being piled in front of the door. Then came the sound of doors being slammed, a car starting.

One of my feet was not securely tied to the chair. I pulled it lose and stretched my leg to push Mom's chair upright. "Are you okay?" I looked her over; a little blood trickled from her eyebrow.

I walked my chair by twisting the legs first one, then the other back and forth until I was against the door. I threw myself and my chair against the door. Nothing budged. I tried it again. God that hurt! But the door was not going to give.

I slid my chair next to the back of Mom's. I tried untying her hand with one of mine. It was slow going, maybe impossible.

"Have they left before?"

"No. Are you sure you want to undo me? They'll just get angry. There's no way out of this room."

True. There was only a slit of a window above the tub. Could I squeeze through there? Not likely.

"We could open the window and scream for help?" I suggested still fumbling with one tied down hand to untie mom's hand.

"They'd probably be the only one's to hear us."

"Worth a shot. Have you got a better idea?"

"If you break the window open and they're gone all night, we'll freeze."

"Just hold still while I work on these knots." I tried to pry a finger into the knot. "Who are these guys?"

"No idea." Mom sighed. "But I know they weren't supposed to shoot you. They were supposed to get some papers before you read them, and when they didn't, they took it upon themselves to kidnap me to keep you quiet. Then they got the idea to kill you so you couldn't talk . . . all of which was way beyond what they were asked to do. They've been trying to figure out how to get back in the good graces of the person who hired them ever since we got here."

"Mom, the papers are Dad's file on the Zodiac killer. When we get out of here, you're gonna tell me everything you know about Lexi's murder and a girl named Jennifer."

"O-o-oh." Mom sighed, caught a sob.

"I think . . . I've almost got one of your hands undone. Can you use your fingers to hold this piece of rope? Here, feel that?"

"Al, think of something else, we can't get out of here."

"Please. Don't give up so easily."

"So easily! What?" Mom twisted around to glare at me. "I've been tied up for four days. They let me go to the bathroom three times, gave me water twice, and I haven't given up. I've fought to stay sane, but look at that window. Neither one of us can get out that thing, and yesterday, the last time they let me go to the bathroom, I could barely walk."

I looked around the room. "I'll take the top off the toilet and use it to break out the window frame as well as the glass. These old walls aren't that strong. Dad's always complaining about the amount of work this place needs, how much dry rot there is in the wood. Maybe the walls will break."

I dropped the knot I'd been working on and fumbled to find it. "You can watch for them to come back. I'll scream and break. Just help me get this undone."

"Lock the door. If we get in the tub, and put that toilet top on us, maybe we can withstand them shooting at us," Mom said.

"Mom, help me. Hold on to the rope and hold still." I didn't want to admit it, but Mom was right. Even if I could untie her hand, which wasn't going very well, what then? The cord kept slipping from my fingers, and then I had to start over finding the piece to pull. If my hands weren't shaking, it would help. I took a deep breath.

I twisted my two fingers around the cord and tried to wedge my fingernail in between the sides of the knot. I persisted. I broke the nail but I kept pushing. Finally I felt a little give, I pushed harder, got it, and pulled another strand. I pulled Mom's hand free.

Mom shook her hand, bending and stretching her fingers.

"Get your other hand. I'll help. Then you do mine," I ordered.

"I need to get circulation going in this hand before I can do anything with it." She wiggled her fingers faster. "Can you reach the drawer in that dresser?" Mom asked.

"I can try, why?"

"I think there's a pair of shears in there."

"Now you tell me that." I'd just spent what seemed like hours getting her one hand undone. Maybe not really that long, but at least half an hour. If they'd gone to eat, they shouldn't be much more than an hour.

I twisted my chair from leg to leg, scooted next to the antique dresser, and used my teeth to pull on a knob. I leaned my face into the drawer and tongued a pair of nail scissors. With my teeth, I held them up for Mom to see. I grunted to get her attention; she was concentrating on untying her other hand.

"That'll work." She grabbed them with her free hand and used the small blade to saw at the cord.

"Mom, do you remember a girl named Jennifer from Jamie's farm around the time Lexi was killed?"

"Sweetheart, I didn't go to the farm until months after Lexi died."

"Why was Uncle Tom asked to pick a guy out of a line up?"

She slipped from where she was sawing, groaning when she stabbed herself with the small blade.

"Sorry, never mind. Don't talk, concentrate."

"Got it." Mom had two hands free.

She untied mine, then we both undid our feet.

"Now what?" Mom asked.

I lifted the toilet top, swung it thru the window. Glass flew at us.

The first couple times Mom tried to stand, her legs collapsed. I rubbed the circulation back into one leg while she rubbed the other. Finally she succeeded in holding up a towel so that the next swing sent glass sliding down the wall, not at us.

We used bloodied fingers to pull shards of glass, and broken wood frame from the opening and tossed them into the tub. Frigid air streamed into the room.

"You better be right about this," Mom teased. She stuck her head in the opening and we both screamed, "HELP! HELP! HELP!"

"Get back, Mom." I took a huge swing, and broke free a chunk of the pine paneling.

"Stop. Hear that?" Mom asked. "I hear a car." She pulled the towel away from the window.

Time's up already?

I looked at the hole. Maybe I could get out, although I would do a lot of damage on the jagged bits. But Mom could barely stand. She'd never be able to get up and through there.

54

I looked out the window and saw Nancy's Range Rover in the circular drive. Steven and Nancy, each holding a gun, crept towards the house.

I screamed out the window. "Steven! Hurry! Get us out. They'll be back any minute."

Steven ran to the house and burst through the back door.

"Hurry! Hurry, they'll be back," I screamed.

We heard them both struggle to pull furniture away from the door.

I heard the chair scrape away, the door shook.

"Unlock the door Al!"

Shit!

Steven picked Mom up in a fireman's carry; we piled into Nancy's car just as Mom's car pulled into the drive.

"Get down," Steven yelled. He gunned the motor down the circular drive and screeched through the gate without checking the traffic.

Mom's car was right on our tail.

55

"Go to the sheriff's station," I yelled. "It's just off North Lake Boulevard."

"Where are they?" Steven asked.

Shots hit the rear window frame, then the tailgate.

"Get down! Lie down on the floor back there," I screamed at Mom and Nancy. "Right behind us," I told Steven. "The guy on the passenger side has a gun trained on us."

"Not stupid enough to follow us into the sheriff's substation are they?" Steven asked.

"Just drive."

"Where is it?" Steven asked.

"Turn left off of Lake Boulevard just past the road to Ron's condo," Nancy said looking at the map on her iPhone. "I've seen it before, it's way past the golf course." She dialed 9-1-1.

"It's the same place you go to pay traffic tickets. It's the courthouse and substation all in one building," Mom said.

Steven screeched the car into the asphalt parking lot. The building looked like a ski chalet with its steep roof and dormers covered in gray horizontal siding and white trim. One closed door displayed the traffic court hours on a hand painted wood sign.

"Other side," Mom said.

Steven hit the brakes next to a Sheriff's black SUV. Nancy and I jumped from the car and jerked open a wood door. Steven carried Mom into the building. I slammed the door to the station closed behind us.

"Uh, this is not a public area. The court is closed for the day." A frowning middle aged woman behind a desk stood to shoo us away.

"Get out of the way!" we all yelled at her at once. "Where's the sheriff? We're being chased by killers. They have been holding our mother captive."

"The sheriff is expecting us," Nancy said.

Steven got on his phone, "Detective Schmidt, we couldn't wait for you. The bad guys left, then we heard Mom and Al screaming. We have Mom and Al. Now we are at the Tahoe City Sheriff's Sub Station on North Lake Boulevard. How far away are you?" Steven listened, then hung up the phone. "He thinks he's five minutes from Tahoe City, coming in from the Reno airport."

A petite woman in a sheriff's uniform rushed out of an inner office. "Detective Schmidt is on the phone with my boss. He says to keep you secure." She ushered us through a doorway to a hall, then into an office.

A heavyset uniformed man, with hair too black for the wrinkles and sags in his face, came from behind a desk to shake our hands. "Detective Schmidt has had us on standby, ready to go get you upon his arrival. Glad to see you're ok."

"The guys who were holding Mom and Al followed us here," Steven said. "In Mom's Lexus."

Three uniformed men in the room jumped to attention, pulled their guns from holsters, and ran out to the parking lot.

"Actually, the last time I saw them was when we crossed Fanny Bridge," I yelled from inside the doorway.

Steven gave the sheriff the make, model, color and license plate of Mom's car, which was broadcast to patrol cars with instructions to approach with caution, suspects armed, dangerous.

"They were right behind us as we came across Fanny Bridge into Tahoe City. I was looking for the turn off into your parking lot and stopped watching'em then. I didn't see them once we got into the lot," I explained.

"Would they have another car in the area?" the sheriff asked Mom.

"I don't know. They were both in my car on the drive up here from Berkeley. I was tied up in the back seat. I didn't see another car when we arrived at our place up here."

A sharp rap on the office door announced the arrival of Detective Schmidt. He nodded at me, then his eyes lit on Mom. "Mrs. Nichols, I'm glad to see you. Are you okay?"

"Mom, this is Detective Schmidt. He has been heading the search for you," Steven explained to Mom.

Mom extended her hand, "Thank you Detective."

"Your husband sent his friend's plane to bring me up here from Oakland. I believe the plane returned to the city for him. So come to think of it, he should be here in less than an hour."

"Thank you," Mom said with a nod.

The Sheriff explained that he had deputies looking for Mom's Lexus and confirming that the kidnappers were not at our compound.

"Are you up to returning to your place?" Detective Schmidt said to Mom, "It would be helpful if the two of you," a nod indicating Mom and me, "could show us where best to check for fingerprints and so on."

"I need to stretch my legs a bit, get my circulation back before getting back in a car. Can you give me a few minutes?" Mom had been limping around on Nancy's arm; although Nancy was so slight she couldn't possibly be holding Mom up. Steven finally noticed and offered his mother his arm.

"We'd both like to use a ladies' room. Mom needs water and food," I said. "And warmer clothes."

"Of course," Detective Schmidt said. He turned to the Sheriff. "Is there a hospital nearby, or a medico who could check out the ladies? Make sure they're okay."

"I'll go to my place and pick up clothes for Lauren," Nancy offered.

"Thank you Mrs. Burns. Sheriff, please have two deputies take Mrs. Burns to her place. Be on alert. The kidnappers could be lurking around there," Detective Schmidt said.

We excused ourselves, used the facilities, and splashed water on our faces. When we returned to the sheriff's desk, a doctor waited in the office. He checked Mom's vital signs, then mine. I left the office closing the door behind me to give Mom some privacy while the doctor further examined her.

I turned to speak with the detective. He ushered me into an adjoining office.

I told him what I knew, not telling him exactly how I knew some of it. I hoped I'd never have to testify to any of this.

I explained that one, if not all of my so-called "uncles," had probably hired these guys to get Dad's file. The hired guys had failed to get every piece, so they decided on their own to kidnap Mom, and when that didn't seem like it would shut me up, they shot at me. Or at least, that's how I saw it.

"How do you think they knew you were still on it?" Detective Schmidt asked.

"Maybe someone had an intercept on my phone, heard me tell Dad I knew what was going on? Dad warned me to get rid of my phone. So maybe that's also how they knew where to find me. Also, one of my "uncles" was on the phone with Dad when I asked for the file. We need to find out from my Dad who he was talking to. Whoever that was probably hired the guys."

"Why'd they want the file?"

"I'm not sure," I said. "Something to do with a girl named Jennifer. Maybe she was the Jane Doe. The one body thought to have been moved by the Zodiac."

The detective raised his eyebrows. "I looked over the Zodiac case. Your dad thought there might be a tie-in." He stopped speaking and looked at his shoes. "As it happens, I know a little about the Zodiac case. I was in the vicinity the night the taxi driver was shot in San Francisco. I got the call and was first on the scene. Wasn't my case, but I did follow it closely after that."

I wondered why he hadn't mentioned that before. I hesitated, but then went ahead and asked him. "You worked on the Zodiac case?"

"No."

"But you . . ."

"I was a brand new detective. My wife was a nurse at UCSF hospital. I used a police car to pick her up and we were on our way home. I was embarrassed to have her in the car. That was a long time ago."

I nodded, not sure what that story had to do with him not mentioning his connection to the Zodiac much earlier, but so what?

"Is it possible to exhume that body? The Jane Doe." I asked, "Would it still have DNA in semen? I mean, how long does it take for DNA to degrade?"

"They have technology that can use mitochondrial DNA. That's a more stable component to at least demonstrate familial relationships, perhaps not DNA fingerprinting, not always enough to tie a suspect beyond a doubt, but thirty-six year old semen was used to eliminate a suspect in 2000." Detective Schmidt said. "But, I don't get something. The Zodiac wasn't known to rape his victims. Why check semen?"

"I think, from overheard conversations, that Jane Doe was actually a girl named Jennifer who possibly, just prior to her death, had sex with four of my uncles." I hoped he would assume the conversations to which I referred had perhaps taken place while I was captive, definitely more recently than forty years ago.

The sheriff entered the room. "Doc has given Mrs. Nichols a clean bill of health. She's got just some mild dehydration. She's eaten, had water, and is in warm clothes. Ready to head out?"

We drove back to the cabin in a caravan of Sheriff's SUVs. I showed the authorities around, pointed out where one of the men had slept on the sofa and the door they had both touched. I couldn't remember if Fatty had touched anything without his gloves, but Mom showed them a glass in the kitchen that he had used.

Steven got boards out of the boathouse and used them to close up the bathroom window. "Wow, Sis, you really did some damage."

I shivered to think of the close call if Steven and Nancy hadn't been nearby.

"How did you guys happen to be close enough to hear us scream?" I asked.

"Despite your doubts about my use of voicemail, I checked my text messages when you didn't come back. Then I called Detective Schmidt and Dad. Dad arranged for Uncle Dave's plane to pick up the detective near where he was in Oakland so he could coordinate a rescue. Guess Dad didn't have much faith in local sheriffs pulling off a rescue without Mom getting hurt. Nancy and I parked on the road behind bushes, against the wall. We saw Mom's car drive out with two guys in it, but we didn't know how many were involved, and if there was anyone in here with you."

"And you had guns!" I said.

"Yeah, Elliott keeps a few at their place." Steven's face reddened. "I doubt we had the safeties off, but they looked good, huh?"

Tires on gravel announced a new arrival. Dad jumped from a sheriff's vehicle, ran to enfold Mom in his arms, and without letting her go made his way to where Steven and I surveyed the bathroom damage, gathering us all in a family hug.

Detective Schmidt held back for a few minutes, then spoke to us. He shook Dad's hand but refused to take any credit for our rescue. "Your family took care of themselves and each other. Come to think of it, it was all over by the time I got here. Wherever you are staying tonight, two sheriffs will keep watch. I'd rather you didn't stay here, though."

"They're staying with me," Nancy volunteered.

"When you're through here, Detective, at some point to-morrow hopefully, Steven and I need to check out the winter-izing," Dad said.

"I'll give you a call later this morning. And I'll send a stenographer over to the Burns' to take statements from Alexandra and Mrs. Nichols in the afternoon."

The sun was peeking over the snow covered mountain's on the far side of the lake as Dad, Mom, Steven, Nancy and I loaded into two Sheriff's vehicles and were driven to Nancy's. As soon as we arrived, Mom went to soak in the tub. After hot drinks, Steven and Nancy headed off to bed.

Flickering flames from the living room fireplace cast a golden glow on Dad and I as we sipped hot cocoa laced with brandy.

"Okay Dad, time to come clean."

56

"Sweetheart, time to get some sleep, we'll talk in the morning."

"You're not getting out of it. You're talking to me now."

"You just got out of the hospital. You've had a very strenuous few days—especially the last twenty-four hours. Off to bed with you."

"NO!"

The look Dad gave me used to scare the shit out of me when I was little.

"Not working Dad. I can't go to sleep with all this on my mind, and I think you know the answers to some of the questions that won't stop running around my head."

Dad sighed and squirmed farther into the down chair. "What do you want to know?"

"How long have you known that your friends living at the ranch had a connection to the Zodiac killer?"

"No. No, I didn't *know*." Dad took a deep breath. "But I suspected. I've always suspected there was a link. I was freaked to think it might have been one of my friends who was the Zodiac. But it wasn't. I know that now."

"Did you ever ask?"

"Of course, Christ! Al, I am an officer of the court, I take my responsibilities quite seriously. Do you think I would knowingly let murderers run free no matter who they were?" Dad stood, paced in front of the window that overlooked the lake. Dawn sun sparkled off the snow and the water.

I pretended that was a rhetorical question and said nothing. I didn't want to admit I had suspected the worse of my father, who was once my best friend.

"I was in a state of shock when Lexi was killed. It was years before I realized that Tom, Jamie, Elliott, and Ron had acted strangely afterwards. They came to the funeral, I think, then stayed for the week, but then they stayed away for months. Lauren and I went out to the ranch some weeks later. I wasn't sure if it was because I had Lauren with me, or because Lexi's death had changed the dynamics of our relationships in some way, or what—but it wasn't the same. We only went there one more time. They were not the comfortable, easy friendships they had once been."

I sipped my cocoa and let him talk.

"When I went to work in the district attorney's office, I had access to police files. I was even allowed to copy some of the reports. Lexi's murder had never been officially solved, but there was a suspect. I was determined to prosecute the case, bring her the justice she deserved. She was the reason I went into criminal prosecution." He cleared his throat.

"I found things in the file that seemed strange. Lexi had been killed in Berkeley on Tuesday. Her date, Derek, had never been located. Disappeared right off the face of the earth. If he'd been shot or stabbed—as had all the others thought to be Zodiac victims—there were no signs of it at the site. The same week a Jane Doe body turned up in Marin. She'd also been shot in the head, but hadn't bled from the wound. That indicated she was already dead when she was shot. She also had some postmortem carving on her chest. Those two incidents were the only ones in the entire file that were different from the others. These were the only two people who were removed from the scene. It didn't make sense."

"But how did you tie them to the farm?"

"Jane Doe was found just down the road. There weren't a hell of a lot of other things on that road in those days."

"And how did she get tied to the Zodiac?"

"A chunk of hair had been cut from her head with a knife, the carved chest, a shoe print; the bullet was consistent with those found in the other Zodiac victims—and the Zodiac claimed responsibility in a letter to the newspaper telling them where to find the body. But there were the anomalies—she was wearing a nightgown, that combined with the location on a creek bed in the middle of nowhere, and lividity pointed to her having been moved postmortem. And the bullet was fired from a shorter distance than the other victims—"

"How did the lividity indicate she had been moved?" I asked my father.

"You know, at death, the heart stops beating, blood stops moving. Stagnant blood goes to where gravity leads it. In this Jane Doe's case, she evidently was lying on her back, on a soft surface, after she died as she developed lividity on her back and buttocks."

"I had trouble understanding that in the file. I didn't get the significance of her being found on her side."

"It appeared that she remained on her back for at least some eight to twelve hours after she died because no secondary or shifted lividity was found. If she had been moved within four to six hours of her death, a certain amount of blood would have shifted to the new body position."

"And she was on a soft surface for those eight to twelve hours?"

"Yes, probably a soft mattress such as a feather bed . . . or a water bed."

"How did they know that?"

"Any part of the body that presses against a hard surface appears pale and is surrounded by lividity. Her lividity was uninterrupted."

"Were there waterbeds at the ranch?"

"Of course. They were the latest thing then."

"Did you . . . was that one of the things that had you worried?"

"Yeah." He returned to the chair in front of the fire. "That bothered me."

"What else?"

"The ME estimated she had died on Sunday, or maybe early Monday, and was moved as late as Tuesday. Or really early on Wednesday. She was found on Thursday. It was clear that she had not been exposed to the elements for more than a day or two."

"Because of the letter? A letter telling where to find her body was mentioned in your notes in the file. But I thought she was found by hikers."

"She was, but the letter had been mailed the day before. Seemed odd that the Zodiac was unusually active in those few days. There were otherwise weeks, if not months, in between incidents."

"She wasn't killed by the gunshot. The file said they found lethal amounts of monoacetyl morphine. She ODed on morphine?"

Dad shook his head. "Heroin. Monoacetylmorphine is what is found in the body after heroin has been ingested."

"They had a *heroin addict* staying with them?"

"Probably not an addict. It's not uncommon for first time users to OD."

"Where did she get all the paraphernalia?"

"She didn't need needles and so forth. She ate the heroin. She wouldn't have tracks; they might not have had any idea she was using. Ingested toxins showed up in the stomach, also the lividity color, deep purple, was consistent with asphyxia. That's what heroin OD's die from, especially if they've been drinking alcohol which is also a brain depressant. Opiates suppress the respiratory center of the brain, the user falls asleep, slips into a coma, stops breathing, dies from asphyxia."

"Mrs. Mac described the girl. Her description fits the description of the Jane Doe from what I read in your file. She also said the girl, Jennifer, who had been staying there, had been having sex with all four of the guys. Could they exhume the body for semen samples?" I asked.

"No need. Samples of vaginal swabs would have been taken at the autopsy. They'd be dried and stored."

"So when you read the file, you wondered if there was a connection to the farm?" I watched my father's face.

"I remembered Mrs. Mac complaining about a girl she called a slut who had been there, unusual for Mrs. Mac, she isn't usually critical. And she had mentioned something about the girl's freckles being the ugly kind, or something," Dad said. "I went to see her; she did indeed describe the Jane Doe. Years hadn't dulled her memory—she was pretty shocked by the girl and her behavior."

"So what did you do then?"

"I went to see each of my friends, much like what you've been doing for the last two days."

"And?"

"The bottom line was, I was convinced they hadn't killed her. The statute of limitations had long since run out on any crime the four of them may have committed. Failing to report a death, even a suspicious one, is a misdemeanor. But I did get Tom to look at a line up with the hopes he could ID Allen. He couldn't pick anyone. He said the man he'd spoken with wasn't there even allowing for the passage of time." Dad sighed, pushed back against his chair. "I still had insufficient evidence against Allen, and at the time, I was convinced he was the Zodiac."

"And now you're not?"

"DNA from postage stamps on the Zodiac's letters, wasn't Allen's."

"Right, I remember reading that," I said.

"When Derek came to the Berkeley police, years after the Zodiac was inactive, with this story and said he had evidence, but that his dad was dead, I was contacted. The law enforcement agencies in the Bay Area knew I had spent years on the cases. I advised leave it be, don't dredge it all up again," Dad grimaced, rubbed his forehead. "I was worried about what might happen, if evidence linking my friends would be included. It would only be damaging to their reputations at that point. I thought there was no justice to be served. That it was time to move on."

"How could you?" I'm pretty sure I failed to keep the disappointment out of my voice.

"Sweetheart, I'm sorry not to live up to your expectations."

Tears ran down my face. "How could you still be friends with them?" I rebuffed Dad's effort to put an arm around my shoulders.

"We all make mistakes." He sat back down. "They panicked. They didn't want to be tied to a scandal. They had nothing whatsoever to do with her obtaining, having possession of, or taking the heroin. She didn't shoot up. They had no idea what she was up to."

"How can you be so sure?"

Dad sighed, looked at me with disappointment evident on his face. "We were not any of us heavy druggies. I can't imagine any one of them even knew how to buy heroin. Or that they would want to. No, I'm certain she brought the drug with her when she arrived."

"Okay, whatever . . . I'm still not clear why the Berkeley police ignored Derek's efforts to help with their investigation."

"That was almost two decades later."

"But Dad, Derek said he sent letters to the police while he was still in Italy. That was early on."

"Sweetheart, you can't imagine the flood of letters about the Zodiac that were received by every police department in the Bay Area. It was impossible to follow up on all of them—especially one from Italy."

"You knew he was in Italy?"

"After the fact." Dad stood up, held out a hand to help me from my chair. "Can we get some sleep for a couple hours at least?"

"Which of my uncles was on the phone the day I asked for the file?" I held my position in the chair.

"Tom."

"Did he hire the kidnappers?"

"We'll find out who did, I promise."

57

I woke up a few hours later in a panic until I remembered that Mom was safe. I drifted back to sleep. When I dragged myself out in the afternoon, I found Dad and Detective Schmidt involved in an intense conversation in the living room. It seemed that Detective Schmidt had spent the morning interviewing Ron and Jamie; Tom and Elliott were slated for the late afternoon. Tom had already been picked up by SFPD.

"It's possible that Jamie and Ron had no prior knowledge," Dad said.

"May I join you?" I asked and plopped on the sofa. "Jamie wasn't at all surprised to see Steven and me show up with Ron." I was willing to bet that Jamie was the recipient of the phone call Ron had stepped away from us to make.

"Word must've gotten around that you and Steven were looking for Lauren," Dad said. "I had called all four of them to see if they could be any help. Not all of them returned my call immediately. They probably spoke with each other as well."

"Dad told you that Tom knew I had the file?" I asked.

"Yeah," Detective Schmidt said. "And we already know that one of the men who kidnapped your mother, and presumably shot at you, is occasionally employed by Tom O'Connor's law firm as an investigator. That's why Mr. O'Connor is now in custody. Just a matter of time until we've also picked up the two men, the investigator Mr. Samuels and his accomplice, a Mr. Bubbal. Their fingerprints were on file. Mr. Bubbal has a criminal record."

"So it's over?" I asked, "We don't have to worry about anyone's safety?"

Detective Schmidt nodded. "Just a couple of loose ends. We want to see if anyone other than these three perps could be involved. So we'll be keeping you safe until this is all wrapped up in a neat little package."

"Cool. I'm down with that," I said. "What about the hair in the box?"

"DNA testing is not complete on all of the samples, but from what has been done, looks to be from the Zodiac's victims. And the rifle Derek Hamilton gave us, is one of two guns used by the Zodiac."

"You know, there were some things about the Zodiac file I had questions about. Dad explained a couple of things last night. Maybe you could help me with the others?"

"Shoot," Detective Schmidt said.

"We've explained one thing that didn't fit; the moving of the bodies, cause one wasn't a body at all. He was taken away, and the other, the Jane Doe, wasn't a Zodiac victim, although it seems he—that is the Zodiac—was enlisted to move the body. But what about the other changes in his MO, the modus operandi?"

"Yeah?"

"The earliest victims were shot, right?"

"Yeah."

"But later sometimes he shot them, sometimes he, supposedly the same 'he', stabbed and cut them with a knife. Carved them to be more accurate. Now using a knife is really something different from using a rifle and shooting from a distance. A knife is up close and personal, way different."

"You've got a point, young lady."

"There's also the fact that serial killers tend to operate close to where they live, especially at the beginning. The first killings confirmed as the Zodiac were in Benicia, and the letters were mailed from there, too. The later attacks at Lake Berryessa, Lake Herman Road in Benicia, Vallejo, even Modesto and Berkeley are fairly close especially as chronologically those attacks came later, but Presidio Heights is in San Francisco, then Half Moon Bay, the Sunset district again in the city, Noe Valley, in the city. Those in San Francisco don't follow a pattern that profilers would expect. And the ones in the city all involved a knife."

"Except the taxi driver. Keep in mind MO's have been known to change; signatures don't."

"Signature? The hair?"

Detective Schmidt nodded at me, but his body language clearly said he was not anxious to re-open the Zodiac case with all the attendant publicity and public hysteria. "Yeah, the hair was always cut with same kind of knife in the city . . . and that was a closely guarded secret."

The front door of the house slammed, Elliott Burns stomped through the entry hall and into the living room where we sat. Detective Schmidt stood. Dad introduced them.

"I thought I'd better come see what the hell is going on up here. Nance has told me some wild tales," Elliott removed his trench coat, exposing his usual stodgy three-piece suit.

I looked at Elliott with new eyes, remembered that he had been sturdily built in college. Now he was bloated, paunchy.

"We've had some excitement, but it seems to be all under control now. I'm glad to see you, Sir. This saves me a trip to Oakland. Is there someplace private where we could talk briefly?" Detective Schmidt asked.

"Sure, right this way." Elliott showed the detective into the den off the entry and closed the door.

Shit! I would've loved to have heard that conversation. I headed to the kitchen and some breakfast.

58

I was still eating my granola and yogurt when Detective Schmidt came into the breakfast room to say good-bye. Elliott was right behind him.

"Mr. Burns says that Tom hired the kidnappers, but only to get the Zodiac file. He called Mr. Burns when the break-in at your house failed to get their objective."

"I told him to back off, to call them off," Elliott said. "I wanted no part of thugs and break-ins. I warned Tom that men criminal and stupid enough to break and enter were too un-predictable. I had no idea he or they had anything to do with later events. Tom started a nightmare when he got those two involved."

"Tom isn't a great judge of character, huh?" I said.

Elliott grimaced and wagged his head. "I guess you all know it wasn't the first time Tom got involved with crazies. And now he's been arrested!" Elliott collapsed into a chair. "You know what that means: it's just a matter of time before the press gets a hold of the story, and probably dredges up the whole sorry mess. I can hear that whiney voice of horrid Nancy

Grace carrying on about it now, 'Pillars of the San Francisco society and business community named in police investigation tied to the Zodiac killer of the late sixties' . . . Oh God." He banged his fist on the breakfast table and buried his face in his hands.

Nancy put her arms around her husband resting her head on the top of his.

I watched this couple, my parents' close friends, with some suspicion I admit. I couldn't help but think that Elliott knew more about this matter than he was letting on, that Tom told him that the thugs had Mom at our cabin. I remembered that he'd taken Nancy aside before he went up to bed. Had he whispered for Nancy to take us to their cabin so that we wouldn't stumble into our own and find Mom there?

I thought about Ron's reaction when Steven and I mentioned going to our cabin. Ron definitely didn't want us going there. Bottom line, I was willing to bet all four of them—Elliott, Tom, Ron and Jamie—knew what the thugs had done. They were squabbling about it, but they all had knowledge. Tom was probably the "he" the dickhead, Samuels, had phoned. At least they had been told to release us, but why wait for twenty-four hours?

"Detective Schmidt, I realize I'm the one person in the room with the least legal knowledge, but . . . isn't Elliott guilty of some kinda crime? Shouldn't he have told you, or somebody, what he knew?"

Schmidt gave me a subtle "no" shake of his head. "He did. He told me."

"Yeah, way too late to be any help in saving Mom." I started to say more, but the Detective glared at me and I finally got the message to shut up.

Detective Schmidt started to speak, but Elliott held up his hand silencing him. "Alexandra, I'm terribly sorry that I wasn't more help in locating Lauren. But I really had no reason to believe that I knew anything that would be helpful. Truly, I never imagined that Lauren's disappearance had something to do with Tom's insistence on getting that file."

I glared at Elliott, disgusted that these four men were going to get a way with the cover up they had kept up for decades.

Yes, they'd tortured themselves. Living with their secrets must have been hard for men of goodwill. Perhaps in some strange way it explained the amount of charitable and altruistic work that Tom and Jamie had devoted themselves to.

Elliott looked like shit. He had failed to balance his guilt with anything philanthropic that I knew of. Perhaps he'd punished himself enough, but I was going to tell the asshole what I thought of him anyway.

The doorbell pre-empted my intended tirade. Detective Schmidt and the sheriff escorted a stenographer into the dining room.

I told the stenographer all I knew to be the facts about recent events, leaving out my opinions, conjectures, and memories that I'd have a hard time testifying to in court.

Now this situation was no longer my problem; it was over to Detective Schmidt and the police to sort out.

"Dad, I need to get back to school, I've missed too much, I'm gonna have a hell of a time catching up."

"Me too," Steven said.

"Not yet," Dad said, "Rest here for the weekend, have classmates email your assignments, I don't want either of you on campus until these guys are apprehended."

"I agree," Detective Schmidt said. "We have yet to arrest Samuels and Bubbal."

"I don't get it," Steven said, "You know who they are, and the car they're in. What's taking so long?"

"We found your mother's car abandoned in a shopping mall parking lot near Auburn."

Steven and I groaned, I bit my tongue to keep from spewing swear words all over the breakfast room. Nancy's not at all understanding about the use of the F-word.

"But we have the license plate of a car stolen nearby. We'll get 'em," Detective Schmidt said. "And rest assured Alexandra; none of the men involved in this crime will get off without legal repercussions."

We spent the weekend at Tahoe, got some assignments that could be done online and had to admit the Burn's "cabin" was well equipped with all the latest wireless tech with computers enough for all.

Steven enjoyed the exercise room with all the bells and whistles including steam room and sauna, and it was good to spend time with Mom after being so scared of losing her. I snuggled with her most of the weekend.

But it was still hard to get my mind off of the Zodiac, which led to thoughts of Derek. Whenever I thought of Derek, I realized he was still damn hot, even if he was the same age as my father.

59

Sunday morning we awoke to the clamor of TV trucks and reporters outside the gates. The media had gotten onto the story with Tom O'Connor's arrest and somehow made the connection to the Zodiac. The Sunday papers reported Tom's arrest and his arraignment scheduled for Monday morning.

Television news ran stories about the Zodiac, and at first, Mom and I, curled up together in the media room, found the TV coverage interesting. But the talking heads came up with the same guesses and suppositions over and over. I was surprised at how close to the truth some came. Not only Tom, but also Jamie, Ron and Elliott were mentioned—even Mom and Dad, and Steven and me. They showed shots outside Nancy and Elliott's Piedmont house, outside Mom and Dad's San Francisco house, outside the gates of our Tahoe place—dubbing it an estate because we had three buildings on the site—never mind the largest was 800 square feet.

No one escaped the media. Ron was attacked by a swarm of microphones as he attempted a Sunday morning bike ride.

Jamie holed up in his office using the county security as a barrier.

Sunday night came without the kidnappers having been located. I was getting worried about blowing the school term.

Mom and Nancy planned to stay put inside the security and gates of the Burns's Tahoe place, but, as comfortable as the estate was, I needed to go back to the city with Dad on Monday morning.

"Dad, Steven and I cannot afford to miss anymore classes. I've probably already screwed my GPA for this semester. We have to go back in the morning." I demanded, then whined while giving him my best imploring look.

"Jeff," Elliott said, "I feel some responsibility for how out of hand this situation has become. I'll cover the cost of bodyguards for the kids."

"I appreciate the offer, but your hospitality is plenty," Dad answered, "And I'm not sure bodyguards are the solution."

Dad called Detective Schmidt. Then told us what he'd learned.

"He says the police are certain of their identities and the vehicle they are using. Found a motel in Vallejo where they were and he expects a break soon. Schmidt strongly recommends that you kids not return to Berkeley. With the media all over this thing, the fact of you being back on campus won't be a secret."

"That's it, guys. No bodyguards." Dad flashed a fake smile at us. "What good would guards have done in front of Kroeber hall? No defense against a rifle. You're staying right here."

"But with Tom arrested why would they bother us?" Steven asked.

"Tom will be bailed out in the morning. With him arrested, they're liable to be more desperate than ever. They won't want your sister or your mother to ID them. No, you're all staying right here until they've been arrested. That's my final word on the matter."

I woke up on Monday morning after a restless night. I used the remote to turn on the TV from the warm, cozy bed. At first glance it looked like the same old footage of the front of Ron's condo, so I guessed the arraignment hadn't started yet as the media didn't have new material to report.

The next thing I saw was a banner along the bottom of the screen. An as yet unidentified bicycle rider had been shot and killed. The incident took place just outside the planned community where Ron Bailey, associate of Tom O'Connor, Elliott Burns, and Jamie Gregg, lived.

"Dad," I yelled. I ran from my room, "Dad, are you still here?"

Nancy wrapped a robe around herself as she came out of her bedroom. "What's the matter? Are you okay Alexandra?"

I headed to the breakfast room. Dad and Elliott were watching a monitor above the banquette. Dad held a phone up to his ear, "Detective Schmidt, who got shot at Ron's place this morning? Call me back at this number." Dad relayed the landline number from Elliott.

"Did you call Ron?" I asked.

"I got Ron's voicemail a bit ago, and now I got Schmidt's. The detective is probably in court. He would've appeared at Tom's arraignment."

"Should we go over there?" Elliott asked. Elliott and Dad had that strange kind of pale that tan people get. They were shocked and scared. They obviously thought the same thing that I thought; Ron had been shot.

"I don't think getting involved with that media circus would be a good idea." Dad's voice sounded flat and tired.

For the first time, I realized what an emotional rollercoaster the last few days had been for Dad. I'd been so pissed at him for letting this happen when it truly wasn't his fault. I'd been totally unsympathetic, and now not only had one of his closest friends of long-standing been arrested in connection with events that had endangered Dad's own family, it looked damn likely another old friend had been killed.

The landline rang. We all froze.

Elliott answered and put the phone on speaker so that we could all hear what Detective Schmidt had to say. "Yes, I'm sorry. Ron Bailey was shot. He died en route to the ER."

"By the kidnappers?"

"We don't think so. But we'll keep Mr. O'Connor in protective custody until they've been apprehended."

"Why?" Dad asked.

"They might be wanting to get rid of anyone who can link them to the kidnapping."

"Then why don't you think they shot Ron?" I asked.

"We have them located. A swat team is preparing to enter a motel room in Albany to take custody of the perps."

"Are you sure that's them?"

"Pretty sure," Detective Schmidt answered. "This shooting seems to be unrelated."

"How unrelated?" Dad asked. The worried tone of his voice made me wonder if he was having second thoughts about having chosen one of the gang of four's house as a safe place for his family.

"Tom's in jail. Well, more accurately, he was bailed out an hour ago, but before he even left the courthouse, we had him back in protective custody."

"Could he possibly have had time to hire a hit man?"

"Pretty far fetched. He would've had to use his attorney's phone. I don't see it," Detective Schmidt said. "And why would he?"

Dad shook his head. "No logical reason that I can see. Unless Ron could've tied him to the kidnapping," Dad hesitated. "Come to think of it, he could. Ron knew what had happened, Tom had been in touch with Ron. I'm sure of it."

"We have statements from both your wife and daughter that the perps clearly said that the person who hired them was upset about the shooting and the kidnapping, told them to release their victims."

"It may not have been premeditated, but doesn't change the fact that Tom failed to notify the police of two crimes, including one in progress." Dad's voice was now tight with restrained anger; I knew that voice from personal experience.

"So who else would get involved? Isn't it quite a coincidence if this is unrelated?" I asked. The cyclist in the trees below Ron's house popped into my mind. Was he carrying anything besides a bike? A gun maybe? And why did he look familiar?

"We've had other times when someone who has been an object of media scrutiny has then been attacked by a stranger who happened to see them on television. And I understand that footage of Mr. Bailey riding his bicycle away from his residence appeared on several channels nationwide. He was shot near there."

I wondered if Elliott had left the house that morning. But the deputies outside would've seen him.

Where was Jamie this morning?

It was pretty hard for any of the men to have made any movements without being seen by the media camped outside each residence and office.

Detective Schmidt continued, "I'm going to double the number of deputies there. Come to think of it, I want all of you to stay inside and close all the curtains. Stay away from windows. I'll call when these two, Bubbal and Samuels, are in custody."

"Elliott," Dad said once Detective Schmidt was off the line, "you could be in danger, too."

Elliott nodded his round gray head. His eyes were filled with tears. "What a mess!"

60

Nancy decided that the best cure for the waves of emotions that swept over all of us was a good hard work out followed by a sauna or steam. Television was forbidden. She unplugged the screens in the exercise facility and cranked up the soundtrack from *Across the Universe*. She was right about the cure. At least I felt less frustrated after working up a sweat.

Dad had one of his staff ask for still another continuance in the trial he was prosecuting. Elliott did the same with his lawsuit. They both tried to put a good face on it, but the strain of grief, fear, and frustration showed in both faces.

"Jeff, join me in a Bloody Mary before lunch?" Elliott asked.

"May I have one too please?" I asked.

"Hell, I'll make a pitcher," Elliott answered.

Dad, Steven, Elliott and I half-heartedly played cards while Mom and Nancy napped after lunch.

Mom was starting to get some color back in her cheeks, but all of the events of the last few days, including Tom's arrest and Ron's death, were showing on her face too.

Dad had the doctor who checked her out at the Sheriff's Station send a colleague over to make sure she was okay. The new doctor brought her a prescription to relax her.

I checked on her while Elliott dealt. She had fallen asleep with a book on her chest. I took her reading glasses off and pulled the covers up. It was good to see her looking peaceful.

Cards were a good distraction. I was beating the pants off the men when I pulled an ace to the front of my hand. For some reason, that sight triggered a flash of memory of Dave—Dave of forty years ago. When did he become such a meticulous dresser?

"Your play, Al." Steven nudged me.

"What's the matter? You okay, sweetheart?" Dad asked me. "You went kinda pale there."

"I'm okay Dad." I played my ace and took the trick.

The unlisted landline rang. Elliott picked up the receiver. "Hello?"

"Yes, Detective Schmidt, we're all still here." Elliott hung up. "He says he'll be here in a few hours."

I wondered what was up, but I didn't get so distracted as to prevent my winning several hands. After sundown, my fellow card players lost interest, having failed to win for most of the afternoon.

Schmidt arrived as we were beginning the evening cocktail hour lounging on down sofas and chairs in front of the crackling flames in the fireplace.

"We got'em. They were holed up in Albany." Schmidt announced as he removed his heavy wool coat.

Elliott slammed his glass on the side table, and jumped up from his armchair. "Let me take your coat. Detective. Please have a seat." Elliott waved to an empty armchair that sat next to the welcoming warmth of the fireplace and carried the Detective's coat to the front hall closet.

Detective Schmidt addressed me, "I brought photos for you and your mother to ID, but I'd rather you looked at a line up."

"Detective, my wife has been through an awful lot," Dad said. "She's sleeping now, and I'd like for her to rest for at least another day or two before we return to the city. The media is liable to be difficult to deal with."

"I can show her photos. What do you say to Alexandra accompanying me in the morning?"

"I could go along, Dad," Steven said. "We could go back to school tomorrow."

Dad nodded.

I was more than willing to look at a line up and anything else I could do to bring them to justice for what they had done to Mom, and especially for shooting Kira.

"May I offer you a cocktail?" Elliott said to the detective.

Schmidt glanced around at what we were drinking. "Just plain soda, or tonic, would be fine. Thank you."

Elliott poured a tonic from the bar set up on the sidewall.

"There's something else that's come up. Maybe you caught it on the news?" Detective Schmidt said.

"We've avoided the news today," Dad said.

Detective Schmidt nodded his understanding. "The *Chronicle* received a letter from the Zodiac today."

"Wha-at?" Dad blanched losing what little color the previous good news had restored.

"From a dead guy?" Steven asked.

"The writing's different, although it looks like an attempt to copy the original," Schmidt said. "The tone and sentence structure are very similar. The letter claims responsibility for Ron Bailey's murder."

"Phew!"

"Fuck!"

"Shit!

"Christ!"

"A copycat, of course, but damn close. The weirdest thing is the bullet that killed Ron Bailey is a match for two that killed Zodiac victims." Schmidt laid that bomb on the coffee table along with his glass.

"Does that mean you're convinced that Derek's father–"

"Stepfather," Schmidt corrected Steven.

"Are you convinced it was him?" Steven asked.

"The hair turned over to us by Derek is from the female victims, from more of them than we had tied to the Zodiac, and the guns are a match too," Detective Schmidt said.

"So Derek's father, uh stepfather, was definitely the Zodiac?" I asked.

"There is definitely a connection. We're doing some more DNA testing. Testing on the stamps has been inconclusive."

"How does that happen?" Steven asked with a frown.

"It seems that more than one person licked or handled those stamps."

"What? On each stamp there is DNA from more than one person?" I jumped to attention in my armchair.

"How does that happen?" Steven repeated.

"Perhaps the Zodiac had another person lick some stamps, and then he licked'em later," Detective Schmidt said.

"Why would he do that? I mean DNA testing didn't start until like twenty years later. How could he have foreseen that the stamps would be tested?" Elliott asked.

"We've no way of knowing that. Maybe it was an accident, a coincidence." Detective Schmidt looked at each of us in turn. "Most of the stamps have one type of DNA. But there are two different types of DNA represented on stamps. Just a couple stamps have two. And the DNA types found on those two stamps are the same as found individually on other stamps. Points to the likelihood of two individuals being involved."

"So you *aren't* convinced of Derek's father's guilt?" I asked.

"Let me explain. We have no doubts that Derek's father committed some of the murders, but we have not eliminated the possibility of another murderer. We've got the hood that Derek found. It fits a description given by a survivor. That's being tested, but it's been handled by both Derek and his son Lian, so results certainly wouldn't be admissible."

"But they don't need to be if the guy is dead, right?" Elliott asked the detective.

"If the guy is dead, yeah, but the latest shooting muddies the waters. Profilers have always thought that the Zodiac was at least in his late thirties. That put him in his late seventies now, so him being dead didn't seem unlikely. But Ron Bailey was definitely shot with the same gun as two victims who were killed in 1970."

"But Derek gave you the Zodiac guns." I said.

"Maybe he didn't give us all the guns. He could've hidden one." The detective answered.

"But didn't you search the house?" I asked.

"Not thoroughly. We had no reason to think he was holding out on us. We've got Crime Scene over there now."

"Does that mean that you suspect Derek was the Zodiac killer?" Steven asked.

Detective Schmidt shrugged with the corners of his mouth turned down.

"Wait, wait. Are you sure that Lexi was killed by the Zodiac?" I jumped up from my chair, nearly spilling my gin and tonic.

"Yes, right gun, right MO, right signature."

Shit, how would I explain this one? I knew Derek wasn't the one who shot me. He was standing right behind me. We had just kissed. Lexi was shot from the front and from at least twenty feet away, Derek didn't have a gun— no it was impossible, but what could I say? "What about what's-his-name, cousin Harold?"

"Both men have voluntarily given us samples. Harold gave us two guns but he claimed he's missing the third, a rifle."

"Why would Derek come forward with the evidence, the hair and guns if he were the Zodiac?" I asked.

"There's no explaining what some of these nutcases do."

"And what about the handwriting. You said it was different?" I asked.

"It was somewhat similar, and handwriting does evolve over forty years. We got handwriting samples from Derek and Harold. Experts are lookin' at 'em." Detective Schmidt said.

"Derek was in Italy when most of the Zodiac victims were killed. You'll be able to check on that. He said he went to the American embassy shortly after he arrived in Florence. Check that out." I said.

"Will do young lady." Detective Schmidt smiled at me, stood up from his chair, then nodded at both Steven and me. "I'd like to pick you up around eight in the morning. Okay?"

Steven and I looked at Dad for permission.

"Are you sure they'll be safe?" Dad asked the detective.

"They'll be safe with me." Detective Schmidt assured Dad. "And I won't drop them off in Berkeley if there is any reason to believe they're in danger."

61

Detective Schmidt showed Steven and me into a room with a huge window, presumably with one-way viewing, that looked out into a larger room with an elevated platform at one end, a lot of visible recording devices, and a row of metal chairs with vinyl seats. "I'll be back in a minute," he said.

Steven grinned at me, raised an eyebrow. "Tight, huh?"

"Yeah, I'm down with it." I returned his smile, but butterflies fluttered in my stomach.

On the other side of the window, a group of six men were ushered onto the platform by uniformed policeman, and lined up against a white wall. Brawny and Fatty were number three and six.

"Well?" Detective Schmidt asked as he re-entered the room.

"Number three and number six," I said.

"You sure?"

"Totally."

"Good deal. I'll get your statement typed up. You sign it, and we're outta here. Let's take you two back to school."

The process wasn't quite that fast. I spoke with a young officer who typed very fast, but then Detective Schmidt and, I imagined, his supervisor wanted to see my statement. Given the red tape, it took awhile to get something to sign, but by late afternoon we were headed to Berkeley in the back seat of Detective Schmidt's police car. A uniformed officer drove.

We'd missed two weeks of classes. I wondered if there was any hurry, or if we'd already blown it.

"Steven, have we missed the drop date?"

"Whatta ya mean?"

"I don't know about you. But I don't think I can miss this many classes and still do okay."

"You mean, maintain your stellar GPA?"

I frowned at my brother. With my hand out of view of the front seat, I flipped him off. "Like you don't care about your grades," I said.

We drove onto the Van Ness entrance to the 101 headed for the 80 and the Bay Bridge when Schmidt got a call.

He hung up and turned around to speak to us. "Sorry guys, just a little detour. Something's come up. You're gonna stay in the car." He motioned to the driver who took the next exit and headed back to Van Ness and over to Pacific Heights. We drove up California Street.

"We're getting close to Derek and Lian's place," I said.

No response from the front seat, but three minutes later we pulled up across the street from Derek's house. The huge second floor window had the curtains drawn. No other windows were visible from the street. Two uniformed policemen sat on the wall that surrounded the courtyard entrance.

"Detective Schmidt, what's going on?" I asked.

"Stay here." The detective and his driver exited the car slamming the doors shut.

"Steven, what the hell?"

"You think I know?" Steven leaned back in the seat.

"Are you still smarting over a remark I made ten minutes ago? Get over it." I leaned over him to see, if I could tell who answered the door. "I'm not staying here. I wanta know what's going on." I flipped the door handle down, but it didn't budge. "Shit, we're locked in here."

Steven tried his door. "Yep, we sure are."

62

What the hell were we doing here? I couldn't see past Schmidt and the uniformed driver in the courtyard, or the two officers on the wall.

Detective Schmidt looked ready to spring into the house. Somebody with dark hair, maybe Derek, stood in the shadowed entry hall, blocking the entrance. The two figures in the doorway were animated, agitated.

What the hell were they talking about? I reached across Steven again and tried to put the window down. "Trade places with me?"

Steven slid across the bench seat; I climbed over his legs. The window went down exactly one inch but at least now it was possible to hear the heated discussion taking place in Derek's entry court.

"There's no need for your involvement here," Derek said. "It was an accident, I tell you. Nobody is hurt, no harm done." Derek blocked the entrance.

"Where is your son? Is he here?" Detective Schmidt demanded.

No answer.

"We will not leave here without seeing your son, without verifying that he's okay."

"He's not here."

"The gunshot gives us probable cause to search the premises." Detective Schmidt pushed Derek out of the door and went into the entry hall. Derek stumbled, recovered and followed.

The quiet of the neighborhood was broken by what sounded like a gunshot. A second gunshot rang out. The body of the uniformed driver jerked. He fell onto the courtyard paving.

A third explosion, the force of a bullet hitting his chest, knocked one of the uniforms backwards off the wall. The other officer dropped into the shrubbery that ringed the inside of the courtyard.

63

Steven and I exchanged startled looks.

"Where did those shots come from?" Steven asked.

"I think from over there. " I pointed to a yard behind us. "In that hedge."

"He was hit, right? The cop?" Steven looked from the officer to where he imagined the shots were fired.

"Either that or he was ducking out of the line of fire." Remain calm. Stay cool. My god, we were like ducks in a barrel, trapped in this car.

Schmidt ran from the house. He motioned with his arm, yelled, "Get down!" from where he crouched behind the courtyard wall.

We ducked down, but when a loud thud hit the car, Steven jumped off the seat and grabbed my arm. He yanked me down to the floor, on top of his legs.

"Two hit." Steven said as he punched 9-1-1 into his phone. He didn't wait to be asked questions. "This is Steven Nichols, I am with Detective Schmidt, SFPD, at California and Scott in Pacific Heights. His driver and another officer have been shot. He needs back up. We need paramedics. Officers down."

The rear window shattered at the same moment we heard the bang. The bullet entered the back of the seat above our heads. A bullet slammed into the trunk, another bounced off the rear bumper.

Steven pulled me tighter to the floor then threw himself on top.

We heard the percussion of projectiles striking the body of the car, the whack of slugs on metal.

Detective Schmidt fired from behind the low courtyard wall drawing attention away from the car. We heard the thud of bullets hitting the concrete courtyard wall.

"Who the hell is that?" Steven asked, his voice tight with fear.

"Lian, probably. Or Harold, but I'm betting Lian."

"Why?"

"Why do I think that? Or why is he shooting at us?" I didn't even try to control the quaver in my voice. "I think whichever one it is, he sees himself as carrying on for the Zodiac. Lian could've got the missing gun from Harold."

I clinched my teeth to stop them chattering. "And he is scary weird." I remembered the cyclist who was outside Ron's townhouse and realized why he looked familiar. It was Lian I saw there and in Pacific Heights. Had he followed us to Ron's condo? Why would he carry on where his step-grandfather, a man he wasn't actually related to, left off? Perhaps it was pointless trying to understand craziness.

Gunfire, sirens, the arrival of a swat team, and paramedics distracted Steven from asking more questions.

Steven allowed me to lift my head to steal a peek out the bottom of the window just in time to see a barrage of bullets hit the hedge. Lian's bullet ridden body fell forward out of the shrubbery, down the property line wall and onto the sidewalk.

Deathly silence followed when even the usual sounds of the city were muted in ears scarred by gunshot explosions.

64

Detective Schmidt opened the car door. We slid out like snakes on our bellies, then struggled to stand and regain our dignity, but our limbs wouldn't stop shaking.

The detective looked us up and down checking for damage. "As that was going down, I kept seeing myself trying to explain to your father how I managed to get his children shot. You're okay, right?" Hearing his voice tremble made me feel less like a scaredy cat.

"I have to deal with this for awhile." Schmidt yelled over the sirens of numerous vehicles arriving on the scene. "Please call your parents before the media gets here."

I glanced over to where Lian's body lay on the ground, but I had to look away when Derek knelt next to his son's body. He held his son to his chest, and sobbed. Horrible wracking, gut wrenching sobs. The sight ripped my heart. My tears couldn't relieve my pain.

Crime scene investigators swarmed the area to document the justified, unavoidable killing. Paramedics tended three wounded officers who all looked like they might make it.

Fog rolled in obliterating the stars and black evening sky. Mist haloed the streetlights and wrapped the half block of the incident location in an obscuring haze that shut out the rest of the city. Damp cold caused us to shiver and our teeth to chatter severely as we stood around watching, waiting to leave.

Detective Schmidt had ignored us once he determined we were not hurt. An hour later he stood next to me, handed me a handkerchief to wipe my nose and face instead of the sleeve I'd soaked with snot and tears. "Back to headquarters, time for another statement, you're getting to be pros. I'll catch up with you soon as I can, and take you home, I promise, straight home."

Steven and I nodded. We allowed ourselves to be ushered into the back seat of another police car. I leaned on my brother and he put an arm around my shoulders. I closed my swollen eyes for the drive back.

The officers who drove us back to the station escorted us to the room where our statements would be taken, fetched us terrible, but thankfully hot, coffee that sat badly in our empty stomachs. We spotted snack machines and bought stale crackers and faux cheese. It had been twelve hours since we last ate.

While Steven was giving his statement, I found a restroom and felt the déjà vu as I used it, splashed cold water on my face, then soaked a paper towel and held it to my eyes. I made the mistake of looking in the mirror and blew out of the room.

Kyle, the young officer who had typed a statement into a computer for me earlier in the day, shook my hand. "Sorry to see you back again."

"Me too," I answered with a heavy sigh.

I described with as much objectivity as I could muster what I had just seen happen in front of Derek's house. Kyle was patient. He waited calmly while I cried, wiped my nose, got water. My hand shook violently enough to slosh and spill the water.

"Thanks," he said when I couldn't think of anything more to say about the shooting.

"Can I ask you something?" I said.

"Sure." Kyle smiled gently, "Shoot." He caught himself, "I mean, please go right ahead."

"Are there ways of comparing or locating similar crimes, crimes with the same MO or signature?"

"Sure, we call it linkage. When forensics or the profile, or really any aspect of a crime links to another crime, there are a number of databases we can access. There's this really long form you fill out with all the info you have about a certain crime and the database finds matches. The one most law enforcement agencies use is VICAP, stands for Violent Crime Apprehension Program. It's an FBI program."

"So is that a national program?"

"Yep." Kyle nodded.

"What about internationally? Is there a way to compare international crimes?"

"Yep, via the International Criminal Police Organization, or Interpol."

"How does that work?" I asked.

"Same way really. We use an access known as I-24/7 to get to the Interpol National Central Bureau that links us to all the national databases throughout the world."

"In southeast Asia?"

"Yes. It's not as instant as with EU or UK, but we definitely exchange data."

"Am I correct in assuming that the Zodiac data has already been entered into Vi-i-i—"

"VICAP?"

"Yeah, that one."

"Yep, in fact I just updated the Zodiac data a couple days ago."

"Did you send it to Interpol?"

Kyle blushed. "No, nobody said anything about that."

"How hard would it be to do it?"

"Not hard at all. I've already filled out the form." His fingers danced across the keyboard. "Southeast Asia you say?"

"Yes, please. Can it go to EU and UK as well?"

"It'll go there automatically. We just have to specify the other countries. So that would be the Philippines, Malaysia, Thailand, Cambodia, Laos, Myanmar, Vietnam, Taiwan, Singapore." Kyle typed faster than I can talk.

"And East Timor and Brunei," I reminded him.

"Okay, sent. But I don't understand, didn't the Zodiac copy cat just—you know—get blown away?"

"Probably. I just want to tie up some loose ends. Questions I can't get out of my mind. Can I look at the form you filled out?"

"Hmm . . . I don't know . . . don't think I'm supposed to . . ."

"Hey, you said it yourself: it's a closed case as of tonight."

Kyle studied my face for a minute. I smiled, started to flirt, and then remembered what shit I looked with my snotty face, red nose, and swollen eyes, not to mention my filthy hair, with one side of my head shaved, and no makeup.

I guess I looked so pitiful that he took pity on me and turned the monitor around so I could look at the screen.

I noticed some things that either weren't in Dad's file, or I had missed.

Two sets of footprints were found in the dirt at the scene of the Jane Doe body dump: one pair of work boots, one pair of REI hiking boots. It was only time both boots were seen at one scene. But the hiking boots were at one other outdoor crime scene at Half Moon Bay, just south of San Francisco. Another stabbing; the knife again.

The work boots showed up at Lake Berryessa, Benicia's Lover's Lane, and Lake Herman Road, both scenes of shootings.

"Kyle, don't the two sets of footprints at this scene indicate there were two people?"

"It could," he thought about it for a second, "but there are other explanations."

"Like what?"

"The perp changed his shoes? Maybe he got blood on one pair. Or the site was contaminated."

"Blood?" I asked, "Whose?"

"The Jane Doe."

"I thought she didn't bleed. The gunshot wound was in-flicted after she died."

"I was thinking from the knife wounds, but you're right, postmortem wounds wouldn't bleed."

"Knife wounds?" My stomach lurched. "There were knife wounds?"

"The Z carved in her chest."

65

I sat in stunned silence. Knife wounds? A **Z** carved in her chest! REI hiking boots? Whoa, wait a minute. Mental pictures flashed through my mind. Snippets of conversations, papers from Dad's file and moments from my childhood swirled in a confusion.

"Kyle, is there a way to track movements of Americans abroad?"

"Through the NSA. You're supposed to have a warrant."

"NSA . . . National Security Administration?"

Detective Schmidt joined us just as I considered begging Kyle to violate the Constitution and hack into NSA records to track movements of my uncles abroad.

Kyle stood, explained to the detective that we had just broadened the search for linkage on the Zodiac data.

Detective Schmidt turned to me with a puzzled look. "Say what? Alexandra, what's going on here? Come in here."

He waved his hand to an enclosed interview room.

"Kyle, thank you. You'll let me know if anything interesting comes up?" I said.

"He'll let *me* know," Detective Schmidt said. "Right, officer?"

"Yes sir." Kyle quickly turned his red face toward his screen.

Detective Schmidt waved me into a chair. He sat down and studied my face for minutes before speaking. "You doin' okay?"

I nodded.

"What made you so sure it wasn't Derek?" he asked.

How could I explain? I ran a few answers by myself. No way, every answer was either nonsense or made me sound nuts. I decided to try one out.

"Could craziness be hereditary? I think this kid picked up the mantle of the Zodiac, like the responsibilities got passed from generation to generation. He maybe had some idea—"

Detective Schmidt stared at me. He looked haggard. "Lian was not a blood relative of his *step*-grandfather."

"Or maybe that sort of insane fantasy of cleaning up the world of promiscuity wasn't hereditary." I didn't mention my real theory, which would probably have made the detective question my sanity. My theory that Lian and his grandfather were one and the same being, that Lian was the reincarnation of his step-grandfather.

I hesitated for a minute while the detective stared without seeing me, his eyes dropped to the tabletop.

"The crime scene guys found a diary in Lian's room. Might explain something," Schmidt said.

A diary? That must have made him really nervous when I was looking around his room, when he saw me re-enter the hall from his doorway. "Lian's diary?"

"Looks to be his grandfather's. But pages towards the back were written in different handwriting. Presumably Lian's handwriting. He wrote about driving up to Tahoe and shooting Ron Bailey."

"Why?" I asked.

The detective shook his head. "Who knows? Can't explain nuttiness."

"Was Ron—was there carving?"

"No. But his hair had been chopped, and a small piece was in the pages of the diary." Detective Schmidt rubbed his forehead and heaved a sigh. "The diary explains how the transfer of info from one perp to another went down. We've got techies on it. Should clear up a lot of questions."

"Detective Schmidt, there's something else I need to talk to you about," I waited until he returned my gaze. "I think there were two Zodiac killers back in the 60's and 70's, and one of them is still alive."

66

Detective Schmidt rubbed his forehead and his eyes without responding. He groaned and leaned back in the metal chair. "What? Doesn't make sense, he hasn't killed anybody in forty years."

"The other men—look, if he were any of the other suspects, they all lived for a long time after the murders without any more killings—that we know of, anyway."

"We thought the Zodiac moved or broadened his field of operation." Detective Schmidt explained to me with hard won patience. "Serial killers tend to start out close to where they live and then go farther and farther away as time goes on."

I nodded. "Exactly. That's what I think this second Zodiac did, except rather than elsewhere in California, he murdered elsewhere in the world."

"That's what you and Kyle were up to?" Schmidt raised an eyebrow at me.

"We were looking for MO's and or signatures like the Zodiac where a knife was used in other parts of the world, like in Southeast Asia. With VICAP. Well actually, with I-24/7."

The detective looked at me, looked away, then chuckled. "Okay, tell me what you're thinking."

"The Jane Doe found in Novato," I said, "who we now know was Jennifer—"

"We think. That hasn't been confirmed by evidence yet," Detective Schmidt interrupted to remind me that I was getting ahead of the results of the DNA testing. "I guess I should light a fire under the lab's ass. They can rush those results when needed." He smiled at me, picked up the receiver of a phone on the table and ripped the poor person on the other end of the line a new one. He wasn't smiling.

"Okay, continue," he said to me as he hung up the phone.

"So that crime scene, the one in Novato, was out of the norm for many reasons. It didn't follow the same pattern that profiler's would expect. One, he was way out of his territory. Two, he shot at two different scenes within 24 hours when usually there were weeks, sometimes months in between shootings. We know that was because Tom O'Connor sent the Zodiac—"

"Allegedly sent the Zodiac." The detective was doing his best to keep me real.

"Okay allegedly, Tom has a conversation with this guy at the Monkey Inn, the Monk, in the sixties." I saw the look on the detective's face and knew he was about to correct me again. "Please, just let me tell you what I think. I've been very good in all my statements, the official shit, to leave out conjectures, opinions, anything I couldn't testify to in court, but I've got these ideas and I really want to tell somebody, somebody who could do something about what I think I know. Okay?"

Detective Schmidt nodded. He folded his arms and leaned back in his chair to listen.

"Tom is drinking in the Monk, sitting at the bar, worried about what to do with this dead girl who has overdosed at Jamie's family's place. Tom feels it's his responsibility because he's the one who picked up the girl hitchhiking and brought her to the farm. He did this in violation of the agreement that he had with the three other men who lived there. All of the men were planning to attend law school, and they knew they needed to protect their reputations. Drugs and a low level of criminality were rampant in the Bay Area in the late sixties, right? And crims justified their petty thievery and drug use by calling it a protest against the establishment."

"But these guys at the farm want to be part of the establishment. They don't want any part of crims. So they made this agreement: never bring or invite strangers to the farm. Only people already a part of their circle of trusted friends. Tom violated the agreement and now there's this body. They don't want to call the authorities to report a death from an overdose of what maybe heroin. That would never do."

I took a swallow of water and continued, "After Tom brought the girl to the farm, she not only manages to OD, but not before she also has sex with all four of the guys, apparently being quite aggressive about seducing them. So the dead body potentially has semen from all of them. Of course in 1969, prior to DNA matching, the semen would only have told authorities blood types, but maybe the four of them have unusual blood types. They're smart enough to know that dumping the body could be a real bad idea. Trace evidence at the scene might tie them to the girl. So what to do?"

"Tom meets this older guy at a bar. They're drinking next to each other and the guy starts talking about the Zodiac murders. Tom's a smart, perceptive young man. He realizes at some point in the conversation that maybe—make that probably—this guy is the Zodiac killer. He gets what seems like a real good idea after a half-dozen beers to get the guy to move the body. Then any trace evidence will point to the Zodiac."

The detective kept nodding, looking less tired.

Encouraged, I continue the story I'd built around all I knew. "Tom tells the guy where to find the body. Maybe helps him draw a map, being careful not to touch the paper. Tom leaves, goes up to Northside Berkeley, to a house where a group of his friends live, and where his housemates are hanging out. He tells them what he's done. But he's overheard talking to his housemates."

Was the detective going to let me get away without saying overheard by whom? He was still sitting back with his arms folded. Listening.

"Later that night, one of the girls who lives in the house is shot and killed. Now Tom is freaked. Did he lead the Zodiac killer to his friends? Is he responsible for Lexi's death? He has to talk to someone so he discusses his concerns with someone else who lives or hangs out at the house. The next day, someone, probably the person he talked to, or Tom, but I don't think so, goes to the ranch and helps the Zodiac move the body. That explains the two sets of shoe prints."

Schmidt nodded, pursed his lips.

"She was the only victim who showed signs of both MO's, both the gun and the knife, right?"

He lifted his eyebrows, shrugged his shoulders. "Yeah, I believe so. That's how I remember it."

"Yeah, I just found out about the **Z** carved in her chest. Then there was the gunshot to the head, neither of which killed her. You see, I think she was the overlap; the way the second killer picked up or was infected with the signature, the cutting of the hair. The signature of the original Zodiac." I slapped the table to emphasize my point.

"Hmm, could be. It's one explanation, that's for sure."

"One of my so-called uncles must have helped the Zodiac to dispose of the body."

"We've been checking into that day in prep for building a case against Tom O'Connor," Detective Schmidt said. "They all have alibis for the day she was moved."

I nodded my agreement. "I figure that was why they stayed in Berkeley. All four guys made a point of being seen elsewhere until after she was gone from the ranch— for the most part, until after she was found. Hell, they were even being interviewed by the police the day she was dumped."

I thought for a minute. "God, they must've been scared to death that the police would decide to go to the farm." I took a deep breath. "Then there was the shit about Mrs. Mac and Tom being sick. Mrs. Mac says she was never sick. It was just an excuse to keep Carol and Nancy away from the farm until they'd cleaned up any trace of the body.

Airing out the room, burning the bedding. That kind of stuff."

"The boys—men—could've paid someone else or somehow got another person to do it—someone other than the Zodiac. Can't help but wonder what will be O'Connor's defense," Detective Schmidt mused.

"One of my uncles made a point of saying he was nowhere near the farm the Wednesday after Lexi died, or any time around then. But Carol and Nancy and Mrs. Mac happened to mention Elliott was around. He told the girls that Mrs. Mac was sick. You could question the three of them. The stories they told me had some conflicts. It's understandably hard to remember exactly after forty years, although Mrs. Mac's got one hell of a memory."

"I'll talk to them all," Detective Schmidt said. "It'll be good to tie up all the loose ends in connection with all these incidents."

"Kyle says you have to get a warrant to track American citizen's movements abroad?"

"If you go through the State department, or NSA, yes, you're supposed to have a warrant. I'll help him with that tomorrow. Meanwhile, there are other ways he can try, I'll have a word with him."

I leaned across the table. "There's just one more thing—now that you know, or at least suspect that the Jane Doe was named Jennifer, can you use databases to find a match with missing girls named Jennifer and matching her description?"

"Yes, we can—and will."

"It would be good to give her family some closure."

"If any of them are still around, yes it would be." The detective stood, "So that's it?"

I nodded and stood also.

"Let's get you and your brother back to school, huh?"

67

The drive to Berkeley was uneventful this time. Detective Schmidt drove Steven and I in his personal car. He was on his way home for the first time in several days.

He pulled the car into the driveway in front of the big, old brown shingle house I shared with seven other students.

"Looks quiet here. Dark in there," he commented.

For once my housemates must have remembered to turn off all the lights. Just the porch light was on.

"The other people who live here won't be home from the library until ten, maybe eleven tonight," I explained.

"Maybe I ought to walk you in?" The detective said without much enthusiasm. He had to be exhausted.

I knew he was really tired, besides I wasn't afraid of my own house. "I'll be fine, it's cool."

Steven got out of the car, opened my door, walked onto the porch with me and waited for me to unlock the door. Once I had the door open, he kissed me on the cheek, gave me a big hug, and waved good-bye as he went back to the car. I leaned out the door to wave to Detective Schmidt. "Thanks," I called out.

What a relief to be home! I could hardly wait to get into my own bed, in my own room, sleep in my own nightgown and rest enough to visit my professors in the morning to see what I could salvage of my classes.

"Nah, nah, nah, da nan, nah, I'm not scared of you anymore, la di da," I said to the full sized taxidermy bear that resided in our entry hall at the bottom of the stairs.

Okay, I am weird, I talk to dead bears, but see, this bear was in the entry hall when I moved into the house. I moved in second semester of my junior year. The house was already full of three girls and four guys. I'd sublet from a friend who was studying abroad. I loved the room I'd rented from her, but that damn bear, which had apparently lived in that hall forever, used to scare me every time I entered the house.

The golden bear was an easy ten feet tall, towering in watch over the front door. He was dressed in a navy blue Cal watch cap, navy and yellow striped scarf, and a letterman's sweater with a block 'C' on the chest. The tattered sweater must have belonged to a very big football or basketball player from many years ago. I suspected the bear had been a school mascot once upon a time and was stolen in some prank. Most students and alums laughed to see the school mascot, the golden bear, Oski in our stairwell.

Not me. I'd always been afraid of bears, even dead ones, and this one freaked me every time I came in the house. But now I was too elated, too buzzed to be scared.

I used to rush up the stairs without turning on the light in the entry so that I needn't look at the bear. This time, I reached out from the stair landing and touched, yes touched, the bear's head. My laugh echoed in the quiet, empty house.

I glanced through the archway into the unlit living room. My laughter caught in my throat, my stomach jumped to join it. The outline of a dark figure, a man sat in the armchair. Was this one of my housemates, sitting quietly in the dark?

"Hello?" I called out.

No answer

"Hey, what's up?" I said.

I crept down to the bottom of the stairs and flipped on the light in the hall.

"Who's there?"

This was a little creepy. I hesitated in the doorway before I decided my imagination was running away with me after all the violence and excitement of the last few days.

I got brave, went into the living room, and turned on a lamp. I turned around to face the dark male figure and nearly jumped out of my skin.

68

"Uncle Dave? What are you doing here? You scared me to death."

My uncle Dave, the meticulous dresser, who always wore the "correct" gear appropriate to the activity at hand; like topsiders for sailing, après ski boots after skiing, high top Converse for basketball, cleats for baseball—even REI hiking boots for climbing around the countryside when disposing of bodies.

Dave didn't answer. He grinned at me, the scariest goddamn grin. In his hand was the biggest, longest, scariest goddamn knife you ever saw. He didn't move.

I backed away, but I was afraid to turn my back to him. I tripped over the ottoman, and plopped onto the floor.

My cell phone flew out of my pocket, landed under the armchair.

The rest of the pieces of the puzzle swirled through my mind and fell into place.

Dave. He was never really an accepted member of the inner circle of the farm. Dave, who always insinuated that he was left out because he grew up poor without the social connections, the advantages of the others. Who was extraordinarily driven by ambition. Dave, who couldn't afford a gap year, or law school, instead went straight to work after graduation. Who, all of a sudden, shortly after Lexi was murdered, found investors for his fledgling waterbed business with enough capital that he was able to quit his day job and concentrate on booming his business. Dave who used his private plane to fly all over the world, especially to southeast Asia where he dealt with factories and suppliers for his furniture lines.

Dave was the knife wielding Zodiac who was happy to let the Zodiac, the original one, take credit for Dave's killings as well as his own. Who learned everything he needed to know the day he helped the Zodiac move Jennifer's body.

And whenever he needed an influx of capital, well, he had four wealthy benefactors, always happy to help out.

Dave, the dandy of the group, always perfectly correct in his dress in the way that those who are worried about fitting in, about being good enough are so careful.

The irony, the dichotomy of his meticulous cleanliness wasn't lost on me. It made some strange kind of sense: it was the very contrast, the release from the constraints of correctness that motivated the messy killing with a knife.

It also required a constant supply of new clothes. Bloody old clothes had to be destroyed. I remembered his housekeeper's comments that he got new suits when he traveled. He never brought home the old ones. Most of his associates wrote that one off to the fact that he traveled to places where new suits were cheap and fast to get tailored. Convenient if you ruined—bloodied—a set of clothes every time you went abroad.

I imagined blood all over the Peter Marino designed white interior of his gulf stream.

All this raced through my mind when I should've been figuring out how to get out of this danger, how to get away from him.

Flat on my back on the floor, the phrase frozen with fear flashed through my mind.

I propped myself on my elbows, slowly pulled my knees up, posed to jump up.

Dave sat in the chair and cleaned his nails with the very sharp, curved tip of the knife. His face twisted ugly with a jack-o-lantern grin. Cold eyes studied his fingers.

Finally he spoke, "That shot to your head did something to your senses, cutie pie. You've been getting some very funny ideas. You gotta cut that out," he chuckled, "or I should say, I gotta cut that out." He cackled at his clever play on words.

"You see, I got a very funny phone call tonight, from my pilot. Someone's tracking my movements abroad for the last forty years. Then I learned that you and that snotty brother of yours have not only spent the last couple of weeks stirring up trouble by going around asking lots of questions, you spent the day at the SFPD headquarters."

Could I reach my cell?

It was less than four feet away, but if I made a move for it, would he pounce on me?

Would I be stabbed, sliced, cut before I got a call out?

"Now, I could threaten to decorate the pretty face of yours if you don't just go back to class and mind your own damn business. Or I could just fix one side, one beautiful cheek, to serve as a reminder, to mind your own god damn business. I think a Z would do it."

Roll it
Pat it
Mark it with Z
And throw it in the oven
For Baby and me

He sang, then he sighed. "But then, I don't think that's gonna work. You're too stubborn for that, too independent, too self-reliant. Reminds me of some one. Can't think who." A scowl replaced the grin.

"You," I whispered. "It was you. You poisoned Carol. You tripped her, wrecked the brakes in the car."

Dave looked startled. "I always hated that cold, beautiful," he spit the words, "arrogant bitch. I enjoyed seeing her suffer when Lexi died. I saw Tom buying drinks for that guy. I was curious what they were up to so I followed that guy, that Zodiac from the Monk and saw him shoot her. Even gave him a hand with drugging that guy she was with." He watched my face for a reaction.

I fought back my revulsion determined not to give him the satisfaction of affecting me.

"I guess I'm not surprised she told you about her, quote, 'accidents.' She has an extraordinary love for you. Has from the day you were born. She's gonna suffer even more this time." He stood up, took a step toward me.

I jumped to my feet.

I ran.

I ran up the curved stairs.

He was only as far as the bottom of the stairs, in no apparent hurry. He must have figured he had me trapped. He'd probably looked around long enough to see there was no way out from the upper floors.

But if I could get to a bathroom, I could lock myself in.

And him out.

At the top of the stairs, I realized what would happen when my housemates came home. He'd stab and carve them.

I couldn't hide in a locked bathroom.

I had to deal with this lunatic.

He grinned at me from the foot of the staircase, that horrid, twisted grin.

He swung the knife in an arc, and cackled, getting off on my fear.

69

I came part way down the stairs and reached out to the head of the grizzly.

I threw out my arms at the ten-foot tall bear, and, with both hands, shoved the massive body towards Dave.

Dave was so intent on cutting me, he never saw it coming. The toppling giant knocked the knife out of his hand onto the stairs and Dave to the floor.

I dashed down the rest of the stairs for the knife and had it in my grip before he got up.

From where I stood on the second step, my eyes were level with his.

He laughed, that horrible cackle of a laugh. "You won't use that. You sweet little cutie pie. You wouldn't hurt anyone. Especially not your old Uncle Dave." He took a slow step toward me.

"I wouldn't bet on it." I waved the blade at his neck. "You shouldn't bet on it either. Bad bet. Remember the odds: I'm one for one."

Dave squinted at me like he thought I'd lost my mind, but I was betting he was scared of knives.

After all he knew how much damage they could do.

He growled at me like a bear, and swung a paw. Asshole thought he could use my fear of bears, the fear my family knew so well, against me.

I scraped his hand with the sharp edge of the blade.

He grabbed his hand, hugged it to him. "You cut me!" he whined.

"And I'll do it again," I blasted at his face. "Next I'll stab you in the throat." A sudden flash of my memory, the mugger in Golden Gate Park. Uncle Dave always in turtlenecks or cravats, it wasn't just meticulous dressing. He had to hide that knife scar.

He grabbed his neck with his good hand.

"Remember that! It was only forty years ago. I almost got you right in the jugular, could've killed you that time." I slashed the knife at him.

He jumped back.

His stupefied look said he didn't remember, but on some level, his unconscious was flashing warning signs.

I swung the blade, aiming for the arm that came up to protect his face.

I wasn't afraid to cut him.

In fact, I wanted to hurt him, to make him feel some of the pain, both physical and emotional, he'd caused so many others.

The blood that spurted from his hand shot a thrill through my body.

Fear that he would get the knife away from me vanished, replaced by an animal lust for revenge.

I charged at him aiming the dagger at his chest.

He turned sideways like a matador.

I slid by, turned back, and glared.

His eyes bugged. He clutched his wounded hand to his waist and grabbed the door handle to get the hell out of there before the crazy woman cut him—again!

He opened the door and collided with Schmidt. Steven was behind the Detective.

Dave tried to push past them. "I've got to get medical attention. She's crazy. She cut me."

"Not so fast." Detective Schmidt pulled out his handcuffs.

Dave shoved the Detective down the porch steps then broke into a run for his Porsche.

Steven chased him. He jumped on Dave's back, wrestled him to the ground in the front yard, but couldn't hold him there.

Detective Schmidt caught up to them and pulled his gun. He trained it on Dave.

"Back up, son!" Schmidt ordered Steven.

"DO NOT KILL HIM!" I screamed, "Whatever you do, don't kill him."

70

Detective Schmidt cuffed Dave and read him his rights while Steven and I collapsed on the steps of the front porch and watched.

Steven had his arm around my shoulders, trying to comfort me while I shook violently. "I . . . I really would've stabbed him. I didn't want to . . . but all of a sudden I was overwhelmed with anger at all the pain and emotional suffering he's caused countless people."

Detective Schmidt shoved his prisoner into the back seat of the car and returned to where we sat. "You gonna be okay?" he asked me.

I nodded in answer to his question, but the violence of my shaking hadn't subsided, and I doubted I was very convincing. I was mostly shocked at what I had almost done. At what I had wanted to do.

I handed him the knife. "That's his."

"I didn't figure it was yours, but you looked pretty intimidating the way you held it." Detective Schmidt chuckled as he put the knife in an evidence bag.

He dialed his headquarters. "I need a patrol car at Piedmont and . . ." he looked at the street sign, "and Rose in Berkeley. A prisoner needs transport back to the city."

"Do you want me to take you to your parents?"

I shook my head.

"We better give them a call, let them know you two are both okay before the media blows everything that happened since we left them all out of proportion." He grimaced. "Well, come to think of it, maybe they won't need to exaggerate much. And to think I assured your father that you'd be perfectly safe with me." He shook his head, smiled at the irony, but quickly stopped as though he had thought of something totally awful.

"God Damn. Come to think of it, we're gonna have to go back to the city, back to headquarters. You gonna make it okay?"

I nodded, after several deep breaths.

"What are you guys doing here anyway?" I asked once we were back in the car.

"Got a call from Kyle. Your I-24/7 got lots of hits, lots of matches all over Southeast Asia, even a couple in EU. He couldn't get anything out of the State Department, but he was able to get some data from the log of Dave's plane with several links. We were just coming over to tell you that you were right." Schmidt turned the car onto Ashby Avenue. "There was a second Zodiac killer."

EPILOGUE

NOVEMBER 2008

There was no point in going back to school: I'd missed too much. I retook my classes in the fall. I did some research into reincarnation too but what I learned, well, that's another story. But I do know I'm a girl with a past.

As it turned out, I was ok with taking the term off because that left the spring and summer free to work on the Obama presidential campaign. And even after getting back in school, I snuck off to North Carolina for the five days leading up to Election Day to get out the vote. I caught a plane as the polls closed in the East and, thanks to the time difference, managed to get back to Berkeley in time to dance in the streets, wave American flags, sing the *Star Spangled Banner* and chant U-S-A with the tens of thousands of Cal students and Berkeley residents who took to the streets, not to protest this time, but to celebrate. To celebrate one more forward step in the dream of equality.

I assumed I was one of the few students with enough perspective to fully appreciate the contrast between the tears of joy that November night in both Sproul Plaza, where students celebrated, and Grant Park, where Obama accepted the election, with the tears from gas in those same two locations forty years earlier. In those forty years, we had gone from Jack Weinberg being arrested for talking about racial equality to electing an African American president.

ACKNOWLEDGEMENTS

Thanks for encouragement from my fellow writers including members of Mystery Writers of America and the teachers and students of UCLA Extension Writer's Program especially my first mystery writing instructor, Jerrilyn Farmer.

Thanks to my writing group, Shari Shattuck, Mark Hosack, and Sharon Doyle for the laughs, advice, gentle criticism, and putting up with a newbie.

My brave early readers, Joan Goddard, Del Boles, and Elisabeth James deserve special gratitude for their kind comments.

Editors Candy Samoza and Alison Farr Brisker rose to the challenge of dealing with an inexperienced author and are much appreciated.

Michael James suffered through every version of this story and then applied his usual meticulous attention to details to do the final preparations for publishing.

Kate James not only designed my covers, website, and Facebook banner, she patiently answered gazillions of questions about computers, the internet, eBooks, and all the other gadgets that were barely dreamt of in 1969.

David Oh demonstrated extreme patience by reworking cover art until the color picky designer in me was happy.

Berkeley in the sixties was an experience for which I am still grateful. With our shared ambition to make the world a better place, my fellow idealists encouraged a direction in life that had adventures and disappointments, but ultimately brought me all that I hold dear: my husband, children, grandchildren, extended family, and good friends. Thanks guys!

33969167R00231

Made in the USA
San Bernardino, CA
15 May 2016